"Informal, colloquial, sassy . . . Liz and Jack are likeable protagonists, and Susan Kelly does a nice job with the Boston and Cambridge background."

Grounds for Murder Newsletter

"A page turner with action and suspense."

SSC Booknews

"A quick, pleasing read . . . Kelly's Cambridge is wonderfully real, Connors and Lingemann continue to be delightful, and true to form, Kelly provides a high-tension climax that gives Connors a chance to show her stuff."

Drood Review

Also by Susan Kelly:

THE SUMMERTIME SOLDIERS
THE GEMINI MAN*

**Published by Ballantine Books:*

TRAIL OF THE DRAGON

Susan Kelly

BALLANTINE BOOKS • NEW YORK

Library of Congress Catalog Number: 87-25404

ISBN 0-345-35749-3

This edition published by arrangement with Walker and Company.

Manufactured in the United States of America

First Ballantine Books Edition: July 1990

1

Professor DiBenedetto leaned back in the swivel chair and linked his hands over his midsection. His midsection had expanded quite considerably since I'd last seen him. With his well-trimmed short white beard and mustache, he looked like a Neapolitan Santa Claus in mufti. The resemblance was probably carefully cultivated.

"I'll get right to the point," DiBenedetto said.

I leaned forward and looked at him expectantly.

"I think I have a problem," he said.

A statement like that called for only one response, and I gave it. "I'm sorry to hear that," I said.

DiBenedetto nodded and closed his eyes. He seemed to sink further back into his chair. It was as if the mere act of speaking had wearied him beyond acceptable human limits. "I'm not sure what to do." His head drooped so that his chin was pressed against his breastbone. I hoped he wasn't falling asleep.

"Carl?" I said.

He raised his head swiftly and said, "Would you like some tea, Liz?"

The question was sufficiently disconnected from his earlier remarks to startle me a little. "Sure," I said. "If it's no trouble."

"Trouble," he repeated. He opened his eyes and gave me a small smile. "No trouble at all, I assure you." He heaved himself up out of the swivel chair.

I watched him leave the room. His tread was heavy and slow, more so than could be accounted for by his age and bulk. I wondered what was bothering him. But more than that, I wondered why he'd want to tell *me* about it. We weren't close friends. We were just barely acquaintances, if that. Not two people who'd trade confidences.

I'd met Carl DiBenedetto three years ago when he'd hired me to ghostwrite the instructor's manual for a textbook he was editing on Elizabethan tragedy. I'd done the work, apparently to his satisfaction, gotten paid for it, and that had been that. Ours had been a purely professional—and very limited—relationship. We'd had no contact at all since he'd handed me my check.

Which was why his phone call this morning had come as a surprise. He'd gotten me out of bed with it at eight. And all he would say, after my brain had started functioning and we'd exchanged the usual pleasantries, was that he wanted to see me as soon as possible. I'd assumed he had another writing job lined up for me. It didn't occur to me to wonder why he'd been so cryptic, yet urgent, on the phone. I didn't *know* the man, but you didn't have to have that intimate an acquaintance with him to understand that he loved being mysterious. Or, even more so, dramatic. And why not? His field *was* the history of the theatre.

DiBenedetto was about sixty-five, I guessed, and had spent forty of those years teaching in the English departments of various colleges and universities in the greater Boston area. At present, he was the director of the freshman composition program at a small college in Newton, an institution the name of which I could never remember. He'd been at Northeastern when I'd worked for him.

The room I was sitting in was the study of DiBenedetto's house on Garden Street in Cambridge. It looked exactly the way you'd imagine a professor's retreat ought to. Wainscoting, floor-to-ceiling bookshelves on two of the walls, threadbare Oriental rug, a couple of comfortably worn armchairs, an antique camelback sofa, and a massive oak desk littered with papers and scholarly journals. The only false note was the Apple PC in the corner.

I was inspecting the contents of the bookshelves when DiBenedetto reappeared in the study entrance, hefting a laden tray. He hovered in the doorway a moment, glancing vaguely around the room.

"Where can I put this?" he said.

"Would you like me to clear a space on the desk?" I asked.

"Please."

In the center of the desk blotter was a copy of *The Journal of English and Germanic Philology* and a pile of typewritten papers. By the look of them, the latter were student productions. The first sentence of the topmost paper read, "Ballards [sic] or story songs were the television of the Mid-Evil [sic] period." I shook my head; poor old DiBenedetto wasn't ending up his teaching career at one of the top-of-the-line local institutions of higher learning. I pushed the pile of papers to the left side of the desk. DiBenedetto placed the tray in the cleared space and sat down heavily in the swivel chair.

I resumed my place in one of the rump-sprung armchairs. DiBenedetto turned to fuss with the contents of the tea tray.

"So, Carl," I said. "You have a problem. Do you want to tell me about it?"

"How do you take your tea?" he asked.

I sighed internally. DiBenedetto's idea of getting to the point was forty-five minutes of verbal foreplay. Part of his mystique. "A little lemon, if you have it," I said.

He handed me a cup and saucer with a wedge of lemon in the saucer.

"Thank you," I said.

He offered me a small plate of Pepperidge Farm cookies and I shook my head.

He frowned. "Why not?"

"That stuff makes you fat."

"You're not fat."

"I know," I replied. "I want to keep it that way."

He shook his head and picked up one of the cookies and bit into it.

"Carl," I said.

He looked me over his shoulder. There were some cookie crumbs clinging to his goatee.

"What is it?" I said. "You want me to write something for you?"

He shook his head.

"I didn't think so," I said. "So what is it? Your problem?"

He set his cup and saucer carefully down on the desk. Then he spun around in his chair to face me. We gazed at each other for a few moments before he looked away again.

"A month ago," DiBenedetto said to the bookcase, "a young lady came to me and asked me to give her thirty-five hundred dollars."

I sipped my tea. "Oh?"

"She was desperate," DiBenedetto continued. "Terrified."

I sat silent.

"I gave her the money," DiBenedetto said.

I took another sip of my tea. When I'd worked for him, there'd been a rumor going around that DiBenedetto had a fondness for "young ladies." The student body of the college where he was teaching now probably included a reasonable number of women. He wouldn't have worked there otherwise.

"I know what you're thinking," DiBenedetto said sharply.

I raised my eyebrows. "I'm not thinking anything, Carl. I'm waiting for you to tell me what all this is about. You gave a young woman some money. So?"

DiBenedetto took a deep breath and sagged back in his chair. "She told me she had to have it right away. And that she didn't know anyone else to turn to."

Uh-huh, I thought.

"If you could have seen her," DiBenedetto continued. "She looked so helpless. So scared."

I drank more tea. "Why? What was her trouble?"

DiBenedetto closed his eyes. "She told me she had brain cancer. And that she needed the money right away to pay for her treatment."

I stared at him for a moment. Then I set my cup and saucer carefully on the end table next to the camelback sofa and said, *"What?"*

"If you could have seen her," DiBenedetto reiterated. "So pale. So helpless."

I put my right hand up to my forehead and rubbed it, hard. "This young woman," I said. "Was she one of your students?"

He shook his head. "No. She's one of the instructors in the freshman composition program. I hired her last September."

"Is she . . ." I bit my lower lip. "How is she now?"

He gave me a vacant look. "I don't know."

"You don't?"

"No." He inhaled again, long and heavily. "I gave her a cashier's check for thirty-five hundred dollars on April first, and I haven't seen or heard from her since then. No one has."

"No one? In four weeks? Are you sure? What about the other people in your English Department?"

He shook his head.

I picked up my teacup "Carl," I said. "There's a lot more to this than what you've told me so far. Maybe you should tell me the rest of it."

He sat motionless in his swivel chair, staring at the wall opposite.

"Carl," I said sharply.

"I'm sixty-eight," he said. "I'm retiring in June." He turned to face me. "The college tells me I can keep on teaching part-time as long as I want. Maybe one drama course in the fall. Maybe a seminar in creative writing in the spring."

I was quiet for a moment. Then I said, with a kind of cautious joviality, "Well, that sounds pretty good, doesn't it? Just think of all the free time you'll have to write and—"

"Shit," DiBenedetto said.

There was nothing to reply to that, so I swallowed some more tea.

"What they're saying, in the nicest way possible, is that I've outlived my usefulness." DiBenedetto paused a moment. "And they're right."

I finished my tea and set the cup and saucer back on the end table. "Tell me about the young woman, Carl," I said.

He stared at me and then laughed, a hard curt sound. "Right."

"She asked you for thirty-five hundred dollars for medical treatment," I said. "Did she tell you what hospital she was going to?"

"No. She was very adamant about that. About *not* telling me that."

I furrowed my eyebrows. "Was she employed full-time by your college?"

"Yes."

"Well, then, she would have been eligible for one of the school's medical insurance plans, wouldn't she?"

He nodded.

"What kind of coverage do they give?"

He shrugged. "Very good. The best available. You have your choice of eight plans."

"And this woman *was* covered by one of them."

"Yes."

"Had she been sick for very long?"

He gave me another blank look. "As far as I knew she was perfectly healthy till the day she came to me asking for the money. Why?"

I hesitated a moment. "Oh, nothing, really. It's just—well, if she'd only recently discovered she was ill, and had to go into the hospital, whatever kind of medical plan she'd signed up for surely would have paid for most of her treatment. At least initially. Who knows what kind of bills she might run up eventually, but at least in the beginning, if she had to have an operation, Blue Cross or whatever would have picked up most of the tab . . . wouldn't they?"

DiBenedetto was looking at his clasped hands.

"Carl?" I prodded. "Wouldn't they?"

He leaned back in his chair and shut his eyes. "It was a

special treatment she'd signed up for,'' he said. ''Not covered by regular medical insurance.''

''Oh?''

''Yes.'' DiBenedetto blinked his heavy-lidded eyes at me, like an old turtle. ''She told me she needed thirty-five hundred dollars to give to someone by four o'clock the following day to reserve a place for her in a course of treatment that would begin on the first of May. I gave her the money.''

I just managed not to blurt out, *you idiot*.

DiBenedetto read the expression on my face correctly. ''I know,'' he said. ''I know. I should have insisted she tell me more about it. At least give me the name of the doctor who was treating her.''

''Why didn't you?''

''I couldn't.''

''Why not?''

He unclasped his hands and threw his arms wide. ''She was frantic. I couldn't press her. All she would say was that she had to have the money. And that this doctor had told her that an essential part of the treatment was that she not tell anyone his name or talk about it at all.''

''What?''

''She wasn't supposed to reveal the doctor's name,'' he repeated. ''Or any details about the treatment.''

''Whoooo,'' I said softly and gave my head a single vigorous shake.

''I don't know what to do.''

''I understand that she hasn't tried to get in touch with you,'' I said.. ''But have *you* tried to get in touch with her?''

He nodded. ''I've called her at her apartment, oh, I don't know how many times. Maybe twice a day for two weeks now.''

''And?''

''I always get a busy signal.''

''Have you tried her at night?''

He gave me an anguished look. ''I get her roommate. Who hangs up on me.''

''Carl,'' I said. ''I don't know anything about medicine,

but I think I do know that there isn't any kind of legitimate treatment for brain cancer that asks the patient for thirty-five hundred dollars and then delays the treatment for a month. Tumors don't get smaller with the passage of time."

"I know," he said. "I asked my own doctor those same questions."

Must have been some conversation, I reflected.

"Carl?"

"Yes?"

"This young woman could be in very serious trouble. In fact, I'm sure she is, if she's sick and has gotten hooked up with some quack. What's her name, anyway?"

He stirred in his chair. "Bonnie."

"Bonnie what?"

"Bonnie Nordgren."

"Good *God*," I said.

DiBenedetto glanced over at me in dull surprise. "What's the matter?"

"I know her."

2

It wasn't accurate to say that I *knew* Bonnie Nordgren. I'd met her twice, the first time at a dinner party in Boston about a year ago, and the second time last March at a local writers' conference here in town. On each occasion, I'd spent a grand total of maybe five minutes in conversation with her. Still, I'd been able to form some distinct impressions of her. And they weren't particularly favorable ones.

The first thing you noticed about the woman was that she was gorgeous. Hers was the kind of beauty that derived from spectacular coloring rather than fine bone structure. She had the longest, thickest, curliest, real blonde hair I've ever seen, worn Brigitte Bardot fashion spilling halfway to her waist. Her eyes were vivid blue, with an almost Asian slant to them. She had the kind of fair skin that tans to the shade of teak after a single weekend at the beach.

What spoiled her looks, according to my aesthetic anyway, was her facial expression. She apparently had just one—a withdrawn, sulky look that verged on an outright pout. Even when talking, the woman seemed unable or unwilling to smile, frown, grimace, or produce any of the other facial contortions most of us use to punctuate our speech.

Not that she talked all that much. At the dinner party she'd sat virtually silent, gazing mostly at her plate and picking now and then at its contents. Most of her responses to various attempts to draw her into the conversation had been monosyllabic. Curt, too. I suppose that had been what had put me off her. There had been something almost contemptuous in her refusal to be even minimally sociable. I found myself wondering why she'd been invited to the party, and why she herself had accepted an invitation to an event she seemingly found boring or distasteful. But since I didn't know the hostess or indeed any of the other guests very well, there was no discreet way I could ask.

The second time I'd met Bonnie Nordgren, at the writers' conference, she'd been slightly more forthcoming. I'd been asked to participate in a panel discussion about the problems of free-lancing. Nordgren had been in the audience. Afterward, she'd come up to me and asked a few innocuous questions about breaking into magazine writing. There was something erratic about her speech, I noticed, as if she weren't quite sure how to articulate her thoughts. And she'd seemed nervous—oddly so, under the circumstances. I found myself hoping that she wrote better than she talked, which is true of a great many writers.

DiBenedetto's voice broke in on my recollections. It took me a second to redirect my attention to him.

"Sorry, Carl," I said. "I didn't catch that."

"I was asking you to help me." He leaned forward in his chair and gazed at me intently, almost pleadingly.

A little red warning light flashed on in my brain. "Oh?" I said carefully. "What would you like me to do?"

"Find her," he said, in tones nearly as melodramatic as his words. "Find out what's happened to her."

Happily, I wasn't holding my teacup, or else I would have dropped it. Instead, I just stared at DiBenedetto. Apparently he mistook the expression of disbelief on my face for one of acquiescence, or at least interest, for he smiled as if relieved.

"Carl," I said, bemused. "How on earth could I do that?"

He was all airy unconcern now. The man was an emotional chameleon. "Well, I don't know. You'll think of something."

"I can't imagine what," I said.

"Oh, you'll figure something out," he replied.

I gave him another incredulous stare. Clearly, it was time for me to try to take control of the conversation.

"Tell me," I said, in as neutral a voice as I could manage, "why you think it is that *I'll* be able to get hold of this woman when *you*, her boss, and her colleagues can't."

He looked somewhat taken aback by the question. "Well, you're a crime writer, aren't you?"

"So?"

He shrugged. "So you know about those kinds of things."

"*What* kinds of things?"

"Missing persons," DiBenedetto said impatiently. "About finding them."

I took a deep-cleansing breath and let it out very slowly. "Okay," I said. "I think we have to straighten something out here. Yes, Carl, I *do* write articles about crime. And yes, I *have* written articles about missing persons. But I do not *find* missing persons. The police do. They—"

"No police," DiBenedetto interrupted.

"Why not?"

He shook his head.

I sighed. "If you really think that something bad has happened to this woman, Carl, then I would say you have what amounts to an obligation to report it to the police."

"No." He made a fist and thumped it on the arm of his chair. His face had grown quite red.

Oh, boy, I thought. "I really would like to help you, if I could," I lied, making a gesture with my right hand that was supposed to signify helplessness. "But I honestly can't imagine how I'd go about it. I'm a writer, not a detective."

"But you investigate things," he said quickly.

"I research them," I corrected.

"Same difference," he replied.

"Well, not quite, Carl."

"Please," he said. "I need help."

I peered at him. His eyes seemed to be wet. I was horrified. If he broke down, I knew I wouldn't be able to handle it. I sagged back in my seat, put my left elbow on the chair arm, and cupped my forehead in my hand. DiBenedetto blew his nose loudly. When I looked up, he was stashing a crumpled linen hankie in his pants pocket and looked reasonably under control.

"All right," I said. "I'll see if I can do something."

Feminism had certainly turned some curious tables. Now men were using tears to extort favors from women.

"Thanks," DiBenedetto said huskily.

"Don't expect any miracles," I warned. "In fact, don't expect anything at all."

"Whatever you can do," he said.

I nodded gloomily. And wondered, not for the first time, how in hell I got myself into these things.

3

DiBenedetto reiterated his thanks. Lavishly. For a moment I was afraid he might try to kiss my feet, but he restrained himself, for which I was deeply grateful. The situation was embarrassing enough as it stood.

We talked for another ten minutes. DiBenedetto gave me Nordgren's home address and telephone number, and after some persuasion, the addresses and phone numbers of the other people in the Thatcher College (*that* was the name of the damn place) English Department. He didn't seem happy with the thought of my talking to Nordgren's colleagues about her, although he refused to say why. I pointed out to him, as temperately as possible, that as far as I knew, it was customary to open a missing persons investigation by interviewing those who'd last had contact with the person missing. Judging by the expression on his face, I don't think he believed me.

Refusing, graciously I hoped, an invitation to join DiBenedetto and his wife for drinks and dinner, I finally managed to escape. Out on Garden Street I looked at my watch. It was just four-thirty. Perfect. I was supposed to meet Jack at the police station at five, and the walk from Garden Street to Central Square would take just about half an hour.

Jack is Detective Lieutenant John Lingemann of the Cambridge Police Department. He is my . . . I don't like to use the word *lover* because, to my ears at least, it implies that the only thing between us is sex. Which isn't true by a long shot. Jack is the best person I know. We met about five years ago, when I'd just begun to write for publication and was interested in doing a series of articles on crime in Cambridge. I'd gone to the police station looking for information and had been directed to Jack. As I recall, the questions I'd asked him had to do with missing persons investigations. Sweet irony, in view of my latest assignment.

Jack is forty-four. I'm thirty-six.

My name is Elizabeth Connors. I used to be a full-time college English teacher. I still do teach part-time now and then, but only when I really need the money. I like writing for a living a lot better. My dog Lucy and I manage quite comfortably on what I make.

Jack is a widower. I've never been married.

Today was the kind of spring day that made Garden Street more than live up to its name. Even the squirrels looked as if they were smiling. I trudged across the Cambride Common and into Harvard Square. Going from Harvard Square to Central Square is like going from Juan-les-Pins to Hoboken. En route I got panhandled three times, which is about par for the course.

The police station is on the corner of Green Street and Western Avenue. Directly across from it is the Division of Employment Security. For some reason, this conjunction amuses me. I wish I could figure out why.

Jack's office is on the third floor of the police station, in the Criminal Investigation Division. You can take a temperamental elevator up there or use the cigarette butt-littered stairs. I always use the stairs. That way I stop on the second floor and wave hello to the chief's secretary and the SWAT commander and the guys in the Crime Analysis Bureau.

Jack was on the third floor landing, leaning against the wrought iron railing and talking to a vice-narcotics cop who looked like Lon Chaney halfway through the transformation to the Wolfman. All the guys in vice looked like that except for the lieutenant, who looked like a children's book editor.

Whatever Jack and the Wolfman were discussing had them so engrossed that they didn't notice me coming up the stairs.

I paused five steps below the landing and stood watching them. Jack looked the way he always did to me—terrific. He was six-three and still as lean as he must have been at twenty-two. His eyes and hair were the identical shade of light brown, although the hair was starting to gray. Oddly, the gray made him look younger than he actually was. The bones in his face were pronounced and well-defined, like an Indian's. The world's only Cherokee Hun, I had once called him.

Jack and the Wolfman finished up their conversation on a burst of laughter. The Wolfman prowled away down the corridor, and Jack turned to me and smiled. "What are you doing down there?"

"I didn't think you noticed me," I said.

"I notice everything," he said. "Especially tall red-headed women."

I joined him on the landing and put my arm around him. He gave me a discreet squeeze and we separated. Neither of us is much into public manifestations of affection.

"You ready to go?" I asked.

He nodded. "Just let me get my jacket."

We pushed through the swinging doors of the CID. His office was the first on the left, next to that of the captain of detectives. It had a panoramic view of the Division of Employment Security.

Jack took his suit coat from a hanger behind the door and shrugged into it.

"How was your day?" I asked.

He grimaced. "Wonderful. Jam-packed with administrative bullshit from beginning to end."

"Sorry," I said.

He smiled at me. "Not your fault. How was your day?"

I grinned back at him. "I have a beaut of a story to tell you."

He stopped in the act of straightening his tie and looked at me curiously.

"It's better told over a drink," I said. "However, I will tell you this much now—it has to do with what I think might be a crime-in-progress in Cambridge."

''Oh, hey, great,'' Jack said. ''Just what I need more of.''

''No, no,'' I said. ''You don't understand. You're not going to have to investigate this one. All you have to do is sit back and listen to me tell about it, and savor it.''

''Savor?'' Jack repeated. ''Savor? The day I start savoring more crimes-in-progress in Cambridge is the day they institutionalize me.''

''Trust me,'' I said. ''You'll love it.''

''Let's go get that drink,'' he said.

We walked back to Harvard Square, to a bar on Church Street. It would have been stupid to take his car; there's never any place to park in the square.

The bar—a large, light, airy one—was virtually empty. Jack nodded at a table for two in the corner. ''That okay?'' he asked.

''Fine,'' I said. He likes to sit in the back-to-the-wall seat at corner tables, where he can keep an eye on what's happening in the rest of the room. I do, too, but when I'm with him I let him have the observation post. He's the cop.

The waitress took my order for a vodka martini and his for a bourbon.

''So,'' he said. ''What's your story?''

''Wait till the drinks come,'' I said.

He rolled his eyes at the ceiling, and I laughed and reached across the table and patted his arm. With his free hand he reached for the bowl of sesame stick-nut mix.

The waitress brought the drinks. I took a big sip of mine and gave a contented sigh. ''You know who the next great benefactor of the human race will be?'' I asked.

''I have no idea,'' Jack said. ''Who?''

I smiled. ''The person who invents diet vodka.''

Jack drank some of his bourbon. ''Tell me your story,'' he suggested.

I did.

There isn't any tale you can tell about human behavior that will shock or even surprise a cop with almost twenty years' experience. He's heard them all. All the same, when I finished speaking, Jack was gazing at me with his head slightly tilted and his mouth very slightly open.

"So," I concluded lightly. "I've just been handed my very first detective assignment."

Jack finished his bourbon. He set the glass down carefully on the table, directly in front of him. "Let me get something straight."

"Certainly."

He poked the air before me with his right index finger. "What you're telling me is that this DiBenedetto character handed over thirty-five hundred bucks to some woman because she said she needed it right away for a brain cancer cure."

"Uh-huh."

"Without asking any questions."

"He told me he couldn't."

Jack's lips pursed in a soundless whistle and he shook his head slowly. "What a *bozo*," he said.

I laughed.

"You want another drink?" Jack asked.

"Okay."

"Amazing," Jack said.

I was fairly sure he wasn't referring to the fact that I wanted another drink.

"Would you like to take this case?" I asked. "The Mystery of the Missing Blonde?"

"Christ, no," he said. "I already have more than I can handle."

The waitress brought our fresh drinks and cleared away the empty glasses.

"You know," I said. "I've met this Bonnie Nordgren a few times."

Jack raised his eyebrows. "Oh? What's she like?"

"Hard for me to say." I shrugged. "Quite good-looking. Sort of flaky, I think, though that might be a false impression. I doubt it, though."

"What's DiBenedetto like?"

I smiled. "That's easy. He really *is* a flake."

"Yeah, sounds like it," Jack replied. He picked some almonds out of the sesame stick-nut mix and popped them one by one into his mouth. The look on his face was inward and abstracted.

"What's on your mind?" I asked.

"Huh?"

"What are you thinking about?"

He sipped his drink. "Oh, nothing much. It's just that this business about quickie cancer cures rings a bell, but I can't quite . . ." He set his glass on the table and frowned. "Wait a sec."

"What is it?" I leaned forward slightly.

"There was something that happened here about three years ago . . ." He stopped speaking and, slowly, the frown on his face eased into a great, happy grin.

"Tell me!"

"Son of a bitch." Jack shook his head, still grinning. "Those two old witches must be back in business again."

"*What* two old witches? *What* is this?"

"Gypsies," Jack said. "The gypsies. Sister Shirley and Sister Rose."

I gazed at him, mystified. "Who on earth are they?"

"Like I said," Jack replied, "a pair of gypsies. They used to operate a fortune-telling parlor over on Cambridge Street a few years ago."

"Used to?"

"Yeah. We shut them down." He took another sip of his drink. "At least, I thought we had."

"Okay. But what's that got to do with brain cancer cures?"

"Well," Jack said. "That was one of their scams. Peddling miracle cures to the terminally ill."

"Good God."

"In fact," Jack continued. "That was the reason they got shut down finally."

"What happened?"

Jack scratched his head. "I'm a little fuzzy on the details, but as far as I can remember, it went something like this—a couple of kids from MIT decided it would be fun to have some real live gypsies read their palms or their tarot cards or some such garbage. So they made an appointment to see Sister Rose and Sister Shirley."

"And?"

"Well, so they went, and they got their palms read. After that, they had their fortunes told. So it's all a big joke up until this point, right? Okay. The kids are just about to leave when Sister Rose goes into some kind of trance and starts mumbling and waving her hands in the air and rolling her eyes back into her head. The two kids are a little freaked, but what the hell, it's still a pretty good laugh."

"Ha, ha," I said.

"Yeah. So then, Sister Rose comes out of her trance and announces to one of the kids that he has stomach cancer."

"Jesus," I breathed.

"Uh-huh," Jack said. "So, next thing—Sister Rose gets up and goes into the kitchen and comes back with a little bottle of some kind of salve. She hands it to the kid and tells him to rub it on his gut that night before he goes to bed."

"Oh, boy," I said. "I bet I can guess what happened next."

Jack smiled at me. "Shall I finish?"

"Of course."

"Right. So this little jerkface goes back down to his dorm room and smears himself with the glop in the bottle and, naturally, wakes up the next morning with blisters all over his stomach. He panics and runs back to Sister Rose, who tells him that's the disease coming to the surface."

I was silent and saucer-eyed.

"Anyway," Jack continued. "Old Rosie tells the kid that if he wants to be cured, he should get three thousand dollars and bring it to her by that afternoon and she'll take care of everything."

"Jack," I said. "You're *not* going to tell me . . ."

He nodded. "Yup. This little jackass empties his bank account and goes running back to Rosie and hands her the money. She closes her eyes, mumbles a few magic words, waves her hands, opens her eyes, and tells the kid he's cured.

The kid goes back to school and Rosie laughs all the way to whatever mattress she keeps her money stuffed in."

"Unbelievable," I said. I drank some of my martini. "How'd you find out about it? Did the kid tell you?"

Jack smiled. "Not exactly. What the kid did do was write home to his parents to ask them to send him some more money. So of course they called him at the school right away to find out what the hell happened to the three grand they'd just given him for clothes and books and all."

"And he told them."

"Uh-huh."

I started to laugh. "What happened next?"

"What do you think?" Jack picked up some more almonds out of the bowl. "Mom and Dad hit the roof. After that, they caught the first plane up to Boston and stomped over to MIT and dragged the kid down to us to make a complaint."

"Beautiful," I said. "And so Sister Rose and Sister Shirley got busted."

"Yup."

I reached for some nuts. "Tell me, did the kid ever get the three thousand back?"

"Yeah," Jack said. "That's the best part of the whole story."

"Oh?"

"Sister Rose wanted to know if she could pay it off in installments. Like a car loan or something."

I let out a hoot of laughter and collapsed back in my chair. A couple at a table a few feet away glanced at me. I put my hand over my mouth and giggled into it, feeling tears start in my eyes. The couple at the next table gave me another odd look.

"That's priceless," I said, when I could talk. I picked up the little paper cocktail napkin that had come with my martini and dabbed at my eyes, carefully so I wouldn't wreck my mascara.

"Want another drink?" Jack asked.

"Thank you, no," I replied. "I'm already sufficiently

light-headed, I think.'' I let out a final giggle and folded up the napkin into a tiny square and placed it in the ashtray.

''There's an unfunny side to all this, you know,'' Jack said.

The comment made me feel a lot less light-headed. ''Yes. There must be a lot of very sick, desperate people out there who get taken in by cons like that.''

''All the time.''

''People you would think would have more sense. Only . . .''

''Yup.''

I sighed, and stirred the dregs of my drink. ''You think Bonnie Nordgren got ripped off by some gypsies who told her she was dying?''

''How would I know?'' Jack said. ''All I'm saying is I've heard of stuff like that going down. Maybe that was what happened with this Bonnie. Maybe not.''

''It sure sounds like it,'' I said.

''Maybe.''

''Well, more than maybe, Jack,'' I argued. ''Carl DiBenedetto told me Bonnie came to him pleading for thirty-five hundred dollars to give to somebody by four o'clock the next day so she could be cured of brain cancer.''

''Yeah. That's what he told you. You don't know that that's what happened.''

I stared at Jack. ''But . . . it must have.''

He looked amused. ''Why *must*?''

I shook my head in irritation and bewilderment. ''Because why on earth would DiBenedetto invent a wackola story like that?''

''Don't ask me, sweetie,'' Jack said. ''I don't know the guy. You do. You yourself told me he wasn't wrapped too tightly. Maybe he gets off on fantasizing about rescuing sick beautiful blondes.''

''But why involve me in it? If it's just a fantasy?''

''Maybe he digs redheads too, babe. Anyway, ask him, not me. If you're really serious about finding out, that is.''

I stared at him. ''Maybe I will.''

He smiled at me. "Right on."

I returned the smile, very sourly. "My first detective assignment's really starting to look like a lulu, isn't it?"

Jack raised his empty glass to me. "Don't they all," he said. "Welcome to the wild and wacky world of criminal investigation."

4

After breakfast the next morning I retrieved the list of Thatcher College English Department faculty from my purse, spread it open on the kitchen table, and sat down to study it. There were nine names. None was familiar. Well, I couldn't be expected to know everyone in eastern Massachusetts who taught or had taught college English, could I?

The names were in alphabetical order. Five men, four women. Whom should I call first? I could start at the top and work my way down the list, but that was boring. Or I could pick the person with the most euphonious name. I got a pen from my purse, closed my eyes, and stabbed the paper with the penpoint. I looked back down at the list of names. I'd poked a hole right through the "o" in Linda Rosenberg.

I've had a lot of experience calling total strangers to ask them for interviews. Even so, the act never fails to make me feel like a bit of a horse's ass. There's always a shadow of a hope that the person I'm calling won't answer the phone.

Linda Rosenberg picked up her office phone on the second ring. I introduced myself and told her that I'd gotten her name from Carl DiBenedetto.

"I know this is going to sound peculiar," I said. "But I would like very much to talk to you about one of your colleagues. A woman named Bonnie Nordgren."

There was a moment's silence on the other end of the line. Then Linda Rosenberg said, "Is this in reference to her work?"

"Well, no," I said, feeling like even more of a fool than usual. "I understand that she's dropped out of sight. Professor DiBenedetto asked me to look into it."

"Are you a detective?"

Jesus. "No," I said. "I'm not. I'm a crime writer."

"I see," Linda Rosenberg said.

She was one up on me there.

"If there's a time that would be convenient for you . . ." I began.

"How about today?" Ms. Rosenberg said crisply. "At, say, three-thirty?"

I blinked at the receiver in my hand. "Fine," I said. "Do you have a particular place in mind where we could meet?"

"Could you come here? To my office?"

"Sure."

"Okay, I'll see you at three-thirty, then. My office number is four-thirteen. On the second floor of Harrison Hall."

I wrote that down. "Got it."

"Do you need directions out here?" Ms. Rosenberg asked.

"No, thanks." I glanced at the list of English faculty names. "Could you tell me if any of the rest of your colleagues will be around this afternoon? I'd like to speak to as many people as possible while I have the opportunity."

"Hmmmm," Ms. Rosenberg said. "Let's see. I'm pretty sure Chris Cameron will be here. Would you like me to ask her to join us?"

"That'd be terrific," I said.

"No problem," Ms. Rosenberg replied. "See you at three-thirty."

"Right."

"Good-bye."

I hung up the phone and frowned to myself thoughtfully.

I'd expected that Linda Rosenberg would have shown some reluctance to accept an invitation from a total stranger to gossip about a co-worker and, possibly, a friend. Instead, she'd seemed downright eager to do so. Interesting.

On impulse, I called Bonnie Nordgren. The line was busy. Fifteen minutes later, I tried again. Still busy.

I was between writing assignments, so to pass the rest of the morning constructively, I went to the public library and rummaged around in the reference room until I located a copy of the most recent Thatcher College catalogue. I wanted to get some minimal background information on Bonnie Nordgren. And on Linda Rosenberg and Christine Cameron, for that matter.

Bonnie Nordgren had a B.A. from Emory University. (Was she a Southern belle in addition to being a Swedish blonde bombshell? I hadn't noticed any accent. But the other peculiarities of her speech might have concealed one.) She had a Ph.D. from Brown. The date of her college graduation indicated that she was about thirty. Her doctoral dissertation had been written on William Carlos Williams. For some obscure reason, I found myself pleased that she hadn't picked a poet I *really* liked. Her field was described as, surprise, surprise, modern poetry. She was listed, however, as teaching only freshman composition, which jibed with what DiBenedetto had told me.

It was bare bones data, but it said a great deal if you knew how to read it. I fancied I did. I believe, firmly, that people are drawn to their professions or avocations not so much out of intellect or talent as out of temperament. Take a group of ten people, all of whom have I.Q.'s of a hundred and thirty-five. In addition to being outstanding academically, they've always been pretty good at accomplishing whatever variety of practical tasks the world had thrust upon them. So why, then, does one grow up to be a lawyer, another an archaeologist, another an English professor, another a detective, another an accountant, another an obstetrician . . . and so forth.

I have a good mechanical aptitude. So why did I study

fourteenth-century literature in graduate school? And why did I end up writing for a living rather than designing engines for Porsche?

I read the information on Christine Cameron and Linda Rosenberg. According to their college graduation dates, they were about my age. Cameron had done her doctoral work on Virginia Woolf. Rosenberg was into John Keats.

I killed the early afternoon trying to dream up some intelligent-sounding questions to ask the two women. At two-fifteen I walked to the subway station and caught a Red Line train to Park Street in Boston. From there I took one of the Green Line Riverside streetcars out to Newton.

It was a twenty-minute walk from the streetcar stop to Thatcher College. The college was a cluster of six red brick buildings atop what looked like a man-made hill. I recalled from my reading of the Thatcher catalogue that the school had moved out here from a downtown Boston site about ten years ago. The campus still had an air of raw newness about it that made me think of an upscale suburban housing development. There were a lot of strategically planted trees, but they were mostly saplings. And the ivy had just the barest start on climbing the brick walls.

A student-type in jeans and Thatcher tee shirt gave me directions to Harrison Hall, which was, of course, the building farthest away from where I happened to be. Room four-thirteen was at the far end of a long corridor on the second floor. The office door was open.

A black-haired woman in her mid-thirties in a pink linen skirt and yellow-and-pink-striped cotton sweater sat at a desk, leafing through a stack of typed papers that appeared to be student themes. Even in profile, her face looked dispirited, I thought. I tapped on the doorjamb. The woman glanced up at me.

"Linda Rosenberg?" I said.

"Yes." She rose slightly from her chair. "Elizabeth Connors?"

I nodded.

She smiled. "Come in." There was another chair beside her desk, and she gestured at it. "Have a seat."

I did so. "Thanks for seeing me."

She shook her head. "You're doing me a favor. Otherwise, I'd have had to spend this time correcting those things." She made a face at the pile of papers on her desk.

I laughed. "I know how you feel. I used to be a college English teacher myself."

"And you got out," Linda Rosenberg said. "Lucky you. *Smart* you."

A small, slender woman, also mid-thirtyish, appeared in the office doorway. She had shoulder-length brown hair, very curly, and vivid green eyes. Their color matched perfectly the background of her flower-print cotton dress.

"Hey, Chris," Linda said.

This, obviously, was Christine Cameron. I smiled at her as she came into the room. Linda Rosenberg made the introductions. Christine Cameron and I shook hands. Then she sat down on the floor beside a filing cabinet, waving away Linda's offer to fetch another chair from the hall.

When we were all settled, I said, "You know, I was a little surprised that you were so willing to talk to me."

The two women exchanged glances.

"Why do you say that?" Linda Rosenberg asked. She looked as if she were trying not to smile.

I raised my eyebrows. "I'm a total stranger to both of you. How can you be sure I don't have bad motives for wanting to know about Bonnie Nordgren?"

"Did Carl *really* ask you to find her?" Christine Cameron asked.

"Yes," I said. "He really did. Does that surprise you?"

Rosenberg and Cameron exchanged another look.

"Nothing Carl does, ever, would surprise either of us," Cameron replied.

"That's right," Linda Rosenberg said. She looked about to say something further, but instead giggled. So did Christine Cameron.

The giggles became laughter. Linda hunched over her

desk, shoulders shaking. I folded my arms and sat back and gazed at the two of them, feeling like the butt of a joke I didn't understand.

After a moment Linda Rosenberg said, "Sorry." She gave one last little snort of amusement and then sat up straight.

"You have to know the situation to see the humor in it," Christine explained.

"Well, why don't you tell me about it?" I suggested.

Linda nodded. "The first thing you have to know is that Carl is absolutely enraptured with Bonnie. Or maybe obsessed would be a better word."

"Oh, for God's sake," Christine said. "The old idiot was in love with her."

I widened my eyes at the two of them.

"They weren't having an affair or anything," Linda added quickly. She looked as if she wanted to laugh again at the very idea.

"But he *did* think she was wonderful," Christine said. "How he feels about her now that she's extorted all that money from him and disappeared, I couldn't say."

It occurred to me that neither Rosenberg nor Cameron seemed to share DiBenedetto's warm opinion of Bonnie Nordgren, and I said so.

"Let's put it this way," Linda said. "Bonnie wasn't my favorite colleague."

I looked at Christine Cameron. She shook her head in agreement.

"Tell me," I said.

"It was like this," Linda said.

Bonnie Nordgren had been the last faculty member hired by the Thatcher College English Department, at the beginning of last September. The lateness of her appointment and her unusual looks hadn't been the only things to set her off from the other instructors. From the first, there'd been something off-key about her attitude.

"We're a pretty close-knit department, except for Carl," Linda said. "We have lunch together most days, and go for drinks after work maybe once a week. But Bonnie would never join us. At first, I thought maybe she was shy.'' Linda paused and made a face. ''Then I realized that she was just weird.''

''How so?'' I asked.

''Well,'' Christine said. ''Little things. But they added up. Like she'd come to work, go to her office, shut the door, and lock it. And you'd knock on the door, knowing she was there, and she wouldn't answer. The only time she ever came out of that damn office would be if she had to scuttle off to class.''

''She was just a strange person all around,'' Linda said. ''On the rare occasions when she'd say something to me, her conversation . . . well, it didn't exactly not make sense, but it was sort of . . .''

''Disconnected?'' I supplied.

Linda looked at me curiously. ''That's exactly it. How would you know?''

''I met her very briefly,'' I said. ''Twice. She seemed sort of skittish to me. And remote.''

''Yes,'' Christine said. ''Remote like the planet Venus is remote.'' She crossed her eyes and tapped her left temple with her index finger.

''She had some peculiar interests, too,'' Linda said.

''Like what?''

''Astrology. Tarot. The I Ching. Palmistry. Tea-leaf reading. Crap like that. Oh, I know a lot of people read their horoscope in the paper each day—I do for one, but Bonnie seemed to take it all very seriously.''

I felt a small internal jolt at Linda's words. Maybe Bonnie believed in gypsy fortune-tellers as well. But I said nothing, not wanting to interrupt the flow of recollection.

''And yet for all her flakiness,'' Christine said. ''There was something quite cool and rational about her.'' Christine paused, looking thoughtful. ''Manipulative would be the way to describe her, I guess. I had the sense that an awful lot of that flakiness was contrived for effect.''

''Well, she certainly jerked DiBenedetto around like a trout,'' Linda said drily.

''How'd she do that?'' I asked.

Linda smiled. "In the traditional way. By playing helpless little girl who needed a big strong man to look after her. God, it was nauseating."

I grinned. "Can you give me an example?"

"In a way, it was really funny," Christine said. "I mean, funny in the comical as opposed to the strange sense. Bonnie'd walk into a department meeting an hour late, and DiBenedetto would start to get huffy. So Bonnie would sashay up to him and fiddle with the knot of his tie and bat her eyelashes and say, in this little-girl voice, something like, 'Oooh, pwease don't be mad at me.' And then flutter her eyelashes some more. And Carl would just melt."

"Maybe you thought it was funny, Chris," Linda said, in a voice edged with disgust, "I thought it was sleazy."

"Well," Christine said. "Bonnie once told me that she intended to play Carl for all he was worth."

Linda turned to her with widened eyes. "Really? You never told me that?"

Christine shrugged. "I forgot until now, I guess. It was sometime last October she said this. On one of the rare occasions she wasn't incommunicado."

Linda sighed. "Well, it certainly didn't take her long to scope out poor old Carl, did it?"

Christine snorted. "Ah, she probably had him sized up as a sucker five minutes into her first job interview with him."

"I heard he has a weak spot for attractive young women," I remarked.

"To say the least," Christine said. She grinned at me nastily. "Nobody but Carl would be foolish enough to hand someone thirty-five hundred dollars just because she fluttered her eyelashes at him."

"She told him she needed it because she was desperately ill," I said.

"Yeah, I heard," Christine replied. "And I'm Princess Di." She wrinkled her nose.

I turned to Linda Rosenberg. "You mentioned earlier that Bonnie was very interested in palmistry and astrology."

"That's right."

"Do you think she was seriously enough involved with the occult to visit a fortune-teller and take seriously what the fortune-teller would say to her?"

Linda looked surprised by the question. Well, it *was* a strange one. She ruminated for a moment. "It's possible," she said slowly. "Why?"

I repeated to the two women Jack's story about Sister Shirley and Sister Rose.

"My Lord," Christine said when I'd finished. "I didn't know things like that went on around here."

I smiled at her. "Well, they do. The point is, could Bonnie have been taken in by a scam like that?"

Linda and Christine looked at each other.

"Hard to say," Christine said. "Bonnie was such an operator herself, you'd think she'd see right through another con artist."

"Oh, I don't know," Linda said. "After all, she was really into all that occult crap."

"Well, maybe." Christine sounded dubious. "I'm positive she made up that story about being sick. Although I believe the part about her needing a lot of money in a hurry."

"Really?" I said. "What would she need it for?"

Christine smiled. "Drugs."

"Oh?"

"Sure. It's the only answer that makes sense. She had to have thirty-five hundred dollars right away to pay off a drug dealer. Or else get her legs broken."

I looked at Linda. "What do you think?"

She frowned. "It could be."

"Oh, it *has* to be," Christine said. "A drug habit explains everything about Bonnie. Her funny behavior, the urgent need for money . . ."

"That's true," Linda said. "Yes. I can see that."

"It would also explain why she disappeared," Christine added. "She'd want to hide out if she were involved in some kid of drug mess, I suppose. I know I sure would."

"Carl told me that none of you has heard from her in a month."

"I tried to call her a few times," Linda said. "But all I got was either a busy signal or her strange roommate. Who more or less told me to bug off."

Christine slapped her hand on her thigh. "My God. I'd forgotten about her. *Yes*. What a weirdo *that* one was."

"Stranger than Bonnie."

"Almost," Christine said. "Hard as that would be to achieve." She leaned sideways and reached into her handbag for a pack of cigarettes. She waved it at me and said, "Mind if I smoke?"

"Go ahead. And tell me about Bonnie's roommate."

Christine lit a cigarette. Linda handed her a small ceramic dish, into which she dropped the dead match. She set the ashtray on the floor beside her, blew out a large cloud of white smoke, and said, "Actually, I got the impression that she was more Bonnie's keeper than Bonnie's roommate."

"Interesting," Linda said. "I got the same impression."

I looked from one to the other. "Were they lovers, do you think?"

"I don't know," Christine said. "They could have been. Whatever their relationship was, it was very, very close. Gayle—that was this other woman's name—even came to work with Bonnie sometimes."

I wrinkled my forehead. "What on earth for?"

"Well, it only happened a few times," Christine said. "But I remember once that Bonnie brought her to a department meeting."

"But why?"

Christine shrugged. "Damned if I know. All this Gayle creature did was sit in a corner and watch Bonnie. Very closely. She didn't say much of anything to anyone else."

"How bizarre," I said.

"Yes, that's the word," Christine replied. She frowned. "I can't tell you exactly why, but I sort of got the impression that she was there to keep an eye on Bonnie."

"Like a guardian?"

"Sort of," Linda said. "I had the same feeling as Chris,

that this Gayle was hanging around to make sure Bonnie didn't do anything or say anything ultra-strange.''

I sighed and shook my head. ''DiBenedetto must have thought all this very odd.''

Christine waved her cigarette. ''Oh, Carl would have let Bonnie ride a circus elephant to class if she'd wanted to.''

I laughed.

Linda said. ''Well, if Bonnie really were heavily into drugs, then she probably did need a keeper.''

''But why would this Gayle person be willing to play a role like that?'' I asked.

Christine shrugged again. ''Who knows? Maybe she and Bonnie *were* lovers. Who but a lover would go to that kind of trouble.''

Linda grinned. ''That would be a good joke on Carl, wouldn't it? If his little darling turned out to be gay?''

She and Christine glanced at each other and started giggling again. It was obvious that they found the whole situation to be the source of the most delightful kind of camp humor.

Neither of them evinced the slightest bit of concern for Bonnie's welfare.

I gazed consideringly at the two women. Although I'd double-check (to whatever extent that was possible) the things they'd told me, I had no reason at all to doubt them. They were clearly intelligent and observant. And both were sufficiently physically attractive so that whatever animus they had against Bonnie Nordgren wouldn't have been inspired by jealousy.

Besides, they hadn't really said anything that didn't tally with or enlarge upon what I myself knew of the woman.

Christine stubbed out her cigarette. ''This has been fun,'' she said. ''But I really have to get back to work.''

Linda nodded. ''Yes, me too.'' She looked at her watch. ''I have a class in ten minutes.''

I smiled at them. ''I want to thank you again for seeing me. It was very nice to meet you.''

"Same here, same here," Christine said. "If we can be of any more help, just let us know."

"Oh, I will. Don't worry."

"You can do us a favor," Linda said.

"What's that?"

"We want to know how this whole thing turns out even worse than you do. So . . ." She looked at me with raised eyebrows.

"I'll keep you posted," I promised.

"Every detail," Christine said. "The more sordid, the better."

I laughed. "My pleasure."

On my way out, I looked for Bonnie's office. I found it, five doors down from Linda's. Surreptitiously, I tried the door. It was locked, of course. I went home.

5

That night I learned something else about Bonnie Nordgren.

"Your girlfriend doesn't have a sheet," Jack said.

"My *who* doesn't have *what*?"

"Bonnie Nordgren," Jack said. "She's never been arrested in Cambridge. Or anywhere else, far as I can tell."

I raised my head a little and stared at him. "You devil," I said. "You *are* interested in this business."

He shrugged to the degree of expressiveness you could if you were lying on your back in a bed with a sheet over you.

"I had a free moment, so I punched her name into the computer. Came up empty."

"Well, thank you," I kissed him. "That was nice of you."

He turned over on his side to face me. "That's not to say she hasn't committed a crime sometime, somehow, someplace."

"Of course she has," I said. "She extorted thirty-five hundred dollars from somebody."

"That's not extortion," Jack corrected. "That's larceny by false pretenses."

"Oh. As felonies go, is that a big deal?"

"All felonies are big deals."

I nodded. "So when do you make the arrest?"

He smiled. "Who do I arrest? And for what? Nobody's complained to me about being ripped off by a beautiful blonde."

"It's not likely he will, either." I sighed. "DiBenedetto was very firm about not bringing the cops into this."

"Probably too embarrassed," Jack said. "He'd rather lose the money."

"That occurred to me. It also explains why he wasn't that enthusiastic about my talking to any of Bonnie's colleagues. What do you think of the notion that she needed the money to pay off a drug dealer?"

"It could be."

"Linda Rosenberg and Christine Cameron seem to think so."

"You seem to be tending in that direction yourself," Jack said. "Wasn't it only yesterday you were convinced that Bonnie was the victim of a gypsy swindle? That maybe she really believed she had brain cancer?"

I looked at him. "Do you think I'm jumping to conclusions?"

"Not exactly," he said. "But you're at the point where you have to keep an open mind. Even if the two women you talked to today are more reliable witnesses than DiBenedetto, and they probably are, you've gotta remember they're only speculating. And, what's more, they're speculating on the basis of what DiBenedetto told them about Bonnie. You still don't know that he didn't invent that story about her coming to him for money, or even if she did, that he didn't invent the reasons she asked for it."

I was silent for a moment, mulling over his words. "You're right," I said finally. "I'm not being objective." I sighed. "I really don't like the woman, so I suppose I'm inclined to believe the worst about her."

"Well, at least you recognize that, so you can compensate for it. A lot of people wouldn't."

I smiled at him again. "Thank you again."

"You're welcome," he said formally, and I laughed. "You're the detective," I said. "Sort the wheat from the chaff for me, and tell me what it is out of all I've heard these past two days about Bonnie that I can take to the bank."

"Hmmmm," Jack said. "Well, I think you can accept that she hasn't shown up for work for a month."

"And?"

"That's all. The other stuff you'd have to put in the category of probability, or possibility, or wait and see."

"Oh." I must have sounded discouraged, or disappointed, because he said, "It's better than nothing."

"I guess."

"And," he added. "Remember you're just starting your background investigation."

I wriggled a little closer to him and put my right hand on his stomach. "Any suggestions about how I should proceed from here?"

"Yes. Just move your hand a little lower down."

"Twice in one hour?" I said. "You must have had oysters for lunch. I was asking you about where I should go with the Bonnie business."

"You mean you want me to act in an advisory capacity?"

"Let's say as a special consultant."

He smiled and then looked thoughtful. "Okay," he said. "If I were you, here's what I'd do."

* * *

The next morning I called Christine Cameron at her office and asked her if it would be possible for her to get hold of Bonnie Nordgren's personnel file.

"Sure," she said. "No problem. All the files are in an unlocked cabinet in the department secretary's office. Should I make a photocopy and send it to you?"

"If you would," I said gratefully. "Are you sure it's no trouble?"

"None at all. All I have to do is wait till the secretary goes to lunch. It'll take me two minutes."

"For that you get dinner on me," I said. "Linda, too."

"We accept," Christine replied. "I have a class to get to now. I'll call you back at, oh, three-thirty in case there's a hitch."

"Call me back even if there isn't," I said. "I'll probably have some more questions to ask you."

"Oh? Are you onto something?"

"Not quite yet," I said. "But at least I have a vague notion of where I'm going."

"Well done," she said. "Talk to you later."

I showered and dressed and took Lucy to the park to stretch her legs. For a half an hour, I sat on a bench and watched her gallop around the green sniffing the base of trash cans and tree trunks, and pursue, fruitlessly, the occasional squirrel. Afterward, I took her back to the apartment and left her there with a fresh bowl of water and some dog cookies and an admonition to "mind the house." The admonition was purely rhetorical in view of the fact that Lucy, while hysterically affectionate toward any friend I let into my apartment, would bite the head off anyone who broke into it. The perfect dog.

Bonnie Nordgren lived on Huron Avenue in north Cambridge. Her building was a well-kept dark brown frame three-decker with a front porch and postage stamp–sized yard. I guessed there were six apartments in the house. Bonnie's was number five, which meant it was probably on the third floor.

I went up the steps to the front door and looked at the row of mailboxes next to it. Taped to the box for apartment five was a little white card with "Nordgren" printed on it. Unless

Bonnie's roommate had the same last name, then, she wasn't officially living in the apartment. Or at least, she wasn't receiving mail there. Interesting. But did it mean anything?

I rang the doorbell for apartment five. No answer. I rang it again, pressing the button a little longer this time. The speaker in the intercom remained silent. I tried the front door, a heavy affair of solid oak. It didn't budge.

I crossed the street and walked a block down to a luncheonette. I used the pay phone to call Bonnie. The line was busy, as it had been the other day. It always was in the daytime, according to Carl DiBenedetto and Linda Rosenberg. The phone was probably off the hook, which could mean that either Bonnie or the roommate or both were home. I hung up, retrieved my dime, and left the luncheonette.

I stood for a moment on the sidewalk outside the restaurant, gazing back up the street at Bonnie's three-decker. I had an odd little vision of her huddled up there in her third floor apartment, listening to the doorbell ring, and waiting and hoping for whoever was down there to go away. Far as I could tell, she was less a person missing than a person hiding.

If she were in trouble with a drug dealer, holing up in her apartment wouldn't offer her much protection. If the bad guys wanted her, they'd go in there and get her.

What they would do to her if she'd welshed on a drug payment was something I assiduously avoided thinking about on the way home.

Christine Cameron called me a little after three-thirty to tell me she had a photocopy of Bonnie's personnel file on the desk before her.

"That's terrific," I said. "Thank you, and thank you again."

"You're welcome. I'll just pop it in an envelope and drop it at the post office on my way home."

"Perfect," I said. "Could I ask just one more favor of you?"

"Sure."

"In Bonnie's file, is there the name of somebody who can be reached in case of emergency?"

"Probably," Christine replied. "Let me check." She set the receiver of the phone down on her desk. I could hear, faintly, the rustling of papers. After about ten seconds, Christine's voice came back on the line.

"She's got a Frank Nordgren listed as next of kin. Probably her father. Want the phone number and address?"

"Yes."

Frank Nordgren lived in some hamlet in North Carolina I'd never heard of. When I finished writing down that information, I said, "One more thing."

Christine laughed. "What's that?"

"Bonnie's roommate. Could you describe her to me?"

"Well, I'll try. I only saw her a few times."

"More than I have," I said.

"Okay." Christine was silent for a moment. "Far as I can recall, she was kind of attractive, in a prim way. Like a librarian. Tall, maybe five-eight or so. Sort of average figure."

"How old would you say she is?"

"Well, that's the hard part. She had a fairly young face, but her hair was about two-thirds gray. She could have been anywhere between twenty and fifty."

"But if you had to guess?"

"I'd say mid- or late thirties. She wore her hair short, by the way. And the part that wasn't gray was black."

I was writing all this down in my little spiral notebook. "Eyes?"

"I beg your pardon?"

"Did you notice the color eyes she had?"

"Sorry."

"Don't be," I said. "You've given me plenty already."

"I have?" She sounded startled. "Well, that's good."

I thanked her again and told her I'd call her back in a few days to set up a time for dinner.

"And don't forget," she said. "I want a full report on your findings."

"You'll get one."

After we'd hung up, I looked at the notebook page with Frank Nordgren's name and address written on it. The prospect of what I was going to do next didn't enchant me. I sighed, picked up the phone, and dialed the North Carolina number.

A woman's voice answered.

"Hello," I said. "May I please speak to Mrs. Nordgren?"

"This Miz Nordgren," the woman replied.

"Hi," I said brightly. "My name is Paula Clarke. I'm calling from the Brown University English Department and we're doing a follow-up on some of our recent graduates."

"You mean mah daughter Bonnie," Mrs. Nordgren drawled. "She's not here. She's livin' up in Massachusetts now. She's teachin' at Thatcher College."

"Oh, how nice," I said, with the same inane brightness. "And how is she doing?"

"Verra well," Mrs. Nordgren replied. "Ah had a letter from her just last week, and she sounded very happy."

"That's lovely," I said. I wanted to puke at myself for so deceiving this nice woman.

"Ah kin give you her address," Mrs. Nordgren offered.

It would have sounded peculiar to refuse. "I'd appreciate that."

She recited Bonnie's Huron Avenue address to me.

I didn't want the conversation to end there, where it logically should have, so I said, "I'll be calling Bonnie myself tomorrow, but, if it's no bother, perhaps I could ask you another question or two."

"Surely."

"One of the things we're following up on is the scholarly work our graduates are doing. Has Bonnie published any articles on William Carlos Williams? Is she working on a book?"

There was a brief silence on the other end of the line. "Ah *think* so," Mrs. Nordgren said. "She mentioned somethin' about that when she was home at Christmas."

"Good," I said. "One other question and then I'll let you go."

"Yes?"

"Has Bonnie gotten married?"

"Why, no." Mrs. Nordgren paused again, and then gave a little laugh. "Ah think she has a beau, though."

A *beau*? "How nice," I said, idiotically.

"She told me a little bit about him at Christmas," Mrs. Nordgren continued. "He has a job in government up theah, Ah think."

"Are they planning to be married?"

"Ah don't know," Mrs. Nordgren sighed. "Bonnie's not gettin' any younger."

I wished I could introduce Mrs. Nordgren to my mother. They could sing the lament chorus together.

"It certainly has been nice talkin' to you," Mrs. Nordgren said.

I took that as a sign she wanted to end the conversation. "You, too," I said.

"When you speak to mah daughter," Mrs. Nordgren instructed. "You give her mah love, heah? And tell her to call or write more often. That last letter Ah had from her was the first in six weeks."

"I'll do that," I said, feeling my throat tighten. "Thank you for being so helpful."

"Mah pleasure."

We said good-bye and hung up.

I looked at the clock. It was five after five. The cocktail hour. Good.

I needed a drink to wash from my mouth the bad taste of what I'd just done.

6

It took me a little while to isolate why I felt so excessively lousy over having conned Mrs. Nordgren. I'd run countless similar games on people in the past when I was looking for information for an article and knew I wouldn't get it unless I pretended to be someone other than myself. I'd always felt fine afterward.

Halfway through my drink I figured out that the difference was that all those other folks I'd scammed had been pretty sleazy people themselves. They hadn't been some nice lady lovingly anxious about the happiness of a daughter she wasn't aware was probably mired down in some very deep trouble.

I faced up to the realization that I was an ethical relativist. Then I prepared dinner and ate it, read for a while, watched a rerun of "Mary Tyler Moore" on one of the double-digit channels, took the dog out, and went to bed. The following morning I was walking down Huron Avenue to Bonnie's place, carrying a paperbound copy of the poems of William Carlos Williams.

The brown frame three-decker looked as innocuous as it had yesterday. I rang the doorbell for apartment five out of form rather than out of any expectation that it would be answered. It wasn't. Nobody in apartments six, four, three, or two was answering, either. I rang the bell for apartment one. No response. I was about to leave when the intercom crackled and a voice that sounded like that of an elderly woman said, "Who is it?"

I leaned forward to the speaker. "I have a book to return to Bonnie Nordgren in apartment five," I replied. "There's no one home up there, and I'd like to leave it inside, if I may." I stepped back a little from the intercom, to afford the woman in apartment one a better view of me in case she wanted to peek out the window and make sure I wasn't the Cambridge Strangler.

If there was such an inspection, I apparently passed it. "Just a minute," the voice said. I heard footsteps and then the sound of a bolt being drawn. The heavy door opened about five inches and a small wrinkled face appeared in the crack. I smiled down at it. The door opened a little wider.

The woman who answered it was perhaps five feet tall, at a generous estimate, and pipe-cleaner thin. Her sparse white hair was cut close, like a cap, pink scalp showing through it. The brown eyes that peered up at me were astonishingly bright and shrewd. The woman looked like a geriatric sparrow.

"Hello," I said. I held up the book. "Is there someplace I could leave this? It's too big to put in the mailbox."

The woman pursed her lips. "Well," she said slowly. "I could take it, I guess."

"I'd appreciate that."

"Bonnie's not usually home in the daytime," the woman continued. "She works at some college."

Here was my opening. "I know. But I haven't been able to get in touch with her there, either. And I've been trying for a few weeks now. I hope she's not sick or anything."

The gimmick worked. The woman's bright gaze grew even sharper with interest.

"Have *you* seen Bonnie lately?" I asked in a concerned voice.

The woman frowned thoughtfully. "I *think* . . ." she began. She stopped speaking and frowned harder.

"Yes?" I prodded.

"I *think* I saw her, oh, last week some time. She was on her way out somewhere." The frown relaxed. "She didn't look sick, that I noticed."

"Well, she probably isn't, then," I said cheerfully. "And if she were, her roommate would be around to help out, I suppose."

"You mean Gayle," the woman said.

"That's her."

"I don't see her that much," the woman said. "She only moved in a few months ago."

About a month before Bonnie had pulled her vanishing act, I reflected. "Oh," I said. "Sometime around March first, would that be?"

"That seems about right," the woman nodded. "I think Gayle's staying with Bonnie till she can find a place of her own."

"Not too easy in Cambridge," I said. "All the nice apartments get snapped up very quickly."

The woman smiled her agreement. Then she glanced over her shoulder at her open apartment door. "I have something on the stove . . ."

No hint is too subtle for me. "Then I won't keep you a moment longer," I said, and held out the paperback William Carlos Williams. Tucked inside the front cover was a small, sealed, white envelope with Bonnie's name written on it. In the envelope was a note that read:

> Professor DiBenedetto asked me to get in touch with you. If there's a problem, I might be able to help.

Beneath that, I'd written my name, address, and phone number.

The woman took the book, smiled at me, and closed the door. I heard the click of a deadbolt being shot into place and, a moment later, the soft thud of another door closing.

I had an early lunch in the little restaurant down the street. I took a seat by the window so I could keep an eye on Bonnie's place. No one went in or out of it. After one hour, one bad hamburger, and three cups of worse coffee, I called it quits.

If I'd had a car, I could have parked it outside the brown

three-decker and sat there until a cop came along and told me to move. Since I didn't, I walked over to the branch of the public library two blocks away, used their ladies' room, and killed the rest of the afternoon in the periodicals room reading back issues of *Esquire* and *Harper's* and *Vanity Fair*. None of them had anything to say about Bonnie Nordgren, or about what her problem might be.

At five I went back to the luncheonette, ordered an iced tea, and parked myself at the window seat I'd occupied earlier. The iced tea was a step up from the coffee, but not a big one. I sipped it gingerly and stared out the window. At five-fifteen a silver Volvo sedan cruised down the street, stopped, and then backed into an empty space in front of Bonnie's house. A tallish woman with dark hair that from this distance looked frosted emerged from the driver's side of the car. She was wearing a dark blue suit and carrying a black briefcase with a shoulder strap. She looked as if she were about to argue a landmark case before the Supreme Court.

I put some tip money on the cracked Formica tabletop, left the restaurant, and walked quickly back up the street. As I crossed it, I yelled, "Gayle?"

The blue-suited woman was walking up the flagstone path to the house. At the sound of my voice she halted, then rotated slowly to face me. I trotted the rest of the way across the street, smiling in friendly fashion. If I stopped to think about what I was doing, I would have felt like an Olympic-grade horse's ass.

The woman watched me neutrally as I approached her. The closer I got, the more she resembled Christine Cameron's description of Bonnie's roommate. The hair was mostly gray, not frosted, but thick and expensively styled. Her makeup job looked professional.

I halted when I was about ten feet away from her. "Gayle?" I repeated.

The woman looked me over coolly. I was wearing threadbare Levi's and a U/Mass—Boston tee shirt. An incredible fashion statement. *My* makeup job wasn't Piscasso's Clown, but it wasn't Elizabeth Arden, either. The woman said nothing.

"Hi," I said, still grinning.

The woman gave me another appraising glance. "Do I know you?"

She didn't sound as if she wanted to. "No," I said. "I'm an acquaintance of your friend Bonnie."

It might have been my imagination, but I thought that the woman stiffened slightly, like a retriever on point. "Yes?"

"I've been trying to get in touch with her for a while now," I said. "And I haven't been able to."

Gayle—I was sure that's who she was—stared at me for a moment longer. "When I see Bonnie, I'll tell her you were asking for her." The woman turned and resumed walking up the path to the house. A friendly sort. Ms. Warmth.

"Now, how can you tell Bonnie I was asking for her?" I said to Gayle's retreating back. "You don't even know my name. It's Liz Connors, by the way."

The woman paused with her right foot on the first step leading up to the front porch.

"This is extremely silly," I said. "A number of people are concerned about what's happened to Bonnie. Wouldn't it be the simplest thing to let me see her and talk to her myself and set their minds at rest?"

Gayle turned to face me. As Chris Cameron had observed, she was a nice-looking woman. But there was something eerily robotic about her manner. Her demeanor was too precise.

"Bonnie's fine," Gayle said. "She's very busy."

I folded my arms across my chest and cocked my head. "Oh, really?" I said. "Is that why she disappeared from her job?"

For a moment of frozen silence we stared at each other. Gayle's face was hard and flat. "Bonnie's busy," she repeated. The strap of her briefcase was beginning to slide down over her shoulder, and, impatiently, she twitched it back into place. Forgetting that she had one foot on the step behind her, she moved back a pace and stumbled a bit. She caught herself, then swung around and went up the rest of the steps to the apartment building. Actually she ran, as if she were eager to get away from me. I was sure she was.

I watched as Gayle took a key from her purse to unlock the front door.

"Whatever Bonnie's situation is," I called. "Your attitude is not doing a hell of a lot to improve it."

The woman fumbled a second with the key before she got it into the lock and turned it. I'd really upset her. She opened the door, stepped inside the house, and slammed the door behind her. The lower-floor windows rattled.

"Bitch," I mumbled. Nonetheless, I wasn't particularly displeased by her reaction. I had the feeling I'd stirred things up, and thereby made some kind of headway. Too early to tell what, though.

I dug in my handbag for something to write on. All I came up with was a supermarket check. Good enough. On the back of it I copied down the license plate number of the silver Volvo. Then I went home to feed the dog.

7

I gave Jack the license number to run through the police department computer for me. The silver Volvo was registered to one Gayle Patricia Lydecker, who had a Waltham address. There were no warrants out for Lydecker, nor had she accumulated any traffic violations. She hadn't looked like the kind who would.

I found a phone number for G.P. Lydecker in the western suburban directory and called it. I got a recorded message that the number had been disconnected. The information didn't exactly come as a surprise.

Bonnie's personnel file arrived in the morning mail. I curled up on the couch to read it with the kind of anticipatory pleasure I'd feel opening a new novel by one of my favorite authors. *The Life and Good Times of a Con Artist*, by B. Nordgren.

Bonnie had three letters of recommendation, all glowing testimonials to her scholarly brilliance and teaching ability. Two were from professors at Brown and the third from a professor at Emory. All three referees were male. That made me grin to myself.

I leafed through the rest of the file, carefully studying each page, but found only one other interesting piece of information. According to her curriculum vitae, Bonnie had received her doctorate two years ago. After that, she'd had a part-time teaching job at Currier College in Lexington. I knew a guy on the faculty there, Dan Fowler. I'd give Dan a call and ask him what he had to say about dear old Bonnie.

Apparently he had plenty, but he refused to divulge any of it over the phone.

"Why?" I teased. "Is your office bugged?"

"Let's put it this way," he said. "Around here, anything is possible."

I laughed, and asked him if we could get together somewhere else to talk.

"Well, I have to go to the Widener Library this afternoon. We could meet there, if you want."

"Fine."

"Better still," Dan said. "Why don't I do what I have to do in the library, then meet you at the Fogg Museum?"

"Great," I replied. "I haven't been there in ages."

"Okay. See you around four, huh?"

"Sure."

As soon as I hung up the phone, it rang. The caller was Linda Rosenberg.

"Hiya," I said. "Nice to hear from you. How's things at Thatcher?"

"Sucky," Linda said. "So what else is new?"

Business as usual in academe, I supposed.

"Have you found Bonnie yet?" Linda asked.

"No," I said. "But I'm closing in. By the way, you were quite right about there being something fishy with her roommate."

"You mean you've spoken to Gayle?"

"Face to face." I described to Linda my confrontation with Gayle Lydecker. "She reminds me of a sort of well-groomed android."

Linda laughed. "That's a very good description. Listen, I have a tidbit for you."

"Oh? What's that?"

"Bonnie's been fired—terminated is the word they use—by Thatcher."

"Oh," I said. "Oh, my. Who did the canning. Not Carl?"

"God, no," Linda replied feelingly. "No, the dean wrote her a letter telling her that her services would no longer be required."

"Well, she hasn't been providing them for over a month now, has she?"

"No," Linda said. "But I think they were giving her the benefit of the doubt in case she really was sick. Physically or mentally. About a week after she took off, the dean wrote to her asking if she'd have her doctor send him some kind of medical excuse or whatever."

"And?"

"Bonnie never answered the letter."

"What happened after that?"

"The dean wrote her another letter making the same request."

"And she didn't respond to that, either."

"Nope."

"Wow," I said. "Heavy."

"Uh-huh."

"So who took over teaching her classes?"

"Who do you think?" Linda asked, in a voice leaden with disgust.

I smiled. "You and Chris?"

"Me and Chris. The Sap Sisters."

"Maybe you'll get a bonus."

"From this place? Fat chance."

I could sympathize.

After we hung up, I did some housework. The living room badly needed a vacuuming. The dustballs under the couch were as big as Lucy. In fact, the only way you could distinguish dog from dustball was that the latter didn't have tails to wag.

Someday someone will have to give me the scientific explanation for the origin and growth of dustballs. I swear mine appear the size of volleyballs a half hour after I've finished a major league cleaning.

The Fogg was very quiet on a midweek afternoon in early May. I was just inside the entrance, reading the schedule for the museum's concert series, when Dan Fowler arrived.

Fowler was what the originator of the phrase "tall, dark, and handsome" must have had in mind when he or she invented the cliché. His tan was permanent from skiing in the winter and swimming in the summer. Today he was making the most of it with a white broadcloth shirt. The guy was so dazzling that you had to blink when you looked at him.

Oh, yes. He also had a brilliant mind and an outrageous sense of humor. Of course.

He bounded up to me and we hugged in the warm, asexual way of old friends.

"Good to see you," I said.

"And you," he replied.

We drew apart and smiled at each other.

"Did you get all your work done at the library?" I asked.

"No," he said. "But the hell with it."

"Shall we walk around?"

"Sure." He glanced up at the second floor gallery. "I think there's an exhibition of the English pre-Raphaelites up there."

I made a dubious face.

"Oh, come on," Dan said. "Holman Hunt's always good for a chuckle or two."

I laughed. "Okay."

We went up the stone staircase with its vaulted ceiling and out onto the colonnaded gallery. I felt as if I ought to be wearing a green velvet surcoat rather than denim skirt and gauze blouse. I always had that feeling when I went to the Fogg.

"So," Dan said, as we paced slowly down the right side of the gallery. "You want to know about Bonnie Nordgren, do you?"

"Please."

He looked at me curiously. "What's your particular interest in her?"

I went through the whole saga for him. It took us three turns around the gallery. I kept my voice hushed, as befit the setting.

"Lawsie me," he remarked when I'd finished.

"Exactly," I replied. "So? You worked with the girl for a year. You must know stuff about her that I don't."

We were standing in front of a most peculiar Burne-Jones painting entitled *Depths of the Sea*. It featured a submerged nude couple with bubbles coming from their mouths.

"Your assessment of Bonnie sounds about right," Dan said.

"Come on."

He smiled at me, then glanced at the Burne-Jones and seemed to recoil just slightly.

"Bonnie's first real job after graduate school was at Currier," I said. "But I noticed when I was looking through her personnel file that she doesn't have a reference from anyone there."

"No," Dan said. We resumed walking. As we passed *The Blessed Damozel*, he added, "It's not likely she would."

I widened my eyes at him. "Oh?"

"We had a bit of trouble with her. Nothing as outlandish as what you've described. She was sort of erratic about showing up for class."

"That's a cardinal sin in the teaching profession, Dan."

"Uh-huh."

"How were your relations with her?"

"Mine?" He shrugged, then laughed in a sort of self-conscious way. "When I first met her, I had the feeling she was trying to come on to me."

"Who would blame her?" I reached up to pat his shoulder. "I'm sure she did make a play for you."

"Yes, well," he said. "If she did, she stopped doing it very abruptly. I suppose someone else in the department took her aside and whispered in her ear that I'm gay."

"Let me guess," I said. "Following *that* revelation, she ignored you."

"More or less." He gave me a wry smile. "How did you figure that?"

"Isn't it obvious?" I asked as we strolled by a pair of G.F. Watts oils. "You weren't the kind of guy who'd be useful to her."

"No," he agreed. "But there were others to take up the slack."

"I'm not surprised," I said. "Who?"

"Well, there was one unbelievably unattractive guy who used to hang with her."

"Yeah?"

"He was"—Dan stopped abruptly before a frenetic Holman Hunt canvas entitled *The Miracle of the Sacred Fire*—"her friend, or whatever he was, didn't look like the kind of friend your typical lady English professor would have."

"No?"

Dan narrowed his eyes thoughtfully. "He was kind of thuggy-looking, I guess. Sort of heavyset. Grubby dresser. Doughy face."

"Be still, my heart," I said. "A real dese-dem-dose guy, huh?"

Dan laughed. "Not a bad way of putting it."

"You're right," I said. "He and Bonnie *do* sound like an unlikely duo. The two of them must have raised some eyebrows strolling arm in arm around the Currier campus."

"Oh, it was nothing like that," Dan assured me. "I only saw this stud maybe four or five times over the whole year. Probably nobody else ever noticed him. Only reason I did was that I had the office next to Bonnie's. The thug picked her up after work one day, I remember."

"Do you think he was a student of hers?"

"Gawd," Dan said. "I hope not. Currier isn't too selective in its admissions, but I don't think we're at the stage where we have to accept Piltdown Man just to foot the bills."

I laughed.

"Nah," Dan said. "He wasn't her student. Too old."

We had completed our fifth circuit of the gallery.

"Can we go downstairs and look at something decent for a change?" I asked plaintively. "Like the medieval and Renaissance stuff?"

Dan looked amused. "Certainly, dear."

We went back down the Gothic staircase and into the room that housed thirteenth- and fourteenth-century Italian paintings. In the far left corner was a group of perhaps ten students, being lectured to by a pleasant-looking late-thirtyish woman on the use of light and color in the quattrocento. Each kid was armed with a notebook and was assiduously scribbling down everything the instructor said.

"Anything else?" I asked.

Dan was inspecting a triptych. "About what?" he replied absently.

"About Bonnie. How she behaved. You said she was sort of erratic about coming to class. What else was there?"

Still gazing at the triptych, he shrugged. "Hard to say. I never got to know her. I don't think anyone in the department did. She was careful to keep everyone at arm's length."

"Did you ever meet a woman named Gayle Lydecker?"

He looked at me, then, and frowned. "Don't *think* so," he said slowly. "Nope. Name doesn't ring a bell. Why?"

"She lives with Bonnie. Babysits her, actually."

He raised his eyebrows.

I smiled. "I don't know. Somebody suggested to me that

she and Bonnie could be lovers, but I couldn't say. How could I?''

''Neither could I. I assumed she was straight.''

''Maybe she alternates.''

He laughed softly, so as not to disturb the scholars, and shook his head.

''Seriously,'' I said. ''Do you have any other impressions of her that you could give me?''

''Like what?''

''Anything at all.'' I hesitated a moment. ''Okay, I'll be blunt. Did you ever spot any sign in her speech or behavior, no matter how slight, of mental instability?''

''My dear,'' Dan said, as we walked into the sixteenth-century Italian room. ''Are you asking me was sweet Bonnie cuckoo?''

''Yeah. I guess I am.''

He blew out a long breath. ''Hooo. I don't know. What's crazy, these days? Okay, yes. She seemed a little flaky to me. Not a raving lunatic, you understand. But she wasn't playing with all fifty-two cards. There was one thing . . .'' His voice trailed off.

''Yes.''

He sucked in his upper lip and then released it. ''Even on such a minimal acquaintance, she struck me as possibly the most self-absorbed person I'd ever met.''

''Like narcissistic?''

''Not that.'' He grimaced. ''Beyond that. It's very hard to describe.''

''I think I know what you mean.''

He shook his head. ''No, you'd have to see something like that in operation in order to appreciate it.'' He raised his hands and held them about two feet apart, like someone measuring a fish. ''It was . . . she was completely engrossed in herself. So much that as far as I could tell, external reality didn't impinge. She didn't seem to have any, oh, I don't know, *involvement* with anything.'' He shook his head again, almost angrily. ''I'm not making myself clear.''

''Clear enough.''

"I don't think she could be like that, and still be entirely sane."

I nodded. "What about drugs?"

"What about them?"

"Did you ever have any reason to think Bonnie might be doing them?"

He blinked at me. "Well, dear, I never noticed any free-basing equipment or bhongs lying around her office."

"I don't think even Bonnie would have gone quite that far. But other than that?"

He shrugged. "It wouldn't surprise me."

"Okay. Did you ever get any sense that she might be unusually interested in the occult?"

He threw me a look of comically exaggerated astonishment. "Jesus, what is this? Next thing you'll be asking me about black masses in the college chapel and midnight orgies in the gym."

"Dan."

"I don't know."

"Okay."

We strolled into the Baroque room, which seemed a strikingly appropriate setting for the kind of conversation we were having.

"Can we go back to a previous point?" I asked.

"Sure."

"You suggested that Currier wasn't all that pleased with Bonnie's work."

"No. If a full-time position had come up, and she'd applied for it, I don't think they'd have considered her for it. In fact, I *know* they wouldn't have. They didn't even ask her to come back on a part-time basis."

I shook my head slowly. "So she really screwed up, huh?"

"Well, yes. Not on the grand scale she apparently did at Thatcher, but yes. She did."

I scowled at a portrait of an attenuated seventeenth-century brunette. "Funny," I said.

"Why?"

We drifted out of the Baroque room, past the Graphics rooms, and into Baroque and Rococo.

"Well, look," I said. "The woman went to the trouble to get a doctorate in English from a good school. That presumes that she wanted a college teaching job. There aren't many of those jobs available nowadays. You get one, you hang onto it. Or at least, you try to do decent work so you can get good references to get a better job someplace else. Right?"

"Uh-huh." Dan nodded.

I turned to face him. "So why would Bonnie sabotage—knowingly, as far as I can tell—her own career?"

"I already told you that?"

"You did?"

"Sure." Dan grinned. "She was nuts."

8

Out of all the things Dan had told me about Bonnie, the information that interested me the most was the stuff about her male buddy. Dan was right; one thug and one William Carlos Williams scholar made a notable, if vividly improbably, combination. It was hard to believe Bonnie would date a character like that. How desperate for male attention could she be? She was certainly physically attractive enough to appeal, at least initially, to a nicer type of man. And the fact that she was probably semibananas wouldn't discourage even some of them. A lot of guys like ditsy women. The Marilyn Monroe syndrome.

I called Dan at home the next evening. I could hear television noises in the background when he answered the phone.

"Busy?" I asked.

"Nope. Just watching 'Wheel of Fortune.' I try never to miss it."

"I can call back later."

"That was a joke, dear," he replied. "What's up?"

"I wanted to pursue something we talked about yesterday."

"What's that?"

"Bonnie's boyfriend. The thug."

"What about him?"

"Well, that's just it. Did you really think he was a guy she was going out with? A romantic interest? Or were you just being snotty?"

He was silent for so long I thought the connection had been broken.

"Dan?"

"I'm thinking. You know how hard that is for me, Liz."

"Oh. Sorry."

A few more seconds passed. Then he said, "Okay, I see what you're driving at. You want to know if I could tell from the way she acted around that guy what her relationship with him was."

"Uh-huh."

"All right. Well, yes, I *was* being snotty when I implied that they were lovers."

"I see."

"I had the sense she was close to him in some way. Not necessarily sexual. I mean, she didn't start throwing off sparks when he showed up. He went into her office one day, and they stayed in there with the door closed for about an hour. I'm sure they weren't having at it on the desk, though."

"Did he ever act nasty toward her?"

"Not that I noticed. Why?"

I laughed. "I was thinking he was the drug dealer showing up to collect payment."

"Well, I never heard him threaten to bring on the propane torches."

"Did you ever overhear *any* kind of conversation between them?"

He was silent again for a moment. Then he said, "Just bits and pieces."

"And?"

"All very casual and innocuous. Meaningless to me."

"Can you remember any of it?"

He laughed. "No, honey, I can't. I didn't dedicate myself to eavesdropping on them."

The fact that he couldn't recall any of the conversational passages between Bonnie and her friend probably meant that there wasn't any substance to recall.

"What else?" I said.

"Nothing," Dan replied. "He was obviously a guy she felt comfortable with, that she had some close connection with. I'm pretty sure it wasn't sexual, and I'm damned sure it wasn't intellectual. That dude wasn't a metaphysician."

"I wonder what the bond was, then?" I said, half to myself.

"I couldn't say."

"I know, but thank you for trying."

"My pleasure, love."

"I'll let you get back to 'Wheel of Fortune.' "

When we ended the call, I was more mystified than I had been before I'd made it.

I looked up Chris Cameron's home phone number and dialed it. A man I took to be her husband answered and told me that she wouldn't be in for another hour or so. I left a message for her to call me back when she got home, if it was convenient. Then I tried to call Linda Rosenberg's number. No answer.

Jack was in New Haven, attending a two-day seminar on organized crime. He'd be home and at work tomorrow morning. If he'd been here now, we'd have been having dinner together and I'd be sharing my perplexity with him.

Lucy and I went for a stroll around the neighborhood.

When we got back to the apartment, I opened a can of the liver-flavored grayish slop she favors for dinner and made some scrambled eggs and salad for myself.

I took the food into the living room and switched on the television to catch the world and national news program. It was a few minutes before seven, and the local newscast was still in progress. The entertainment reporter did a movie review and then ran the tape of a piece on a benefit fashion show and cocktail party held at the Copley Plaza. The reporter was waylaying the guests as they arrived at the hotel entrance.

She ambushed a nice-looking dark-haired man and his even better-looking date, and said, "Good to see you here this evening, Senator Levesque, Mrs. Frattiani."

"Nice to be here, Kitty," the man replied, flashing a white-toothed grin. "Especially for such a worthy cause." He glanced fondly at the woman beside him. "Camille here organized the whole thing, you know."

"And you did a wonderful job," the reporter said to Mrs. Frattiani.

The woman smiled. "It was a pleasure." She certainly was gorgeous. She also looked sort of familiar to me. Well, if she were some kind of heavy-duty socialite, I'd probably seen her picture in the papers before.

"Senator, any truth to all the rumors we've been hearing about your plans to move beyond the state legislature?" the reporter asked. "To some higher office?"

The senator laughed and shook his head. "My only plan at this point is to keep doing the best job I can for the folks in my district."

The film ended. I ate my eggs. "World News Tonight" commenced. The lead story was an upbeat number about famine conditions in Pakistan. Maybe all the folks boogying down at the Copley Plaza could send their leftover canapés there.

The phone rang a little after eight. It was Chris Cameron returning my call. She wanted to know if I'd heard that Bonnie had been fired by Thatcher. I told her that Linda had already supplied me with that intelligence. Chris said that as far as she understood, even the notice of dismissal hadn't prompted Bonnie to get in touch with anyone else at the school.

"Why would she?" I asked. "Who would intercede for her, except maybe Carl? And from what you say, no one would listen to him anyhow."

"I suppose," Chris said in reflective tones. Then, in a more animated voice, she added, "How's your investigation going?"

"Okay," I replied. "Got a minute?"

"Sure."

"I have another question or two for you."

"Go ahead."

"All right. The first thing is, did Bonnie ever have any men visitors at the school?"

"Men visitors," Chris repeated. "You mean like boyfriends?"

"*Any* kind of guy visitor," I said. "Except students or faculty, of course."

"Hmmmm. Let me think."

I waited.

"No," she said. "At least, I never saw anyone like that with her or around her office."

"Oh."

"You sound disappointed."

"Not exactly," I said. "It's just that somebody I know who worked with Bonnie before she got hired by your place told me she was on very good terms with a really unsavory character who would drop in to her office every so often."

"*Really?* Oh, tell me about it."

I repeated to her what Dan had told me. I was beginning to feel like the gossip columnist for the *Boston Herald*.

"A drug dealer," Chris said with a great deal of conviction.

"Maybe," I temporized. "But there's another element in this."

"Oh?"

"When I talked to Bonnie's mother, she told me that Bonnie'd said something to her about having a steady boyfriend. In fact, she referred to him as Bonnie's 'beau.' You know anything about that?"

"Not a thing," Chris replied. "She never breathed a word of it to me. But then, as I told you, she and I never talked about much of anything, let alone personal stuff."

"Yeah, I figured," I said. "Oh, well. Just thought I'd try."

It occurred to me as I was getting ready for bed that evening that the more information I uncovered about Bonnie Nordgren, the more enigmatic a figure she became. One half of what I'd found out about her contradicted the other half. To her mother, she was "very happy," absorbed in her work and in a relationship with an eminently suitable man. To her colleagues, past and present, she was a borderline crazy, possibly a drug addict, almost certainly on intimate terms with a creepy person. *And* she was a crook.

I fell asleep trying to make some sense of this dichotomy. I didn't, of course, and it woke me at three. And again at five. Yet again at seven. At ten I got up, feeling logy, and shuffled off to the kitchen to make coffee.

I had showered and dressed and was putting on eye makeup when the phone rang. It was Jack, and the sound of his voice was like a shot of amphetamine.

"Sweetie," I cried happily. "You just get back?"

"No. I drove in about one this morning. Too late to call you."

"How was the seminar?"

"Okay. Listen, Liz, are you dressed yet?"

The question took me aback a little. Automatically, I glanced down at my shirt and jeans. "Yes. Why?"

"I have to talk to you. Here. At the station."

"Well, of course," I said, puzzled. "What about?"

"I'm sending somebody to pick you up. Can you be ready in about five minutes?"

"Sure. But—"

"I'll see you." He hung up, not even saying good-bye.

Bewildered, and just a tiny bit anxious, I scowled down at the phone.

I hustled Lucy outside to relieve herself and, when she'd finished and wanted to play, dragged her back inside and consoled her with a cookie. Then I grabbed my shoulder bag and trotted down to the street to await whoever it was Jack had sent to fetch me.

A minute later, a blue-and-white cruiser rolled down the street and pulled up in front of my house. Behind the wheel was a very young blonde cop. I knew him. He'd been a student of mine a summer ago, when I'd taught report writing at the police academy. He smiled at me and raised his right hand in greeting. I slid into the passenger seat. The young cop's name was Molinari, I recalled. Tommy Molinari. He'd done pretty well in the writing class.

"How you doing?" he asked as I shut the cruiser door.

"Fine," I said. "Nice to see you, Tom."

He smiled again and nodded and put the cruiser in gear. We backed down my street and out onto the main thoroughfare.

"So," I said. "What's the big emergency?"

He glanced at me with raised eyebrows and shook his head slightly. "Don't know that there is one. They just asked me to pick you up."

I nodded. He'd answered me just the way I'd supposed he would. Maybe he knew what was going on; maybe he didn't. Either way, he'd be neutral. Just the facts, ma'am. We made occasional conversation about non-police stuff all the way to Central Square.

Tommy dropped me off at the Green Street, or service, entrance to the police station. I went up the stairs to the CID without stopping to say hello to the people in the Crime Analysis Bureau.

The CID was mobbed. Or maybe it just seemed that way to me because normally there weren't more than three or four detectives present in the office at any one time. Everybody was supposed to be out on the street solving crimes and arresting bad guys, not sitting around shmoozing over coffee the way they do on cop shows. Crowd scenes in the CID were definitely out of the ordinary.

I paused beside the secretary's desk. About half the people directly in my line of vision were Cambridge detectives. Another two I vaguely recognized as investigators from the Middlesex County District Attorney's Office. I couldn't place any of the others.

Jack's office door was closed. I rapped on it, and his voice yelled, "Come in."

He was on the phone. With his free hand, he beckoned to me and nodded at the chair across from his desk.

"Yeah, I understand all that," Jack was saying. "No. They're not ready to move on this yet. Yeah. All right, I'll talk to you later." He hung up the phone, shook his head slowly, and said, *"Jesus."*

"Jolly mood you appear to be in," I remarked.

"Uh-huh." He made a motion with his mouth that somewhat approximated a smile. "Hi."

I cocked my head at his office door. "What's with the Crimebusters Convention out there?"

If he thought the question was funny, he didn't manifest any amusement. He leaned back in his chair, gazed at me flat-eyed, and said, "You know what we've had so far? One bank robbery, one rape, and one attempted murder. And that's just this morning. I can't *wait* to see what happens this afternoon."

"That's awful," I said. No wonder he'd been so curt with me earlier."

"However," Jack continued. "None of that has anything to do with you."

"Well, I should hope not," I said lightly.

He looked at me very seriously and said, "I have some . . . well, some bad news, I guess, for you."

I react to those words exactly the way anyone does. The noise from the outer office seemed, suddenly, to become dimmer. I sat still and silent, staring at Jack.

"That woman you've been trying to track down," Jack said. "Bonnie Nordgren."

Whatever I'd been expecting to hear, it wasn't her name. I could feel the anxiety ease up a little.

"She's dead," Jack said.

9

I stared at him for another few seconds. Then I turned my face aside and muttered. "God." I pressed my right hand to my mouth.

The office was very quiet. I let my hand fall to my lap and looked up at Jack. "What happened?" I said.

He shrugged. "Can't say, positively. It looked like an OD."

I let out my breath. "That's horrible. When did . . . ? Who . . . ?"

"Around eight-thirty this morning," Jack replied, correctly interpreting my ellipses. "The landlord."

"My God."

"Bonnie or her roommate had apparently complained to him about a leak in the kitchen sink," Jack continued. "So he went up there this morning to take a look at it. He knocked on the door, and didn't get any answer, so he figured they were both out. He let himself in with his passkey."

"And?"

"She was on the living room floor."

I winced.

"It looked like maybe she'd been sitting or lying on the couch. And rolled or fell off after she went under. Her nose was broken."

I furrowed my eyebrows at him.

"That probably happened when she hit the floor," Jack explained.

I could imagine the scene quite well. I hunched forward a little and crossed my arms over my chest.

"You okay?" Jack asked.

I sat up straight, quickly. "Yes."

He smiled at me. "Glad to hear it. 'Cause a couple of people want to talk to you about Bonnie."

I pulled my head back, turtlelike. "Me? Why? What do I know about her?"

He shrugged. Then he pushed back his chair and got to his feet. "Come with me."

I stood up, feeling apprehensive, and followed him out of the office. The Crimebusters Convention was still going strong. The two investigators from the district attorney's office zeroed in on us the moment we emerged from Jack's cubicle. I stepped back a pace, purely reflexively. All state cops look nine feet tall and menacing to me, even if they're only five-eleven and wearing three-piece suits. Jack noticed my reaction and rested a hand lightly on my shoulder.

"Liz," he said. "This is Joe McFadden and Bernie Carr."

I gave the two detectives a small smile. They smiled back at me, much more expansively.

"Where?" Carr said to Jack.

"Use the captain's office," Jack replied. He took his hand from my shoulder and patted the center of my back, half reassuring me, half shooing me along.

McFadden held the office door for me. I went into the room, Carr directly behind me as if he were afraid I might try to bolt. One of the Cambridge detectives joined us.

The captain's office was large, paper-strewn, and elegantly decorated with maps of Cambridge. The maps were divided into police sectors and studded with different colored drawing pins. Each color represented a particular crime. Red for housebreaks, green for muggings, blue for rapes, yellow for murders. Certain colors seemed to be clustered in certain places. None in *my* neighborhood, thank God.

McFadden parked me in a chair across from the captain's desk. Then he went to lean against the office door. He folded his arms and looked at me. The Cambridge detective, Bill Wallace, assumed the seat behind the captain's desk. He was a heavyset guy, about five-eight, with slicked-down wavy black hair. He shoved back the chair and set his feet on the desk blotter. He reached into the inside pocket of his suit coat, extracted a cigar, and stripped the cellophane from it. He dropped the cellophane on the floor, stuck the cigar in the center of his mouth, and lit a match. He was meticulous about lighting the cigar, turning it slowly to insure that it was evenly ignited.

Carr swung a ladder-backed chair from its resting place next to a file cabinet and planted it backward before me. He straddled it and crossed his arms across the top rung. Then he leaned forward so that his face was only about a foot from mine. I blinked, and wondered how many movies he'd studied in order to perfect that technique. His eyes were very blue. He rested his chin on his forearms. Wallace blew a cloud of smoke at the ceiling light fixture. I had the feeling the three of them were waiting for me to scream, "I confess."

"How well did you know Bonnie Nordgren?" Carr asked finally.

"Not at all," I blurted. "I only met her about twice."

Carr smiled at me. He had very white and even teeth. Ravishing.

From the doorway, McFadden said, "Jack told us you were looking for her."

"Well, yes," I replied. "A guy I know asked me to—" I stopped, bewildered. "Wait a minute. You must know all this. If Jack told you what I was doing."

Wallace puffed out another cloud of blue smoke. "You tell us," he suggested. He leaned forward and tapped the cigar into a dirty glass ashtray. "Take your time," he added.

"But . . ."

Carr gave me another blinding smile.

For the next twenty-five minutes, I emptied my head of

what I knew, thought, guessed, or suspected about Bonnie Nordgren. I was very careful to identify speculation as just that. Carr asked most of the questions. McFadden leaned and listened. Wallace wrote things down on a lined white pad and blew smoke around the room. Carr never took his eyes off my face. I had the sense that the other two were watching me just as carefully, although considerably less obtrusively. I had no notion of anyone's reaction to anything at all that I said.

When it was over, I wandered somewhat bemused from the captain's office, feeling as though I'd just had my brain reamed simultaneously by Drs. Freud, Adler, and Jung. Carr and McFadden followed me. Tweedledum and Tweedledee with guns. Wallace gave me a wink and brushed some ash from his lapel.

Jack was talking with one of the other Cambridge detectives. He spotted me standing and looking vacantly outside the captain's office, made a parting comment to the detective, and walked over to me. He was grinning. He put his left arm around my shoulders and his right hand under my chin. He tilted up my face and said, "Ah, now, did big bad Bernie hit you with a rubber hose?"

Carr was standing about five feet away. He shoved his hands in his hip pockets and leaned back slightly. "Nah," he said. "Hard cases like *her*, we go straight to the bamboo shoots under the fingernails."

I burst out laughing, along with everyone else within earshot, except for Carr himself. He gazed at me expressionlessly, rocking back on his heels. I had misread him. He was clearly more than just another pretty face.

Jack said, "Want some coffee?"

"What I'd like," I replied, "is an industrial-strength vodka martini. But it's too early. I'll take the coffee. Thanks."

He led me back to his office, got me settled, and fetched me a styrofoam cup of CID coffee. I stirred some artificial sweetener into it, took a sip, and tried to relax back into my chair. I had the comfortable swivel one behind the desk. Jack had the visitor's chair.

I put my coffee cup down on the desk and said, "What was all that about?"

Jack gave me a curious look, as if he were honestly puzzled by the question.

"Come on," I said. "Why is the DA's office investigating a drug overdose death? You guys get those all the time. What's the big deal here?" I was regaining my spirit, or at least making a show of so doing.

"Now look, Liz," Jack said pedantically. "You ought to know by now that any sudden, unattended death gets an investigation."

"Sure," I said. "But isn't something like . . . well, isn't how Bonnie died self-explanatory?" As soon as I'd finished speaking, I bit the inside of my lower lip. The question sounded far more callous than I'd intended or wanted it to.

Jack hesitated a moment. Then he said, "It's not exactly clear *how* Bonnie died."

I drew in a sharp breath. "But she—it was an accident, certainly."

He didn't say anything.

I stared at him. "It wasn't an accident?" I asked finally. "She killed herself?"

The police and the district attorney's office investigated suicides the precise same way they investigated homicides.

"Did she leave a note?" I said softly.

Jack shook his head. "No note. None that's turned up yet, anyway."

Mechanically, I reached for my coffee and took a gulp.

"I don't think she shot herself up with those drugs," Jack said.

I sat very still, the cup pressed against my lower lip. Then I said, "If she didn't, somebody else did."

"Uh-huh."

Involuntarily, my fingers tightened around the cup, crushing it so that a little of the coffee splashed onto the back of my hand. "But that's—my God, Jack. Bonnie was *murdered*?"

He didn't answer the question. No reason for him to do so; it was purely rhetorical.

10

I was shocked but, oddly, not terribly surprised. Probably on some level I'd been prepared for the possibility that a woman with Bonnie's recent history would come to a bad end at someone else's hands. Maybe I'd even been assuming that she would.

I felt some sadness, too. But it was the kind of abstract sadness you experience on hearing of the sudden, senseless death of any person. Especially a young one whom you'd known, however briefly and superficially. Someone had just blotted out that pretty, troubled girl. A hard thing to accept. Harder even than if she'd killed herself.

I set the coffee cup on Jack's desk and wiped the back of my hand on my jeans. "Can you tell me anything about it?" I asked.

He got up and went over to the office door and shut it. Then he turned back to me. "I really shouldn't say anything."

"You know I'll keep whatever you tell me to myself."

He nodded. "I trust you."

"Maybe I can help in some way," I offered. "After all, I know four people who know Bonnie, which is four more than you do." I leaned forward and rested my elbows on the desk blotter. "There's another thing, too."

Despite himself, he looked amused. "What's that?"

"Bonnie was an academic. And an aspiring writer."

"So?"

"So I have the kind of automatic entrée to academic and writing circles that you and"—I nodded at the office door—"Frick and Frack from the DA's office don't." I smiled at Jack. "I could be a valuable resource. You ought to exploit me."

"That made him laugh. "Have you had lunch yet?"

"No. I haven't even had breakfast."

"Well, come on, then. Let's get something to eat."

I raised my eyebrows. "And talk?"

"We'll see."

We left his office. Carr and McFadden were standing by the secretary's desk, approximately where I'd left them, talking together. Carr glanced up as I passed him. I shot at him with the thumb and forefinger of my left hand.

"Have you worked with those two before?" I asked Jack as we went down the stairs.

"Who? Bernie and Joe? Sure. Lots of times."

"What're they like?"

"They're fine."

"Does that Bernie always come on so strong?"

Jack smiled. "That's his job."

We got sandwiches and soft drinks from a take-out place on Western Avenue across from the police station.

"I'd like to put some distance between myself and the looney bin for a while," Jack said. "Want to go for a ride?"

"Okay."

We retrieved his car from the parking garage underneath the station.

"Where're we headed?" I asked.

Jack shrugged. "Want to go sit by the river for a while?"

"Sure."

We drove down Western Avenue and onto Memorial Drive to Magazine Beach. The name was misleading. You couldn't swim in the Charles. You wouldn't even contemplate trying.

We left the car in the lot by the Metropolitan District Commission swimming pool and walked for a bit on the path alongside the river until we found an unoccupied bench, nicely shaded by a large old sycamore. I handed Jack his tuna sandwich and Coke. Then I sat down and began unwrapping my own salami and provolone on rye.

"Has anyone gotten in touch with Bonnie's parents yet?" I asked.

Jack sighed. "We called the North Carolina State Police," he said. "They—"

I nodded. How long ago had it been that I myself had spoken to Mrs. Nordgren? Five days? Such a short time.

You give mah daughter mah love, heah? And tell her to write more often.

My eyes stung. I averted my face a little and blinked, hard.

"What's the matter?" Jack asked.

"Nothing," I muttered.

He patted my shoulder. I took a sip of my diet ginger ale to ease the tightness in my throat. Jack let his hand slip down my back and rest there, a light, warm pressure.

"You're a nice man," I said.

"You've only just figured that out?" he replied. "After five years?"

We ate our lunch. Afterward, I collected the sandwich wrappings and empty cans and deposited them in a green painted metal trash barrel. Then I returned to our bench and sat down sideways, facing Jack, my legs drawn up so I could rest my chin on my knees.

"Tell me," I said.

"Not much to tell," he said. "At this point."

I nudged him with my right foot. "Come on."

He stretched out his legs and draped both arms along the back of the bench. "When I first saw her lying there," he said. "My immediate reaction was that she'd died of natural causes. That maybe that story your friend DiBenedetto told you about her being sick really was true."

"What made you change your mind?" I asked.

He grimaced. "The drug apparatus in the bedroom."

"What, like a needle?"

"Yeah. A syringe, some cotton balls, a spoon, a web belt—"

I frowned. "Why a web belt?"

Jack put his right hand on his upper left arm. "Handy for tying off the arm to make the vein pop up for the needle."

I shuddered. "Ick."

"Yeah."

"What else did you find?"

"Well, there was a little glass vial with the remains of something in it, which I'm guessing is the leftovers of whatever she shot herself or had herself shot up with."

"What do you think it was?"

He shrugged. "I have no idea. Heroin, maybe, or a mixture of heroin and cocaine. We'll see what the autopsy and lab test results say."

"Uh-huh."

"Apart from the stuff in the vial, we also found a little loose cocaine and what I *think* is more heroin. If I'm right, it's a special kind."

"Oh?"

"Mmmm. It's called Persian Brown. It looks sort of like sand."

"Could she have been shooting up with that?"

"I think she was smoking it."

I wrinkled my nose. "How do you smoke heroin?"

"Oh, it's no big deal. You put a little bit of it on a piece of tinfoil and then heat it over a candle flame or something, and tilt it so the stuff runs and burns. Then you take a little straw that you make out of foil and use that to inhale the fumes." Jack smiled wryly. "Chasing the Dragon."

"I beg your pardon?"

"That's the street name for that way of smoking smack," Jack explained. "Chasing the Dragon."

"Lordy, Lordy," I shook my head slowly. "Persian Brown. Chasing dragons. Who dreamed up all this terminology? Samuel Taylor Coleridge?"

Jack laughed. "Not hardly. A poet wouldn't last long enough on the street to be creative."

"I guess not," I said. "Poor old Bonnie didn't, did she?"

"No," Jack said. "She sure didn't."

We sat in silence for a few moments, watching the cluster of sailboats on the river swoop and glide in a seemingly random pattern against the backdrop of Boston. The way the boats moved always reminded me of a school of fish. And like fish, no matter how close they got to each other, they never seemed to collide.

Jack got up, slowly, and stretched. Then he stood with his back slightly arched and his face turned up to the sun.

"Going somewhere?" I asked.

"Time for me to get back to the zoo," he replied. He looked down at me. "Drop you any place?"

"Central Square's fine. I have some errands to do."

"Okay."

We walked back to his car. Jack unlocked the door on the passenger's side and opened it for me. Then he went around to the driver's side. I stood by the open door, watching him.

"Jack?"

"Hmmm?"

"You still haven't told me why you think Bonnie didn't inject herself with those drugs."

He looked at me over the roof of the car. "Hop in," he said. "And I will."

I yelped softly when I hit the front seat. The car had been parked in a sunny spot and the upholstry was like a griddle.

Jack put the key in the ignition, but didn't start the engine.

"There was only the one puncture mark on her left arm," he said. "No scars or old tracks. This was either the first time ever she shot up or else the first time in a long, long while."

"So?" I thought for a moment. "Wait a sec, Jack. If Bonnie were a novice at shooting, she could very easily have miscalculated the among of drug she was taking and accidentally OD'd, couldn't she?"

"Yeah, that's possible," he replied. "But what happens, usually, with first-time shooters is that they get the shot given to them by someone else. Like the dealer."

"Oh," I said. "Okay. I'll buy that."

Jack rested his forearms on the steering wheel. "Plus there was something funny about the whole setup in her apartment anyway," he continued.

"Really? How so?"

"Well, it was a setup that looked *set up*."

I stared at him.

"The syringe—a nice, new, medically clean one, by the way—the spoon, the belt, the vial, they were just so goddam artistically arranged there on top of the bureau."

"Put there for you to find them, do you think?"

"Maybe." He started the car and backed out of the parking space. We drove out of the lot and edged onto Memorial Drive.

"Something else is bugging me, too," Jack said.

"My God," I said. "There's more?"

"I took a pretty good look at her hands. There were what I'm fairly sure were a couple of little inkstains on the middle and index fingers of the left one. Also a well-developed callous on the inside top joint of the middle left finger. What does that mean?"

I thought for a few seconds, and then shrugged. "That she wrote with her left hand. That she was left-handed."

"Uh-huh."

"So?"

He glanced over at me briefly. "Well, now, sweetheart, you tell *me* how somebody who's left-handed managed to give herself an injection in the bend of her left elbow."

11

Jack dropped me off on Western Avenue outside the police station. We agreed to have dinner together that evening. My place at seven, provided the afternoon didn't bring with it a second crime wave.

I did my errands at the bank and the post office. Then I ambled down Mass. Avenue toward Harvard Square. I had nothing special to do. I didn't have to look for Bonnie Nordgren anymore.

I wondered if the cops had spoken with Carl DiBenedetto yet. Poor Carl. The news about Bonnie would devastate him. Probably I should call him myself and offer sympathy. Maybe apologize to him for not having gotten to Bonnie before her killer had.

I took a deep breath and shook my head vigorously. No point in giving brain room to that kind of thought. Bonnie's destiny had probably been etched out long before I'd gotten tangled up in her affairs. Nothing I could have done would have prevented it. Her roommate wouldn't have let me anyhow.

Her roommate. God.

There was a Mexican restaurant a half block down Mass. Avenue. I went into it and used their public phone.

Jack picked up on the first ring.

"Gayle Lydecker," I said breathlessly. "Where is she?"

He gave a laugh that sounded a little tired. "I was wondering when you'd get to that."

"I'm so *stupid*," I moaned. "I even gave a description of her to Frick and Frack."

"You're not stupid," Jack said.

"Be that as it may," I replied. "Have you spoken to her yet?"

"We haven't found her yet."

"No."

"Well, all we have for her is that Waltham address I gave you. She's not there as you know. Hasn't been since the beginning of March."

I had a flash of inspiration. "Did you speak to her former landlord?"

"Why?"

"Well, he or she might be able to tell you where she works. You could get in touch with her there."

"See, you're not stupid at all," Jack said. His voice sounded as if he were smiling.

"Well, did you? Talk to the landlord?"

"Uh-huh."

"And?"

"Lydecker worked for some outfit in Waltham called MacCrimmon Associates."

"What are they?"

"Sort of a general-purpose consulting, I think."

"Figures."

"Why?" he asked.

"She has that look about her," I said. "That *haute*-professional-no-nonsense-I-am-a-lady-to-be-reckoned-with look."

Jack laughed.

"So what's the deal?" I asked. "I take it you didn't get to speak with her."

"No."

"Why not?"

"She's not at MacCrimmon anymore."

I was silent for a moment, absorbing his last words. Then I said, "So where did she go from there?"

"Damned if I know," Jack replied. "She took a leave of

absence from MacCrimmon three weeks ago. Citing personal reasons."

"For how long?"

"The leave of absence? Indefinite, according to her boss."

"But . . ."

"But what?"

I scratched my head. "That doesn't make sense."

"How so?"

"I just saw Gayle a few days ago. She didn't look like somebody on leave or on vacation. She looked like somebody getting home from a hard day of strategic planning."

"Well, I don't have an answer to that," Jack said. "All I can tell you is that we're, ah, eager to talk to her."

"There's a surprise," I replied, and he laughed. "She appears to get back from whatever it is she's doing now at about five-fifteen. At least, that's what time it was when she showed up at Bonnie's place the other day."

"We'll be waiting for her," Jack said.

"Oh. Does that screw up our dinner plans?"

"If it does, I'll let you know."

"Okay. Talk to you later."

"Bye."

I hung up the phone and left the restaurant and wandered the rest of the way to Harvard Square, thinking hard all the way. If Gayle Lydecker had moved in with Bonnie in order to keep Bonnie out of trouble, as Chris Cameron had suggested, she hadn't done a stupendous job of it.

Then again, maybe Lydecker's function hadn't been to protect. Maybe she'd been Bonnie's live-in drug supplier. Maybe that shoulder-strap briefcase of hers was crammed full of all sorts of chemical goodies. A friend of mine who knew about business once told me that the reason that management consultants and investment bankers got paid such astronomical sums of money was so they could keep up their habits. He was only semijoking, I think. Maybe half Gayle's pay was going up her nose, and she'd gotten into dealing as a way of cutting down expenses.

I laughed out loud at the notion. I could be very wrong,

but Gayle Lydecker didn't strike me as someone heavy into doing coke. Maybe into Poland Spring with a splash of Chablis, but that would be the limit.

Stone druggies just weren't as cool and tight and androidal as she.

Then again, you didn't *have* to be into drugs yourself in order to sell them. Or administer them.

My imagination was really running wild. Best to curb it. Keep an open mind until Jack could enlighten me.

Was Lydecker a suspect? If she and Bonnie were sexually involved, they could have had a lover's quarrel.

Sure. And Gayle, in a fit of rage, whipped out her handy medically clean syringe, loaded it with a killer drug, and stuck it to Bonnie.

I marched myself into the Harvard Bookstore and dedicated the next two hours to browsing in the literature and history paperback sections. It had a calming effect. I found a book on the Civil War that I thought Jack might enjoy. I made a stop at the magazine rack to check my horoscope in *Cosmopolitan* and *New Woman* and *Vogue* and *Harper's Bazaar*. Beyond the unanimous assertion that Aries girls were strong and passionate and had great leadership potential, which I already knew, all the prognostications were contradictory. So much for steering by the stars. I flipped through *People*. Then I paid for the Civil War book and walked home.

I took Lucy out and played with her for a while in the backyard. We went inside and I gave her her dinner and started the preparations for Jack's and mine.

The phone rang. I put the potato I was peeling in a bowl and went to answer it. Christine Cameron.

"Hi," I said. "I was going to call you. I sicced two guys from the Middlesex County DA's office on you this morning."

"I can guess why," she replied.

"Oh. You heard?"

"It was on the noon news."

"Were you surprised?"

"No," she said. "Not especially."

"Me neither. Does Linda know?"

"I don't think so. She took off to New York last night to go to some John Keats jamboree at Columbia. She'll be back tomorrow."

"Oh." I sighed. "Have the cops gotten to you?"

"Not yet." She sounded a little puzzled. "I'll talk to them, certainly, when they show up, but why would they want to talk to *me*?"

"To hear you tell them in your very own words exactly what you told me about Bonnie."

"But that's—not anything, really."

"I know," I said. "That was my reaction when they asked me to talk to them this morning."

"Yes, I was wondering why they'd ask *you* about Bonnie."

"They heard I was looking for her."

Cameron was shrewd. "How would they hear that?"

I hesitated a second. Then I said, "My—a very good friend of mine is a detective lieutenant in the Cambridge police department. I told him about what DiBenedetto asked me to do."

"Oh," Christine replied. "I see. How interesting."

"Yeah," I said. "Listen, do you have any idea if Carl has heard about what's happened?"

There was a brief silence on the other end of the line. Then Christine said, slowly, "Gee, I have no idea. He wasn't in the office today."

"I have the feeling he'll be destroyed when he does."

There was another slight delay before Christine replied. "You're right," she said finally. "He probably will be."

"Mmmm."

"You know," she said, sounding slightly surprised. "Jerk that he is, I think I actually feel sorry for him now."

"Me, too."

"Maybe I should call him."

"I had the same thought," I said. "But I can't bring myself to do it just yet."

"Yes," Christine answered. "You would have to psychically prepare yourself for that conversation, wouldn't you?"

"Yup."

The call ended, and I went back to the kitchen to resume my potato peeling. Lucy followed me and positioned herself alongside the counter and watched me very closely as I worked. I tossed her a long skein of potato peeling. She snapped it up in midflight, crunched it once, and swallowed it.

"You do enjoy your *crudités*, don't you?" I remarked.

She waved her tail.

The salad was made, the potatoes were just starting to pan-fry, and the fish was ready to go under the broiler when Jack appeared at five to seven. He let himself into the apartment with the key I'd given him.

I was in the kitchen making myself a vodka martini. He came up behind me and put his face in the hollow between my neck and my shoulder. With my right hand I reached up behind me and patted the back of his head.

"God, you're so sexy," I said.

He laughed into my neck. He thought I was joking. I wasn't. Even after five years.

He let go of me and opened the cabinet above my head. It was where I kept the booze. He took down the bourbon bottle and got a clean glass from the dish drainer.

"No crime tidal wave this afternoon?" I asked, smiling at him.

He returned the smile. "No, it was pretty quiet." He got some ice from the freezer and put it in his glass. "Thank God."

I tilted my head at the kitchen door. "Go on inside and sit down. I'll be with you in a minute. There's a present for you on the coffee table."

He left the room. I inspected the fish and sprinkled a little more dried parsley on it. And another squirt of lemon. Then I picked up my drink and went to join Jack in the living room.

He was standing by the couch, leafing through the Civil War paperback. He looked up as I walked into the room.

"I hope you haven't read that one already," I said.

"No, I haven't. It looks very interesting." He grinned at me. "Thank you very much, cookie."

"My pleasure." I went over to him and he kissed me. Then we sat down side by side on the couch. He gave the book a final glance and placed it on the end table.

I took a sip of my drink and put my head back and said, "What's new?"

"I have to go to Philadelphia tomorrow."

I turned my head to look at him. "What for?"

"We're extraditing somebody," he replied. "I have to go pick him up."

"Who?"

"Some trashbag that jumped bail on an aggravated rape charge about three months ago," he said. "The Pennsylvania state police picked him up the day before yesterday."

"Good for them," I said. "May I offer a suggestion?"

"Sure."

"Are you flying out there and back?"

"Uh-huh."

"Okay. Here's what you do. Kick the guy out the rear exit of the plane halfway between here and Philadelphia. Save the Commonwealth the expense of a trial."

Jack laughed. "Vengeful."

"Damn straight," I said. "When will you be back?"

"Day after tomorrow. Unless there's a hitch."

I drank some more of my martini. "Want to watch the tail end of the news?"

"What for? It'll all be lousy."

I moved so that I could rest my head against his shoulder. He put his arm around me.

"Did you catch up with Gayle Lydecker?" I asked.

"Nope."

I glanced up at him. "You didn't?"

"She never turned up at Bonnie's place this evening."

"Oh, my," I said. I took another sip of my drink.

"Don't worry," Jack said. "One of us will hang around there until she shows."

I stirred my drink with my index finger. All the bizarre thoughts, I'd had earlier about Gayle Lydecker came stampeding back into my mind.

"Suppose she doesn't show?" I asked.

"Well, then, we'll just have to look for her, won't we?"

"Is she a suspect?"

Jack hesitated a beat. Then he said, very carefully, "Not as of this moment."

12

Jack left quite early the following morning, in order to catch a seven o'clock flight to Philadelphia. I woke up long enough to give him a good-bye kiss and remind him to chuck the rapist out the plane door. Then I went back to sleep until eight-thirty.

I woke for the second time feeling vaguely troubled. It took me a moment to figure out why. Why was that I was going to have to speak to Carl DiBenedetto today, something I couldn't in decency put off any longer. I wasn't looking forward to it. He wasn't the kind of person who reacted stoically to bad news. And I'm not good at handling the distraught.

I showered, dressed, had breakfast, a second cup of coffee, and took Lucy out for an extra-long backyard romp. Then I went inside and looked at the telephone for about fifteen minutes.

Do it and get it over with, dummy.

I sighed, consulted my address book, found DiBenedetto's

number, and dialed it. He answered on the fifth ring, just as I was about to hang up in guilty relief.

It was even worse than I'd anticipated.

Like Chris Cameron, he'd heard about Bonnie's death on the news. I told him how sorry I was. He began to cry in great rasping sobs. I cringed and held the receiver away from my ear so that I wouldn't have to listen too closely. Even muted, the sounds were awful.

I let about two minutes pass. Then I said, cautiously, "Carl?"

"Just a second," he replied chokily. I heard the clatter of his phone receiver being set down on a hard surface and, following that, some distant nose-blowing noises.

When he came back on the line I said, "I want you to know that the police and the district attorney's office are investigating what happened very thoroughly."

"Yes, well," he snapped. "They wouldn't have to if you'd done what I asked you to."

I felt as if I'd been punched by somebody along the lines of Marvin Hagler. "Carl—"

He cut me off. "I *knew* that girl was in serious trouble."

"I—"

"I was depending on you to help her."

"I did what I could," I said.

"I don't think so," he replied in heavy tones. "You've seriously disappointed me, Elizabeth." He paused, and added, "I feel betrayed."

I was silent, stunned by the attack.

"I don't think I want to talk to you," DiBenedetto said. Then he hung up on me.

I curled up on the couch in a vertical fetal position and spent the next twenty minutes staring at nothing. I felt ill. More than that, I felt guilty.

After a while, I started feeling angry as well. The issue was really very simple. I was in the right and DiBenedetto was in the wrong. Completely. He'd ripped into me as a way of dealing with his own feelings of inadequacy. The man was bananas at the best of times anyway. You couldn't take to heart what he said. I had done what I could to find Bonnie. If DiBenedetto had taken my advice and gone to the cops with his story, she might possibly still be alive. Indicted for larceny by false pretenses, but alive.

The rationalization didn't do a lot to soothe my feelings.

I stormed around the house for an hour or so, doing the breakfast dishes and other housework with such concentrated ferocity that Lucy took umbrage and retired under the bed, her favorite hiding place. Usually she did that only when I was vacuuming. I gave a final vicious scrub to the kitchen counter and hurled the sponge into the sink.

Then I took off for Bonnie's place on Huron Avenue.

The long walk did wonders to relax me. If I accomplished nothing else that day, at least I had a well-exercised body. And an exceptionally clean kitchen.

The brown frame three-decker didn't look like a murder scene, but then, most of them don't. There were no police cars parked outside, nor anybody obviously a police officer visible. If the CPD had anyone lurking about waiting for Gayle Lydecker to show up, they were being very subtle about it.

I rang the doorbell for apartment one, hoping that the little old sparrow-lady I'd spoken to the time before last might be in. If she were, she wasn't answering the bell. Maybe she still had something on the stove.

I rang apartment two. A moment later the intercom crackled and a female voice said, "Yes?"

"Hello," I replied. "I'm looking for the landlord. Is this his apartment?"

"He's in three," the voice said, and the intercom went dead.

I rang the bell for three. After a slightly longer wait, a youngish-sounding man's voice said, "Hello?"

"I'd like to speak to the landlord," I said.

"I'm the landlord."

"Fine," I said crisply. "I'm here about Bonnie Nordgren."

There was the briefest of pauses. Then the man said, "I'll be right down."

I waited. I heard faint thumping noises from inside like someone trotting quickly down a flight of wooden stairs. The door opened. Just behind the threshold stood a guy about my age, maybe two inches shorter than I, in jeans and a somewhat grubby-looking Duke University tee shirt. He had receding dark brown hair, cut very short, and a mustache and neat goatee. I smiled at him.

"Come on in," he said, and stepped back to let me over the threshold.

I walked into the foyer, somewhat surprised by how hospitable the reception was.

The man gestured toward the stairs. "One flight up," he said. "First door on the left."

I shrugged mentally and started up the stairs, the bearded guy behind me.

The door to apartment three was open. I stopped outside it.

"Go in and sit down," the man said. "I'd really rather none of the other tenants saw you. They're upset enough as it is."

I wondered why the mere sight of me would disturb anyone. Was it my clothing? I was casually dressed, to be sure, but there was nothing objectionable about my appearance. Certainly not by local community standards.

Bemused, I went into the apartment. The man shut the door behind us. I walked down a short hall into what was obviously a living room.

It was a lovely, if typically *haute* Cambridge, room. The floor was refinished six-inch wide oak planks, with a faded Oriental rug in the exact center. A very high-tech hooded wood stove that resembled a miniature blast furnace dominated one wall; the wall opposite it was taken over by floor-to-ceiling bookcases. On the other walls were chrome-framed Harold Tovish etchings. The furniture was a combination of Bauhaus, Art Deco, and Early American. The antiques looked real. An enormous Areca palm flourished aggressively in one corner.

"Sit down anywhere," the man said.

I took the Barcelona chair cater-corner to the blast furnace. The bearded guy sank down into one corner of the couch.

"Are you an architect?" I asked.

He looked at me in some surprise. "How did you know?"

I glanced around the room and smiled. "It shows."

"It does?" He laughed. "Well, thank you, I guess."

I nodded and smiled some more.

"I figured someone from the police would be back today," the man said.

Oh, God. No *wonder* he'd been so willing to let me into his home. He'd assumed I was one of the detectives. If I hadn't felt so awkward, I'd have felt flattered.

I cleared my throat. "I'm not from the police department," I said.

The look that he gave me was at first startled and then suspicious. Very suspicious. I didn't blame him.

"I'm—I was an acquaintance of Bonnie," I said, stretching the truth a bit. "It's kind of a complicated story, but basically what it is is that a man I know, who was also Bonnie's boss, told me that she had been having some problems recently. He asked me to try and get in touch with her to see if she needed help. I *did* try, but . . ." I let my voice trail off and held out my hands, palms upraised. "I wasn't able to get to her soon enough."

"Are you a private detective?" the man asked.

I remembered Linda Rosenberg asking me the same question. "No," I said. "I'm a writer. For magazines, mostly."

The man looked mystified. Again, I could understand why.

"The person who asked me to look for Bonnie wanted it kept sort of informal and low-key," I explained. "He thought I could help him because I have a background in research. I've done articles about missing persons."

The landlord frowned. "I still don't see the connection. Why would anyone think Bonnie was a missing person? I talked to her the day before yesterday about a leak in her kitchen sink.'' He added drily, ''She wasn't missing *then*.''

''Well, she disappeared from her job over a month ago,'' I said. ''And nobody who worked with her was ever able to get in touch with her. She either wouldn't answer the phone or her roommate would and hang up on whoever was calling.'' I leaned forward and rested my elbows on my knees. ''That's a bit strange, don't you think?''

There was a carved teak cigarette box on the coffee table. The landlord reached over and opened it. He pushed it toward me. I shook my head. He took a cigarette, leaned forward slightly, dug into the hip pocket of his jeans, and withdrew a book of matches. He lit the cigarette and blew some smoke at the ceiling. ''I was making coffee,'' he said. ''Would you like some?''

I nodded. ''Thank you.''

He smiled and got up and left the room.

I leaned back into the Barcelona chair. It was quite comfy. I heard some rattling sounds from the kitchen that sounded like cups and saucers being assembled. I knew that the reason the landlord had offered me coffee was to give himself time to mull over what I'd told him. Fair enough.

He returned to the room bearing a black enamel tray loaded down with two tall, slim trigger-handled white china cups, a creamer and sugar bowl of the same design, and one of those Italian glass coffeepots that has a kind of plunger thing into which you put the coffee grounds. The coffee looked dark and thick enough to be espresso, which I hoped it wasn't. I hate espresso.

The landlord set the tray on the coffee table and took his cigarette from the heavy crystal ashtray where he'd left it burning. He puffed it once, then stubbed it out. ''How do you like your coffee?''

''Cream,'' I said. ''Artificial sweetener, if you have any.''

He shook his head.

''Sugar's fine, then. One.''

He prepared a cup and handed it to me.

"I ought to introduce myself," I said. "My name is Elizabeth Connors."

"Rick Harding." He held his right hand across the coffee table and I shook it. "How do you do?"

"Do you think you want to talk to me?" I asked.

His sipped his coffee and looked at me for a moment over the top of the cup. "I don't mean to be rude," he said. "But why? What's the point? Bonnie's dead. Talking's not going to change that."

"I know," I replied. "But I'd like to get a sense of what she was like over the past few weeks. What her, uh, condition was. I think I owe that much to the guy who asked me to look for her."

Harding took another sip of coffee and then nodded, slowly. "Okay. I can see that."

I smiled at him, and sampled my own coffee. It was wonderful, and I told him so.

"I keep the beans in the freezer. I grind them myself."

"You said you saw Bonnie the day before yesterday. How did she seem to you then?"

He shrugged. "Fine. Same as usual. A little spacy, but that was normal for Bonnie."

"So she was no different from any other occasion you'd seen her?"

"Nope. Although you have to understand I didn't see her all that often, even though we lived in the same building. Maybe once or twice a month, in passing. She'd put the rent check in an envelope and slide it under my front door, usually."

"How long had she lived here?"

Harding thought for a moment. "Since last September."

"Do you know where she's lived before that?"

"Some place in Boston. The Back Bay, I think."

"Was she a satisfactory tenant?" I sounded like somebody checking a credit reference.

"Fine," Harding said. "Quiet. Kept to herself. Very few visitors that I knew of."

"I was going to ask you about that," I said. "If you'd ever seen her with anyone."

"In particular?"

"I was thinking specifically of men visitors."

Harding shook his head. "No. None that I can recall. Doesn't mean she never had any, though."

"No, of course not," I agreed. I was beginning to wonder if the boyfriend Bonnie's mother had claimed she had in fact existed. And what had become of the mug who'd pass the time of day with her while she'd worked at Currier College? Had the two of them simply faded from the picture?

"You know how Bonnie died?" I said.

"Yeah." Harding grimaced. "Jesus. What a way to go."

"Did you know she was doing drugs?"

He gave me a very steady look. "I didn't *know* it, no."

I raised my eyebrows. "But you suspected it?"

Harding lit another cigarette. "It occurred to me, once or twice, that maybe she wasn't naturally spaced-out." He shook the match and placed it in the ashtray. "Guess I was right."

"Apparently," I said.

"Care for some more coffee?"

"It's far too good to refuse," I said, and held out my cup. He refilled it for me, and I stirred in cream and sugar.

"I don't know what else to tell you," Harding said.

"Well, if you don't mind, I'd like to ask you a couple of questions about Bonnie's roommate."

"Gayle?"

"Uh-huh."

He shrugged. "She moved in around the beginning of March. Bonnie told me she was only going to be staying for a few weeks, till she found a place of her own."

"What did you think of her?"

He shrugged again. "There was nothing much for me to think. I didn't see *her* that often, either. She was certainly no trouble as a tenant. I thought she was kind of uptight and unfriendly, but that was her problem."

I nodded. "When was the last time you saw her?"

He frowned thoughtfully. "Let me see. It was—oh, maybe four, five days ago."

I counted back mentally. The last time Harding had seen Gayle was around the time that I myself had first seen her. That could be significant. It could also be totally irrelevant.

"One more thing," I said. "Would it be possible for me to take a look at Bonnie's apartment?"

Harding shook his head strongly. "Sorry. There's a police seal on the door."

I nodded, and finished my coffee. "Well, thank you very much for talking to me. And"—I gestured with the cup in my hand—"for this lovely stuff."

He smiled. "No trouble."

Harding escorted me down to the front door. I couldn't figure out if he was being polite or if he just wanted to make sure I left the building without being spotted by any of the other tenants.

I wasn't.

13

I had another violent attack of domesticity that evening after dinner, so I did my laundry and then went grocery shopping. It probably wasn't as exciting as extraditing rapists from Philadelphia to Cambridge, but it had its own charms.

The point is, I *like* supermarkets, especially the ones that have big exotic food sections. I spent about ten minutes inspecting the canned escargots and packets of saffron rice and instant wonton soup and confiture that cost seven-fifty a jar.

It was like an edible version of Around the World in Eighty Days. Did anyone actually buy seven-fifty marmalade on a regular basis?

I bought some tea, orange juice, milk, and half a pound of fresh cherries, and ambled home. It was a nice night for ambling. Chilly, but that was normal for early May in the Boston area. My street was quiet and dark. A lot of old people lived on it, and they all seemed to go to bed by eight.

I went up the two steps to the outer door of my apartment building and opened it. Inside the door was a sort of landing about three feet deep. A step up from that was the inner door. I set the grocery bag on the landing so I could fish in my purse for my keys.

For about a quarter of a second, I thought someone was playing a very bad practical joke. Then I realized that although I had some fairly eccentric friends, none of them was weird enough to do what happened next.

There was a rush of movement from behind me and slightly to the right. I sensed rather than saw a figure come scrambling up out of the shadows. Whoever it was slapped his right hand over my mouth and his left arm around my body, just below the breasts. Then I felt myself being dragged backward and to the side and pressed down onto the outside steps.

The first thing I did was to jerk my face to the left, freeing it, and begin to scream. The hand that had been over my mouth fell away. I tried to lunge forward and the person put his right arm around me to secure his hold.

I was yelling loudly enough to shatter windows in the skyscrapers in Boston, but the houses on both sides of the street stayed dark. No pedestrians. No cars. Where the hell was everybody? Had they all gone deaf? Or did they just think it was kids fooling around?

Whoever it was holding me made no sound whatsoever.

I crooked my arms and made a side-to-side churning motion with my torso like the agitator in a washing machine. My right elbow made contact with something solid, and the tourniquet grip around my midsection relaxed slightly. I raised my left arm, still flexed, and rammed it backward even harder. The person holding me fell back a step. Taking advantage of the slack, I whipped around in a half-circle to face whoever it was.

I was looking down into the face of a guy two or three inches shorter than I. In the light from the streetlamp fifteen feet away, I could see he had pale skin and straggly reddish brown kinky hair. A short beard and mustache. He was wearing a flannel shirt with a dark check and light background and a Greek sailor's hat set far back on his head. His build seemed to be heavy, but flabby-heavy. His eyes were light and stared directly into mine. Maybe I was mistaken, but he looked almost as frightened as I felt.

I stopped thrashing and shoved at him, hitting his shoulders with the heels of my palms. He jerked away a few inches. I linked my hands, raised them, and let him have it in the nose with a double fist. He let go of me immediately and staggered back a pace, down the last step, and onto the sidewalk. His hat fell to the pavement. I let out a scream that made my throat feel as if I'd swallowed lye. The guy wavered a moment, and, without retrieving his hat, turned and began running up the street. Still screaming, I watched him till he reached the corner, swerved to the left, and disappeared from my sight.

And *still* the front windows in my own building and the others remained dark.

I snatched up the hat, fumbled my key from my purse, unlocked the front door and threw it open, and half-fell over the threshold into the foyer. I slammed the door behind me and shot the bolt. Then I raced upstairs to my own apartment. I closed the door and sagged against it for a moment, my chest heaving. Lucy hurled herself at me, making little keening noises.

I ran for the phone, grabbed the receiver, and dialed 911. It rang just once and then a raspy baritone said, "Police Emergency. Garrison."

"My name is Elizabeth Connors," I said, articulating as slowly and steadily as I could. I gave my address. "I was assaulted outside my front door just a minute ago."

"Are you hurt?" The raspy voice was urgent, but somehow softer. "You need an ambulance?"

"No, no," I said. "I'm okay."

"There'll be somebody there right away."

"Thank you." I hung up the phone and collapsed onto the couch. Lucy jumped up next to me and began licking my face. I hugged her, and she burrowed against me.

There were a pad and pen on the end table beside the couch. With my free hand, I grabbed the pen and began scribbling every detail I could remember of the appearance of the man who'd attacked me. Somehow it seemed important to do that. Not because I was in any danger of forgetting what the guy looked like, though, but because it would keep me from shaking to pieces.

The front doorbell rang. I gasped and jumped and the pen in my hand made a wild volitionless scrawl across the pad. Lucy flew off the couch and across the room, barking furiously. I ran to the front window, twitched aside the curtain, and peered down at the street. A trim gray-haired cop was on the sidewalk. He saw me looking down at him and made an urgent beckoning gesture and mouthed, "Let's go."

Lucy was still yammering at the top of her lungs. "It's okay, little bear," I said, giving her a quick pat that did nothing at all to reassure her. I grabbed my keys and the hat from the hall table where I'd thrown them and whirled out of the apartment. My groceries were still on the front steps. To hell with them.

The cruiser was in the middle of the street, blue lights revolving and motor running. I dashed around to the passenger's side, jumped in, and we were moving before I'd gotten the door completely shut. I tossed the hat onto the dashboard.

"Where'd he go?" the gray-haired cop said.

"Left at the top of the street," I said.

We were in a K-9 unit car. The rear seat was separated from the front by a heavy metal grille. It was occupied by a very large, very handsome, very agitated black-and-tan German shepherd.

We zipped down Gore Street toward the railroad tracks and the Somerville line.

"What's the guy look like?" the cop said.

I ran my hand back through my hair, one of my standard nervous gestures. "Oh, God," I said. "Lemme see. Okay. About five-seven, five-eight."

There was a walkie-talkie lying on the seat between us. The cop picked it up, pressed a little button on the side, and raised it to his mouth. The radio cracked loudly.

"Oh, God," I repeated. All of a sudden, my mind was a blank. "Uh—oh, Jesus."

"Take it easy," the cop said.

I nodded and took a deep breath. "Okay. He was—he was kind of heavy built."

The cop repeated what I'd said into the radio. We turned sharply onto a narrow, deserted side street.

"He was wearing a wool shirt," I said.

"Wool shirt," the cop said into the radio. Back over it, faintly through the static, a voice replied, "Blue shirt."

"No, no, *wool*," I said frantically. "Wool, with dark checks on a light background. Dark pants. Maybe jeans."

"Wool shirt, for Christ's sake," the cop yelled into the radio. "Wool checked shirt. Jeans."

We made a right turn onto Cambridge Street and then a sharp left down another side street. It, too, appeared deserted.

"Ah, okay," I said. "He had like reddish kinky hair, short."

The cop shouted that into the radio. Whatever reply was forthcoming was lost in an earsplitting blowback of static.

"Fuckin' piece of crap," the cop said, and slammed the radio against the dashboard.

"And a beard," I added hurriedly. "And mustache. Not a big full beard. Just a little short one, maybe an inch long."

We made a fast turn onto Gore Street and a quick pass through the parking lot of the Twin Cities Shopping Plaza.

I took a deep, trembly breath. "I'm really sorry," I said. "This description I'm giving you is really terrible."

The cop gave me a quick sideways glance. "You're doin' the best you can."

We pulled to a stop in the lot beside the Metropolitan District Commission Skating Rink. The cop reached down, fumbled for a moment beneath the seat, and pulled out a silver metal clipboard that had attached to it some arrest/incident report forms. He got a ballpoint pen from his shirt pocket.

"What else?" he said, beginning to fill in the blank spaces on the form.

I thought for a moment. "The guy looked like he was in his mid- to late twenties," I said.

The cop stopped writing. "Early twenties?"

I shook my head very firmly. "No. Older than that. Maybe twenty-five to thirty."

The cop raised his eyebrows and resumed writing. I went through the whole story with him, supplementing it with bits of description as they came back to me.

When we'd finished, the cop set the clipboard on the seat between us. "You think you could come over to the station and look at some pictures?"

"Of course," I said.

He nodded and smiled slightly and picked up the radio. "Lemme check and see if anybody's on in Records tonight."

I sat quietly while he established with whoever was on the receiving end of the transmission that there was, indeed, someone available in the Identification Bureau. The static on the radio was considerably less harsh. Maybe being smashed against the dashboard had improved the mechanism. More likely, though, it was that the cop was speaking in normal tones and not yelling. I recalled Jack once telling me that a loud voice distorted the transmission in those radios. In the police academy, the recruits were instructed to speak as calmly as they could while using a walkie-talkie. Which was a reasonable enough request, of course, but it didn't allow for the fact that cop's voices, like everyone else's, tended to rise and increase in volume in moments of stress or excitement.

The shepherd in the backseat whined and pressed its forepaws against the grille. I glanced over my shoulder and it slavered at me, canines gleaming.

"Your doggie's excited tonight," I remarked.

"Yeah, well." The cop shrugged. "He hasn't had a good bust since April eleventh."

I laughed, but I felt like a jerk. At that point, I must have been well on the way to out of it. *Doggie?* The thing behind me could have taken down Godzilla.

"You ready to go?"

"Sure," I said.

The cop put the cruiser in gear and we slid out of the parking lot onto Gore Street.

While we were waiting for the light to change on Sixth Street, the cop said, "This is funny. We don't usually get street crime in this part of town."

"Yeah, I heard," I replied sourly. "That's one of the reasons I moved here."

The cop made a little snorting noise. "Guy was after your purse." It was a statement rather than a question.

It wasn't until that moment that I realized that it hadn't, up until this very moment, occurred to me to wonder what the guy who'd attacked me *had* been after.

"I don't know," I said slowly.

The cop looked at me curiously.

"I don't know," I repeated. I hesitated a moment. "My bag was just swinging off my arm while I was struggling with him. He could have just grabbed it anytime and run off." I stopped speaking and frowned, replaying the incident on my mental videotape. "He didn't—he didn't seem that interested in my bag."

"What do you think he was after, then?"

I was silent.

"Did he touch your breast? Say anything, ah, of a sexual nature?"

I looked at the cop sharply and then shook my head. "No."

"And he didn't like order you to do anything?"

"No."

He didn't say anything at all?"

"Uh-uh."

The light changed.

"Strange," the cop said. "Goddamn strange."

14

In all the mug books I inspected, there were maybe seven guys who looked sort of like the one who'd jumped me. But none that I could point a finger at and say, definitely, "That's him."

I was too enervated to be terribly disappointed.

The only physical evidence of the assault was the sailor's cap. It got tagged and filed away in the property room, in case the police ever picked up a suspect and charged him. Fat chance.

The gray-haired cop and his dog partner drove me home at about one A.M. I wasn't enthusiastic about spending the night alone. What a swell time for Jack to be out of town. There's never a cop around when you need one. On the whole, *I* would rather have been in Philadelphia, too.

With considerable trepidation, I let Lucy out into the backyard for her pre-bed run. Every rustle of the bushes and trees made me jump. I kept thinking that there was a bad guy behind each azalea and rhododendron, just waiting . . .

If there were, they stayed put.

Just as I was about to get into bed, I had what seemed to me an excellent notion. I padded into the kitchen and rummaged through the cutlery drawer until I found the biggest, sharpest carving knife I owned. I brought it back to the bedroom with me and set it on the night table. That way it would be in easy reach if I woke up in the night and found a bad guy looming over me.

I let Lucy sleep on the bed rather than under it, a real first. That warm, furry bundle pressed against the backs of my legs felt very good. But I hoped the dog wouldn't assume that this was the start of a new tradition.

Much to my surprise, I didn't have any horrific dreams. Except for a lingering creepy, violated feeling, and a lot of anger focused on the slob who'd jumped me, I felt okay the next morning.

The first thing I did was run around the building to see if I could find out where everyone else who lived there had been last night.

The woman across the hall, Sue McCreary, came to her door in robe and slippers. She operated a pottery studio in north Cambridge that didn't open until one P.M. I asked her if she'd been home last night around nine-thirty.

She brushed a lock of hair from her forehead. "Nine-thirty," she repeated. "Uh-huh. Sure. Why?"

I told her, and as I did, her face whitened and her eyes grew wide.

"I can't believe you didn't hear me," I said. "I was yelling loud enough to raise the dead."

"My God, Liz," she replied. "I didn't hear a thing. I'm so sorry." She gestured toward the room she'd set up as a sort of home studio. "I was working out back and I had the stereo on."

"Well," I shrugged. "I guess it was just one of those things."

She fiddled with the collar of her bathrobe, a gesture of nervous agitation. "But this is awful. My God. I thought there wasn't supposed to be any real street crime around here."

"Yeah, me too."

Sue gave me an intent look. "Are you okay? You seem okay. He didn't . . ."

I shook my head.

"I'm so glad you weren't—that nothing bad happened." She made a face. "What a stupid thing to say. Of *course* something bad happened."

"I'm really fine now."

She shivered, and then sighed. "You know, I hate violence. And I've always been in favor of gun control. I don't like to think of everyone going around armed." She waved her right hand to emphasize the point. "But something like this makes me wonder if—I mean, I live by myself and all—I wonder if . . ."

"Well," I said drily. "If the guy last night was carrying a weapon, he didn't show it. If *I* had been, even a legal one, and I'd blown him away with it, *I'd* be sitting in jail now, charged with manslaughter."

She looked at me in horror. "For defending yourself?"

"That's how the law reads," I said.

"Well, I'm going to get a dog, anyway," she said. "A Doberman."

Nobody in the other apartments was home, which made sense, since as far as I knew they all had normal nine-to-five jobs. Maybe I'd try them this evening. I probably had some kind of obligation to warn them that they no longer lived in a mugging-free neighborhood.

I acknowledged to myself that there was also a mean little part of me that wanted to scare them as much as I'd been scared. But they could never really know what it was like unless it happened to them.

The loneliest feeling in the world was to be standing on a dark street screaming, and to have nobody answer.

When I got back to my apartment, the phone was ringing. I picked up the receiver and said hello.

"Jesus H. Christ," Jack said.

"Oh," I said. "I guess you heard."

"Nobody told me about it," he said. He sounded as if he

were squeezing the words out between his teeth. "I just happened to read the incident report just now."

"It's all right—" I began.

"No, it is not fucking all right" he interrupted.

"Now don't get your blood pressure in an uproar," I said mildly. "I'm fine."

"I'll kill the son-of-a-bitch."

"Now how can you, Jack?" I said. "I don't even know who he is. He wasn't in any of the mug books."

It probably wasn't the most tactful of rejoinders. I added quickly, "I'll come over to the station right now. Bye-bye." Then I hung up the phone.

I hoped Jack would have calmed down by the time I got to the cop shop. I understood why he was angry. I even liked the fact that he was angry. But I didn't feel up to contending with the overflow.

I took a cab to Central Square. Ordinarily I'd have walked, but I figured I deserved a treat today.

On the way into the police station, I bumped into Bill Wallace on his way out somewhere. He took his cigar from his mouth and said, "Hey, honey, I heard you beat the shit outta some guy last night."

I gaped at him for a moment and then laughed. "Whatever story you heard, it got way exaggerated in the telling."

"So what really happened?"

"I sort of hit him in the nose and he ran away."

"Yeah, well, that can be discouraging." Wallace nodded gravely. "Good for you, tiger. You can ride with me anytime."

"Oh, you're just saying that," I grinned. "If I took the night tour with you and we encountered an exciting crime-in-progress, you'd make me go home."

"The hell I would," Wallace said. "I can use all the back up I can get, honey." He stuck the cigar in his mouth and breezed off in the direction of the police parking lot.

Still laughing, I went upstairs to Jack's office. He was at his desk. I struck a model's hip-sprung pose in the doorway and said, "Ta-da."

"Liz," he said.

I sauntered into the room. "You and the rapist have a nice flight back from Phillie?"

"Oh, cut the crap," Jack said. He got up and came over to me. I looked at him for a moment and then raised my arms.

"It was *awful*, Jack," I said, my face against his shoulder. We stood pressed together for what seemed like a long time.

Jack gave me a final extra-hard hug (I could feel my rib-cage compress), and said, "Sit down."

I took what I thought of as "my chair," the one across from his desk.

"Tell me about it," he said.

As I spoke, I kept my eyes on his face. The lines on it seemed to deepen. At the end of the story, I reached into my purse and took out the description of my attacker that I'd written the previous evening. I handed the paper across the desk. "Here," I said. "For your files."

Jack took the paper and read it. When he'd finished, he looked up at me and said, "This is very good."

I shrugged modestly. "Do you want me to write down what happened? Like a report?"

He studied me for a moment and then said, "Would that be hard for you?"

"No. I don't think so."

He smiled. "Then it would be a very good idea. I'll make a copy of it for you to keep."

I frowned at him in puzzlement. "Why? As a souvenir?"

He snorted. "If—*when*—we catch that miserable bag of shit, you'll have to testify before the grand jury. That may not happen for a while. You don't want to forget anything about what happened."

"Of course I do."

"You know what I mean."

I nodded. "Okay. I'll do it now. You have some paper?"

He took a pad out of the top drawer of his desk and tossed it onto the blotter. "Sit here. Want some coffee? Or a Coke?"

"Coffee."

He got up and left the office. I rose and went around to the other side of the desk.

It took me about twenty minutes to write a two-page account of last night's horror show. As I wrote, it all came back to me. Not just the details, the feelings. I was accurate and objective in my writing, just as I'd preached at the recruits to be in the report class. When I finished, my hands were sweaty and shaking. I wiped them on my jeans.

"All done?" Jack said.

I gave him the report. He read it, tugging at his lower lip with thumb and forefinger, and nodded approvingly. "Fine."

"If it weren't, I'd be teaching in the academy under false pretenses, wouldn't I?"

He photocopied the report and put the original in a manila folder. That went into the top drawer of his desk. The copy he gave to me. I folded it and put it in my purse.

Jack went over to the window and stood there, his hands shoved in his hip pockets, looking out at the Division of Employment Security.

"What?" I said.

He turned to face me. "I should have been here last night."

"I know," I said lightly. "You'd have caught the guy in five seconds, God help him."

"That isn't what I mean."

I took a deep breath. It was important that I be careful in the wording of what I said next. "What happened last night could have happened anywhere, anytime. It was a stupid fluke, that's all."

I could tell from the expression on his face that I'd taken the wrong tack. I was being logical and rational. Unfortunately, I was being logical and rational in an area where those things didn't obtain.

"You're here for me now," I said. "I know you always will be."

Maybe that didn't make things a great deal better. I was pretty sure, however, that it didn't make them worse.

15

We had lunch, and by some kind of silent mutual agreement, didn't talk any further about the preceding night. I was pretty sure the subject would come up again, though.

Jack went back to work, and I blew the rest of the afternoon nosing around Central Square and its environs. I browsed in an antique shop and investigated the Japanese grocery store on Prospect Street. I bought some cotton batting at Woolworth's to stuff a pillow I was making. The Woolworth's in Central Square was one of the original ones, with the big gaudy ornate sign of gold letters on a red background, which was why I like going there. Then I went to the public library and read the papers.

A little after five, I went back to the police station to pick up Jack. We drove to my place, making a stop at the liquor store to pick up some wine and a stop at the grocery store to pick up dinner. We foraged around at the meat counter until Jack found some nice-looking steaks.

"Trying to raise your cholesterol count?" I inquired.

"Yeah, just what the doctor ordered," he replied.

We went to the produce department for some asparagus.

"And I get to cook it all," I said at the checkout counter. "Lucky me."

Thus provisioned, we continued back to my house. Jack took Lucy out for a walk while I washed and trimmed the asparagus and made us drinks.

Jack and Lucy returned from their stroll. I opened a can

of liver by-product glop for Lucy. Jack and I took our drinks and the cheese plate to the living room. The cheese was a sort of hybrid Brie with blue veins running through it like those in Roquefort. Just looking at it made me feel like a yuppie. But I sampled a tiny slice and it tasted very good. I sat cross-legged on the floor by Jack's feet and rested my head against his right knee. He put his hand on my head.

"You still haven't told me about your adventures in Philadelphia," I said.

"There weren't any," he said. "Except that the other passengers on the plane coming back looked kind of funny at the handcuffs on the guy."

"I'll bet they did," I said. "How's the Bonnie Nordgren investigation going?"

"Oh, yeah, that," Jack said. "Well, we got the preliminary autopsy report back this afternoon?"

"What'd it say?"

"She had enough heroin and cocaine in her system to knock down a rhinoceros."

I screwed up my face. "That was the cause of death?"

"As of this point."

I looked up at Jack "They checked for signs of physical illness?"

"Oh, sure." He shook his head. "No sign of a brain tumor, or anything else along those lines. They'll do a little more sophisticated testing, but . . ." He shrugged and sipped some bourbon. "I don't think they'll find anything."

"What about your speculation that she didn't shoot herself up with the heroin and cocaine?"

"I think they're going to pursue it."

I got up from the floor and took a seat on the couch next to him. "So one way or another, for whatever reason, Bonnie was murdered."

"Probably." He set his glass on the table. "This is a very attractive subject for a predinner conversation, isn't it?"

"It's just that I'm interested."

"Yeah, aren't we all?"

I smiled at that. " 'Scuse me a sec. I have to go put some water on for the rice."

When I returned to the living room, Jack was feeding Lucy a cracker liberally coated with cheese.

"That dog eats better than a lot of people in this town," I said.

"She's also a lot better behaved than some of the people in this town," Jack said. Lucy licked the final crumbs off his thumb and forefinger, then settled back on her haunches and gave him a loving look.

I sat back down on the couch and retrieved my drink from the end table. "When you say *they* are going to pursue it, who do you mean by *they*?"

"Your two buddies from the DA's office," Jack said, smiling. "Joe McFadden and Bernie Carr. Frick and Frack, as you call them. And Bill Wallace."

"You mean you're not actively involved in the investigation anymore?"

"Well, I never really was. I mean, I was there in the beginning, sure, but then again so were a lot of other guys, including Bill. Bill's good. So are Bernie and Joe, for that matter."

"Maybe." I sniffed. "They'll have a much better chance of finding out who wasted Bonnie if they let you do the finding."

He laughed. "The captain gave me that bank robbery and two attempted murders to play with. I have more than I can handle as it is."

"Just wait," I said darkly. "They'll come screaming to you for help sooner or later. Probably sooner."

"You're very kind to say so."

"That's me," I said. "Kind." I set my drink on the coffee table. Then I reached over, took Jack's glass from his hand, and set it down next to mine. It was still half-full.

He gave me a curious look. "What are you doing?"

"You'll see." I slid sideways along the couch and bounced myself into his lap. He caught me around the waist with one arm. I bent my head and kissed him.

A minute or so passed. I pulled away, feeling flushed and a little breathless, and gazed down at him.

"How hungry are you?" I asked. "For food, that is."

He narrowed his eyes. "Not very."

"Shall we postpone dinner for a bit?"

"That's not a bad idea."

"Good," I said. "Let's go."

I remembered to turn off the stove.

As we were getting into bed, Jack caught sight of the carving knife on the night table. "What the hell is *that*?" he asked.

"Hmmm? Oh. That's in case a bad guy should break in here."

Jack grinned at me. "He has. And now he's attacking."

We had dinner at nine-thirty. Very Continental, except that we ate in the kitchen. Jack cleaned up the dishes while I sat and drank coffee and watched him.

"Jack?"

"Uh-huh?"

"I had kind of an unpleasant experience yesterday."

He turned to face me. "No kidding, sweetheart."

"No, no," I said hastily. "I didn't mean *that*."

"God," Jack said. "What next?"

I told him about the call I'd made to Carl DiBenedetto, and about the things Carl had said to me. "That stupid old bastard," was Jack's reaction.

"I know," I said. "But it still made me feel bad."

"Which was exactly what it was intended to do," Jack said.

"I know that, too. Even so . . ."

Jack rinsed a plate and set it in the dish drainer. Then he dried his hands on a piece of paper towel. He came over to me and put his arm around my shoulders. "You've been having a swell time lately, haven't you?"

I wrinkled my nose and he laughed sympathetically and gave me a hug. Then he sat down across from me.

"Forget it," he said. "It's not worth worrying about or

feeling guilty over. That DiBenedetto is a jerk. He fucked up and now he's looking for somebody else to blame."

"That was what I thought."

"So?" Jack raised his eyebrows.

I looked at him for a moment, then nodded and smiled a little wryly. "Right."

Jack got up and went back to the sink and resumed washing the silverware.

"Have Bill or Frick and Frack talked to DiBenedetto yet?" I asked.

"I don't know," Jack replied. "I would guess yes. Why?"

"No special reason. It's just that I'd like to hear what their take on him is."

"If they tell me, I'll tell you."

"Okay." I ate a cherry from the bowl on the table, then poured myself more coffee. The smell of it reminded me of the brew Bonnie's landlord had served me. Which in its turn made me think of something else.

I put cream in my cup and said, "Any word on what's happened to Gayle Lydecker?"

"Far as I know, she hasn't turned up yet."

"Why am I not unbearably surprised by that?" I asked.

Jack took a cup from the cabinet over the sink, brought it to the table, and poured himself some coffee. "You think she took off permanently?"

"It would seem so, wouldn't it?"

Jack sat down at the table. "You know, when I was in Bonnie's apartment the other day, just poking around, I had the feeling that only one person had been living in it. At least very recently."

"Oh?"

He stirred some cream into his coffee. "You saw Bonnie a few times. How tall would you say she is?"

I was taken aback by the apparent irrelevance of the question. "What?"

He repeated what he'd asked.

"God, I don't know. Maybe, oh, say—five-six?"

"And Gayle?"

"Five-eight? Five-nine?"

He nodded. "Okay. Would a woman five-six and a woman five-eight or five-nine take the same clothing size?"

I looked up from the cup and at Jack, comprehension dawning. "I don't know. They might. If the shorter woman were a little heavy, or the taller woman on the thin side . . . why?"

"Because all the clothing we found in the apartment was the same size. Eight."

I thought for a moment. "Probably Bonnie's."

"Yeah. That was the size of the shirt and jeans she had on when we found her. Plus, what clothing we did find in the apartment looked like enough for only one person."

I sipped my coffee. "There's something else."

"What's that?"

I set the cup in the saucer. "My sense of Bonnie, both times I saw her, was that she was a fairly funky dresser. You know, sort of artsy-craftsy hip?"

"Yes?"

"Whereas the impression I got of Gayle was that she wears gray flannel pin-striped pajamas. In the shower."

Jack burst out laughing. "Very good."

"What was the clothing in the apartment like?"

"Well, I didn't inventory every single pair of underpants, but what I saw of it seemed to tend toward—what did you call it—artsy-craftsy hip."

"Bonnie's," I said with great conviction. "What about the other stuff in the apartment? Any of it look like it might belong to Gayle?"

Jack smiled. "No way to know for sure. People don't label everything they own, do they? I mean, you don't put a little sign on every dish or ashtray saying it belongs to you, do you?" He drank some coffee. "One thing, though. There was only one toothbrush and one tube of toothpaste, and just one of all the stuff like that in the bathroom."

I ate another cherry. "I'd say it's a fair guess, then, that old Gayle cleared out and took off. Probably before Bonnie died. For whatever reason."

"Maybe."

"Frick and Frack must be *very* eager to talk to her."

"Oh, yes."

I looked at him. "Do *you* think she had anything to do with Bonnie's death?"

"I wouldn't know, sweetie." He yawned, and glanced up at the clock on the wall above the table. "Getting late."

It was just eleven. "By your standards," I said. "By mine, it's early evening."

"Tell me," Jack said. "Was there ever a point in your adult life when you had to get up to go to work before ten A.M.? Like normal people?"

"Oh, sure," I replied. "My first teaching job, I had four eight-thirty classes. And I had to travel thirty miles to get to the school. Those days, I was getting up at six."

"I can't imagine it," Jack said.

"Well, it's true."

He smiled. "I think I'll hit the sack. If you'd like to join me, I'd enjoy the company."

"I guess I can make an exception," I said. I gathered up the coffee cups and saucers and put them in the sink. I felt warm and comfortable and relaxed, full of food and sex. A distinct difference from last night at this time.

"Jack?"

"Yes?"

"I know this is going to sound a little odd, but would it be possible for us to go to your place and spend the night there?"

"Of course it would," he said. "But . . . any particular reason why?"

I hesitated a moment, then sighed. "It's—I don't feel like being here tonight, that's all. Even with the company." I glanced around me. "It's a nice apartment and all that, but I just don't want to sleep in it right now."

"Then we'll go to my place."

I smiled at him. Then I went into the bedroom to throw some necessaries into an overnight case. Lucy saw what I was doing and began capering around in anticipation of going for a ride in the car.

I slung the strap of the overnight case on my shoulder and walked into the living room. Jack was sitting on the couch flipping through last week's *Newsweek*. He glanced up at me. "Ready?"

"Yup. Jack?"

"Yes?"

"I may just decide to move in with you for a few days, not just tonight."

He grinned. "My pleasure."

16

Having gone to bed preternaturally early the night before, I was able to wake up early enough the next morning to have breakfast with Jack. He looked at me with exaggerated astonishment when I wandered into the kitchen yawning and tying the sash of my bathrobe.

"Here's a surprise," he said.

"Oh, come," I replied. I opened the refrigerator and took out the orange juice. "We've had breakfast together before."

"Yeah, maybe five times in five years."

"Maybe that was because I wanted to spare you the sight of me in the morning. Ever think of that?"

He regarded me critically. "You look fine. A little sleepy, but fine." He cracked some eggs into a bowl and beat them with a fork. "Want some of these?"

"Sure."

"Okay. Why don't you make some toast?"

"All right." I took the coffee Jack handed me and my orange juice to the table. The newspaper was beside my plate. I glanced at the front page. All the stories looked to be boring or depressing. Some both. Jack brought the scrambled eggs to the table and we ate in silence, which was just dandy with me. At eight in the morning, I don't qualify as intelligent life.

When we'd finished, Jack asked. "Got any plans for today?"

I shrugged. "Nothing rigidly scheduled. I ought to get started on my writing again. I'll probably go to the library and poke around for an interesting topic. What about you?"

"Oh, I got my little old bank robbery to keep me busy. Plus two attempted murders." He spread his hands. "And when I get finished with those, I can go back and work on all the unsolved cases. After that—"

"Okay, I get the point," I said. "Have fun."

He left. I cleaned up the breakfast remains, then took a shower and got dressed. Lucy came back from boogying around in the enclosed section of the backyard. I put a bowl of water on the kitchen floor for her and gave her a dog cookie. I checked my bag to be sure I had a notebook and an adequate supply of pens. Then I took off for the main branch of the public library on Broadway.

It was true I was going there to do research. On Gayle Lydecker.

I don't know why I didn't tell that to Jack. Probably because he would have asked me what was the point. And I didn't have a snappy comeback to that, because I didn't quite know myself. Was I still feeling bad about my failure to locate Bonnie before she'd died? And trying to make up for it?

I have learned that if you spend too much time trying to figure out the reasons why you do whatever it is you do, sooner or later doing anything seems pointless. I mean, what does it all matter, ultimately? Life is a process of inventing ways of keeping yourself occupied.

The public library had a fairly good business section in its reference area. The person in charge of that department evidently took her job seriously. I told her I was looking for a guide to Massachusetts consulting firms, if such a thing existed.

"What *kind* of consulting?" was her first question. "There are management consulting firms, financial consulting firms, political consulting firms, health care consulting firms, educational—"

I cut off the flow. "General-purpose, as far as I know. The outfit I'm interested in is MacCrimmon Associates in Waltham."

The librarian nodded. "Well, let me check over here in our index to Massachusetts businesses."

I tool the chair beside the information desk. A pile of *Publishers Weekly* sat on the desk blotter. I reached over for the topmost one and leafed through it. About half the magazine was devoted to software, which I found acutely disquieting. I was reading an article about something called interactive fiction when the librarian returned from her diggings.

"MacCrimmon Associates is quite a large firm," she reported. "They have headquarters in Waltham, with offices in London, Geneva, Tokyo, and Athens."

I replaced the *Publishers Weekly*. "I had no idea."

"I believe we have their most recent annual report. Would you care to see it?"

"Please."

"In that bin over there." The librarian pointed at a large gray metal filing cabinet. "It should be filed under *M*."

No shit, I thought. Aloud, I said, "Thank you very much."

The MacCrimmon Associates annual report was large, glossy, and expensively produced. The cover photograph was of five nice-looking people (three whites, one black, one Asian, two women) posed in a smiling group in front of an ivy-covered brick building. Idly, I wondered why it was that so many large American businesses felt moved to make their annual reports look like the Phillips/Andover catalogue.

I found an empty table and sat down with the report. On the first page was the chief executive officer's message to the shareholders, which said nothing in vague yet excruciatingly upbeat language. The next section outlined MacCrimmon's functions. Jack had been correct in describing them as a general-purpose outfit. They did finance, health care, politics, and something called human resource management. A true Renaissance enterprise.

What I was really interested in was a list of their employees, above and beyond the minion category. I flipped through the report and found one, just before the balance sheets and consolidated statements of operation.

Gayle Lydecker was—or had been—a senior associate political consultant. Her credentials were a B.A. from Wellesley and a master of arts in law and diplomacy from the Fletcher School.

I went back to that section of the report that described what it was that a political consultant did. Apparently they orchestrated the campaigns of people who wanted to be elected to public office—they did demographics, made surveys, took polls, interviewed and hired campaign staffers, arranged fund-raisers, and told the candidate how he or she should act. They wrote speeches and served as press liaisons.

Among MacCrimmon Associates' most recent coups in this realm were the elections of a senator from one of the midwestern states and of a representative from Connecticut and a New York State Assemblyman.

I went through the rest of the report. It was lavishly illustrated with black-and-white photographs of various consultants doing their thing, shirtsleeves rolled up to the elbow and ties loosened. Women included. There were no pictures of Gayle Lydecker.

I closed the report and leaned back in my chair. With my eyes closed, I tried to conjure up the image of Gayle Lydecker, girl political consultant, hitting the street and canvassing wards and pressing the flesh and kissing babies and arranging twenty-five-dollar-a-head cocktail bashes and a-grand-a-plate fund-raiser dinners.

It wouldn't come. I returned the annual report to the librarian.

"Did you find what you were looking for?" she asked.

"I think so," I said. "Thank you."

17

Actually, I didn't know what it was that I'd found. What I was wondering about was the origin and length of the connection between Gayle and Bonnie. They probably hadn't met in college or while doing graduate work; they'd gone to different schools. Maybe the association went back further than that. Or maybe not. Maybe when and how they'd met wasn't important.

I walked to Harvard Square and had lunch in a soup-and-salad place. Afterward I wandered back up Mass. Avenue, trying to figure out my next move. The burst of inspiration that had sent me to the public library this morning seemed to have used itself up, at least temporarily.

I was old enough to be used to that experience, and thus able to accommodate myself to it.

I was waiting for a break in the traffic so I could cross Mass. Avenue to Quincy Street when I heard a car horn beep twice at close range. Automatically, I glanced to my right. A nondescript light blue Chevy of late seventies vintage drew up to the curb in front of me. The driver cranked down the window on his side. It was McFadden, the state police detective.

He smiled at me and said, "Where you going?"

"No place," I replied.

"Hop in," he said. "I'll take you."

I gave a startled laugh and then shrugged. "Sure. why not?" I went around to the passenger side of the car and got into it. I shut the door and McFadden pulled away from the curb.

He glanced at me briefly and said, "How are you?"

"Fine," I said. "And you?"

"Good." He shot me another quick look. "Heard you had a bad experience the other night."

I grimaced reflexively. "Yeah. Who told you? Jack?"

He nodded. "Lousy thing to have happen. You feeling okay now?"

"Oh, yes. I'm trying not to think about it."

"Don't," he advised.

We merged with the clogged traffic in the dead center of Harvard Square. McFadden had to brake rather sharply in order not to hit a guy with pink hair on a six-foot-high unicycle. Neither McFadden nor I commented on the sight. It was nothing out of the ordinary in this part of town. A polka-dotted brontosaurus wouldn't have been.

We bore right past Harvard Yard and beneath the underpass in front of the Center for Public Administration.

"Sergeant McFadden," I began.

"Joe," he interrupted.

"Joe," I repeated. "Well, Joe, it's not that I'm not delighted to be riding around with you, but are we going anywhere in particular?"

There was a fork in the road ahead of us. McFadden took the left side onto Cambridge Street.

"I'm glad I saw you back there," McFadden said. "I wanted to talk to you again."

I looked at him curiously. "Oh? About what?"

"Just check a few things." He gave me a slight smile. "You got a few minutes?"

"Certainly."

We passed Cambridge Hospital and went through Inman Square.

"Where are we going?" I asked.

"My office, if you don't mind. I'll give you a lift wherever you want afterward."

"Okay."

For the remainder of the ride, I inspected McFadden as subtly as I could.

He was about six feet tall, I estimated, and looked fairly lean beneath the slightly crumpled tan summer suit he was wearing. His hair was sandy and his eyes light brown. His face was long, and the lines that bracketed nose and mouth were strongly cut.

It startled me to realize that he was a sort of muted version of Jack. I hadn't consciously noticed the resemblance before, but it probably explained why I kind of liked him without even really knowing him.

"We're going to the courthouse, right?" I said.

McFadden nodded.

The Middlesex County Courthouse took up an entire block between Third and Thorndike streets. It was a fairly new building and had the anonymous exterior of most modern high-rises. The original courthouse, now the probate court, really looked like what it was. Columns and all.

McFadden parked the car in a space on Cambridge Street across from a bar appropriately named the Barrister. Ahead of us was a state police cruiser and behind us a Cambridge cruiser. About half the motor vehicles in this part of town belonged to one law enforcement agency or another. The state cops tended to park in tow zones, and the city cops just *loved* tagging them.

I had been in the courthouse maybe two or three times before, with Jack while he was on business. Just inside the main entrance was a metal detector like the kind they have in airports. McFadden went around it. I had to go through it, of course, and have my bag searched by the guard.

"Good job I left the Uzi at home," I said to McFadden as we walked to the elevator bank.

"I figured you more for the Magnum type," he replied, straight-faced.

The State Police Detectives Unit was an enormous rectangular room with three rows of desks running front to back, like a school classroom. Only one of the desks was occupied, this by a young guy with curly blonde hair who was sitting with his feet on the desk blotter and reading the sports section of the *Herald*. He was wearing the only shoulder holster I'd ever seen outside of television. I gave a close look at it. The alignment of the straps suggested that the device hadn't been designed to be worn by women.

McFadden had a desk by the window, which was perhaps a perquisite of being a sergeant. He took a chair from behind one of the desks and pushed it over beside his. He gestured at me to sit down in it.

"You gonna put bamboo shoots under my fingernails?" I asked.

"Never," McFadden said. "I leave that to Bernie."

"Oh, I see." I lowered myself into the chair. "You're the good cop, he's the bad one."

"Well, sometimes," McFadden said, and smiled.

I returned the smile, then leaned back and crossed my legs. "What can I do for you?"

There was a folder lying in the center of McFadden's desk blotter. He flipped it open and leafed through the contents, glancing at each page. Halfway through, he stopped reading and looked back up at me.

"In the matter of Bonnie Nordgren," he said. "Yesterday we spoke to Professor Carl DiBenedetto."

"And a good time was had by all," I said, without thinking.

The left corner of McFadden's mouth twitched as if he wanted to smile but couldn't because this was serious business.

"Sorry," I apologized. "Sometimes I try too hard to be a comedienne."

McFadden closed the folder and rested his left hand on it. "That's because you're nervous about being here."

I looked at him, startled. "Oh, no—"

"Sure you are." He leaned back in his chair and linked his hands behind his head. "That's okay. Natural reaction."

Well, if he said so, I wasn't going to argue with him. Come to think of it, I *did* feel a wee bit ill-at-ease. Maybe the bad guys were used to being picked up off the street and carted down to the courthouse to be interrogated, but I wasn't.

"Anyway," McFadden said. "I'd like to run back through what you told us the other day."

"You mean about how I got involved in the matter of Bonnie Nordgren?"

This time, McFadden did smile. "If you don't mind."

"No, of course not." I pursed my lips and wrinkled my nose, the physical manifestation of my thoughts organizing themselves.

When I'd finished talking, McFadden said, "Okay." His voice and face were neutral.

"Well?" I said.

He looked at me curiously.

"Does my version of events tally with Carl's?"

McFadden didn't reply. I figured he wouldn't. But no harm in my asking.

I hitched my chair a little closer to his. "Have you spoken to the two women whose names I gave you. The ones who worked for Carl? And with Bonnie?"

"Uh-huh." The man was a positive chatterbox.

An incredible thought occurred to me. "Carl's not a suspect, is he?"

McFadden smiled again and made a movement with his head that wasn't a shake and wasn't a nod. Deliberately ambiguous, I was sure.

"I don't mean to tell you your business," I said, and then proceeded to do exactly that. "Carl just loved Bonnie to pieces. He wasn't angry at her for ripping him off and making an idiot of him and then vanishing. I don't think he even saw it in those terms. Besides . . ."

McFadden gave me a questioning look.

"You've met Carl," I said. "Does he strike you as a vicious murderer of young blondes? Can you see him sticking a needleful of deadly drug into somebody?''

McFadden laughed.

"Not easy, is it?'' I asked.

"When was it ever?'' he replied.

He even sounded like Jack. If the imitation was studied, at least he'd picked someone worth imitating.

"Remember the two guys I told you about?'' I asked. "The scuzzy one who hung around Bonnie while she worked at Currier College? And the boyfriend I heard about from her mother? The one who was supposed to have some government job?''

"Sure.''

"Were you ever able to track either one of them down?''

"Not so far.''

"Oh,'' I said. "Too bad.''

"Your friend Fowler gave us a pretty good description of the—what did you call him?''

"The scuz.''

McFadden nodded. "Yeah. But there's probably a million guys that fit that description, and without anything else to go on . . .''

"It's a problem,'' I agreed. "And the government guy?''

"Nothing's come up.''

I wrinkled my forehead. "Bonnie's mother didn't even have a name for him?''

"She said not. Apparently Bonnie was pretty secretive about him, whoever he was.'' McFadden picked up a pencil lying on the desk blotter and drummed it idly on the manila folder. "At this point, I'm not even sure the guy existed.''

I frowned harder at him. "What are you saying? That he was a figment of Bonnie's imagination?''

"I don't know,'' McFadden replied. "Nobody I've spoken to so far has made any reference to any kind of current boyfriend.''

"Strange,'' I said. "A woman as good-looking as Bonnie, you'd think she'd have at least one or two men hanging around.''

McFadden smiled. "Yeah, you would, wouldn't you? Her mom *did* give us the name of a guy Bonnie dated two or three years ago, though."

"Oh, yeah? He a suspect?"

"He was in San Diego the week Bonnie died."

"Well, that's a decent alibi, I suppose."

"Better than some I've heard," McFadden agreed.

"Can you tell me his name?"

I asked the question purely out of form, not in any expectation that I'd get a straightforward answer to it. Which was why when McFadden said, "Koenig. Dennis Koenig." I was nearly enough startled to fall out of my chair.

The reaction must have been visible on my face because McFadden said, "Something the matter?"

"No," I said hastily. "Nothing at all. Koenig? K-O-E-N-I-G?"

"Uh-huh."

I pulled out my little notebook and wrote down the name.

"Why do you want to know?" McFadden asked.

A fair question. I was too embarrassed to tell him that I was running my own independent informal investigation into Bonnie Nordgren's death. "No special reason," I said. "It's just that I'm sort of caught up in this business, and Bonnie's an enigma to me, and I'm a curious person, and I'd like to find out more about her."

"Yeah, join the club," McFadden said, somewhat sourly.

I laughed. "So what's Koenig's address?"

McFadden flipped open the file folder on his desk. He turned a few pages, skimmed one, and then said, "He lives in Quincy. Works at a PR firm right here in town." McFadden read off the name of the agency and its address. I took down it and Koenig's home address.

"Thank you," I said. I shut the notebook and dropped it back in my purse. "You're a doll."

"Oh, yeah," McFadden said. "Everybody tells me that."

I slung the strap of my bag over my shoulder and rose. "I should be running along. Errands."

"Lemme take you wherever you're going," McFadden said.

"Oh, that's okay."

"I said I would," McFadden replied. "So I will."

"Well, okay. Thanks."

"No trouble."

We left the office. The trooper in the shoulder rig was still contemplating the American League box scores.

"Be nice if the Sox won the pennant this year," I observed idly.

"Be nice if I won the Irish Sweepstakes this year," McFadden said.

His car didn't have a ticket. We rode down Cambridge Street with no conversation. When we got to Inman Square, I said, "You're a pretty close-mouthed guy, aren't you?"

He glanced at me briefly. "What do you mean?"

"Only that I was a little surprised that you gave me Dennis Koenig's name."

McFadden shrugged. "Couldn't see any reason not to. The guy's not a suspect. Besides, you've already talked to most of the other people I interviewed, anyway."

"When you put it that way," I conceded.

We continued down Cambridge Street and turned right onto Mass. Avenue.

"Maybe there's another reason, too," I said, as we passed the law school.

"What's that?"

"Oh," I said. "I don't know. Maybe you figure that if I talk to Koenig, he might tell me something he forgot to tell you, and I'll tell whatever it is to Jack, and he'll pass the word back to you."

"Possible," McFadden said judiciously. "Anything's possible."

I looked at him for a moment, shaking my head slowly. "You *are* a shrewdie, aren't you?"

McFadden smiled more broadly than I'd ever seen him do. "Everybody tells me that, too."

18

I gave some hard thought to how I should approach Dennis Koenig. I had to assume that he'd be resistant to the notion of discussing Bonnie with a stranger. A stranger, moreover, who unlike the cops didn't have a legitimate excuse to question him about his relationship with a past girlfriend.

If I were upfront about my motive for wanting to talk to him, there was a good chance I wouldn't get past his secretary's desk.

If I lied my way into his office, there was an equally good chance he'd be so angered by the deception he'd have me tossed out into the street.

Nice options.

In the end, I decided to go the con route, my least favorite pastime when I was dealing with someone I had no reason to assume wasn't nice.

I sort of hoped Dennis Koenig would turn out to be a real twerp.

That afternoon I called Clark, DeAngelis Associates and announced myself to the receptionist as Elizabeth Connors from the Management Communication Department at the Harvard Business School. The latter three words worked their usual magic. The receptionist put me right through to Koenig's office. I repeated the same announcement to this secretary, and after a few seconds' pause, she connected me with the man himself.

"Hello, Ms. Connors, how can I help you?" a very cheerful, youngish male voice said.

"Better hear me out before you make any promises you can't keep," I replied.

He laughed. "Go ahead."

"Okay," I said. "As your secretary probably told you, I'm an instructor in Management Communication at HBS. It's a required course that involves teaching the students how to write more effectively for business and also how to make presentations."

Listening to myself, I couldn't believe how full of shit I was.

"Yes?" Koenig said, sounding interested.

"Another very important part of the course," I continued, "entails teaching the students how to handle press and public relations."

"Ah-hah," Koenig said.

Now *I* laughed. "Yes, well, the reason I'm calling you is that we're trying to arrange a series of seminars featuring guest speakers who are experts in the field of PR."

God, I could lay it on with a trowel.

"And," I added. "I was hoping you and I could talk about the possibility of—that is, perhaps you might be interested in being the featured speaker at one of the seminars."

"Well, that's really nice of you to ask," Koenig said. "I'm honored. But, you know," he went on, in confidential tones, "I don't think I'm the world's greatest expert in the field of public relations. Maybe you want to speak to Mr. DeAngelis. He's a real terrific guy. Knows everything there is to know about the field. Maybe you ought to talk to him."

Despite the modest disclaimer, there was a little note of hope in Koenig's voice that I wouldn't abandon him for Mr. DeAngelis. I stopped feeling like I was full of shit and started feeling like shit.

"Be that as it may," I said. "I'd still like to talk to you. Can we get together sometime soon?"

"Let me check my calendar," Koenig said.

While I waited, I made faces at myself. To myself, but at myself as well.

Koenig came back on the line. "All right," he said. "I have a free hour tomorrow morning. How's that?"

"I'll come to your office," I said, before he could offer to meet me at mine at the business school. "What time?"

"Nine-thirty?"

"Fine," I said. "See you then, Mr. Koenig."

"Please. Call me Dennis."

"And I'm Liz."

After we hung up, I went into the bathroom, looked in the mirror over the sink, and made an especially horrible face. "You sleazy bitch," I said to my reflection.

I didn't have a gray summer-weight two-piece suit and a high-collared white blouse with a maroon ladies' bow tie to wear to my interview with Dennis Koenig, so I settled for a navy blue linen blazer and beige twill skirt with open-collared white broadcloth shirt. Maybe he'd think I was a prepette.

Clark, DeAngelis Associates occupied a large renovated Victorian frame house on Mount Auburn Street across from University Place. I was in the reception area at twenty-five after nine the next morning. At nine-twenty-nine I was ushered into Koenig's office.

A man I guessed to be in his early thirties got up from behind his desk as I entered, smiled, and held out his hand.

I was on an eye level with Koenig, which made him exactly six feet tall, since I was wearing two-inch heels. His body, clad in brown suit, looked painfully thin. His eyes were hazel and slightly magnified behind the lenses of gold-rimmed glasses. He had dark auburn hair, a matching mustache, and very fair skin with a faint pink tinge over the cheekbones.

Purely on the basis of his looks, I wondered if his family name might not have been originally O'Koenig. He was the most Celtic Teuton I'd ever encountered.

He waved me to a chair in front of the desk and returned to his own seat. On the desk was a tray bearing coffee service for two. Very civilized.

"So," Koenig said genially. "You're teaching at the B-School."

I took a deep breath and replied, "No. I'm not."

There was a moment's silence. Koenig looked politely puzzled. "But . . ." He paused, and made a slight throat-clearing noise. "We . . . excuse me." He shook his head and gave me a much closer version of the puzzled look. "You *are* Liz Connors?"

"Yes."

"And we spoke together yesterday on the phone."

"Yes."

"And you told me—"

"I know what I told you," I interrupted. "It doesn't happen to be true."

"Ah," Koenig said. The tone in which he spoke that monosyllable was distinctly ungenial. He sat back in his chair and folded his hands on his desktop.

"I should explain," I said.

"Yes," Koenig replied. "That would be a good idea, I think."

"I'm looking into the death of Bonnie Nordgren," I began.

Koenig's face became very still. "You are," he said. "I see." He shook his head again. "No, I don't see. Is that supposed to have some connection with running public relations seminars at the Harvard Business School?"

"No," I said. "The only reason I told you that I was teaching there was so that I could get in here." I bit my lower lip and added, "I figured you'd be more likely to speak to a total stranger if she came to you with a business proposition than if—"

"Um," Koenig said. "You're not with the police."

It wasn't a question. Even so, I said no.

Koenig nodded. "Anyway, they've already been here." He smiled a brief unpleasant smile. "You're quite right, by the way, in your assumption that I wouldn't be willing to talk to a stranger about Bonnie Nordgren. If that *was* your assumption."

I nodded.

"I see," Koenig said. "Well, here's another thing you ought to know." He leaned forward over the desktop. "I also don't much enjoy being jerked around and lied to and, in general, made a fool of. And I don't like wasting my time, either."

My face was red; I could feel it. I should probably get up and walk out and thereby preserve whatever smidgen of dignity I still had left. If any.

Instead, I said, "May I explain?"

He had the restraint not to say, *it better be good.*

I told him the whole story from its beginning, sparing no detail. I spoke of Carl DiBenedetto. I even threw in Jack's tale about the gypsies and their magical mystery cures.

By the time I'd finished, Koenig's facial expression had gone from grim to bemused.

"So," I concluded. "That's it."

"You're a writer," Koenig said.

"Yes."

"Mmm." He looked away from me and at the wall to the right, focusing apparently on the gallery-framed Motherwell reproduction that hung there. "You must have an excellent imagination," he said finally.

I was silent.

He looked back at me. "But probably not that good. To invent what I just heard you tell me."

"No," I said.

He stood up abruptly, pushing his cushioned swivel chair back hard enough so that it bumped gently against the wall behind him. "Let's take a walk," he said.

Startled, but hopeful, I rose. He held the office door open for me.

"Back in half an hour, Lisa," he said to the secretary.

"Sure, Mr. Koenig." She smiled at me, very brightly.

We walked through the reception area and out of the building onto Mount Auburn Street. Koenig shoved his hands into his hip pockets and gazed down the street, squinting a little in the bright sunlight.

"This way," Koenig said, indicating the direction away from Harvard Square, and began walking. He had a very rapid stride, and I had to hustle a little to keep up with him. Even given the length of my *own* stride.

Three blocks down Mount Auburn, on a corner, was a small shop, a combination variety store and lunch counter called Spiro's.

"Let's go in here," Koenig said.

He held the door open for me. Pissed off at me as he probably was, he wasn't forgetting his manners.

We sat at the counter. The woman behind it took our orders for coffee. Koenig asked for a cheese Danish.

I cleared my throat and said, "I want to apologize again for lying my way into your office. It's not the sort of thing I enjoy doing."

Koenig grunted noncommittally and sipped his coffee.

"Try to look at it this way," I said. "If you *do* talk to me about Bonnie, you will in a way be helping *her* more than *me*."

Koenig's face, in profile, seemed to harden. "Oh?" he said coolly. "How do you figure that?"

I sighed. "There's no kind way to put this," I said. "But most of the people I've already spoken to about her haven't had very nice things to say." I didn't add that my own impressions of Bonnie hadn't been exactly roseate. "I was hoping you might be able to give me a different picture."

"Why?" Koenig said. "What difference would that make now?"

"It might help her reputation," I said gently. "She didn't leave a terrific one behind."

Koenig exhaled softly. "No," he said. "That's true."

"She isn't here to speak up on her own behalf," I continued. "Perhaps you could."

Koenig drank the remains of his coffee and gestured at the counterwoman for a refill. She brought it, and removed the plate containing crumbs of the Danish pastry.

When the counterwoman was out of earshot, Koenig said, "All right."

I smiled and nodded.

"Well, what can I tell you?" Koenig asked.

"How long were the two of you together?"

Koenig furrowed his eyebrows slightly. "About two years," he said, after a moment's reflection. "Yeah. Just about exactly that."

"How'd you meet?"

Koenig smiled a little. "Fix-up," he said. "I had a friend who knew her in graduate school."

"Uh-huh." It was time to move to a less innocuous line of inquiry. I phrased my next question as neutrally as possible. "Was she involved with drugs at that time?"

Koenig glanced over at me. "When I met her?" He paused a second, and then added, "Yeah."

"Heavily?"

Koenig shook his head. "Not like later, no. She was doing coke at parties, and on the weekend sometimes."

"What they call recreational drug use," I mused aloud.

"Yeah," Koenig said shortly.

"You sound as if it bothered you," I said.

"It did," he replied, in an equally clipped voice.

From his tone of voice and his facial expression—indeed, the stiffness of his shoulders—I could tell that it had bothered him a lot.

"But you put up with it for two years," I observed mildly. "There must have been some compensating factors."

"Oh, yes," Koenig said. "Plenty of those."

"Well," I said. "I guess that's what I'm waiting to hear about. The only *objective* information I have about Bonnie was that she was very beautiful and very well educated."

Koenig took the spoon from the saucer beneath his cup and dinged it lightly against the side of the cup. He filled his mouth with air, blowing up his cheeks, and then let the air out, in a series of little puffs. "She knew how to make you feel good," he said.

It wasn't the first time I'd heard a man use that phrase to describe a woman, and I knew that Koenig wasn't referring only to sex. Nevertheless, I asked him to elaborate.

"It was a way she had," Koenig said, "of making you feel like you were *important*. Like you were . . ." He set the spoon back in the saucer and shook his head.

"The most important guy on earth?" I suggested. "And she couldn't manage without you?"

He smiled a little wryly. "In the good times, which were very good times, yes."

"And the bad times?"

His shoulders tightened again, the way they had when we'd talked of Bonnie's drug use. "She also had a way of closing you off," he said. "I . . ." He picked up the spoon again, but this time simply held it poised in midair. "She'd close you off sometimes," he concluded. "Just pull away and shut down."

"Suddenly make herself unavailable?" I said. "Break a date at the last minute? For no good reason?"

He nodded.

"And this kind of erratic behavior went on independent of her drug use?"

"Yeah." He put the spoon on the counter, raised his hands to his forehead, and rubbed it. "I knew I was being manipulated, but somehow that didn't matter."

Koenig and I were having the kind of conversation that should properly have been conducted over a strong drink, in a dimly lit place, in the sad and early hours of the morning. That he was saying such things to me, at ten in the morning, was an indication of the bitterness he still felt.

But I wasn't particularly surprised by his admission. Men tell men things. Women tell women things. Men and women tell each other things. But there's some stuff women say only to women. And there's other stuff men can only tell to women. A lot of times it's stuff they can't even say to themselves.

I had the feeling we were in one of those situations.

It was clear that Bonnie's hot-and-cold attitude toward Dennis Koenig had simply magnified her desirability in his eyes. *Another* thing that didn't surprise me—perhaps because of my age and degree of experience—was that Koenig, like a lot of men, seemed to not only enjoy on some level but encourage being treated cavalierly by women. The fact that this knowledge no longer surprised me didn't, however, mean that it no longer saddened me. That feeling seemed to get stronger with each passing year. All I could do was be thankful that my attraction for Jack didn't depend on my alternately and arbitrarily adoring him and spurning him.

Koenig and I had been silent for several moments, immersed in our individual deep thoughts, so that I was startled when he spoke again.

"I guess you could say," he remarked, in almost idle tones, "that Bonnie was well-trained in the art of Southern womanhood."

"Oh?"

"Sure. I think that was probably the big conflict of her life."

"Being a belle?"

"Being expected to be a belle, yes, but also being expected to be an achiever."

"That's a big conflict for a lot of women of my generation and Bonnie's," I said. "Being demanded to be soft and feminine as well as strong and competent."

"It was harder for Bonnie," Koenig said.

"Tell me."

"She told me, once, that she'd gotten mixed messages from her father."

"Oh?"

Koenig leaned forward and rested his elbows on the counter. "Bonnie came from a very upwardly mobile family. She was the oldest of five kids. All girls. She always felt a lot of pressure to . . . to meet expectations."

I nodded, and said, "I spoke briefly to Bonnie's mother. She seemed like a very sweet person."

"Oh, she is," Koenig said. "I met her once. She's very nice. But she was . . ." Koenig paused for a moment. "I guess the best way to put it is that she was in the background of the family." He hesitated again, as if searching for the right descriptive words. "She was a very pleasant shadow. Devoted to her husband and children. Totally self-effacing."

"I gather Dad was somewhat different," I said.

"An asshole," Koenig replied. "Even given my very slight acquaintance with him."

"Yes?"

"The wife and the daughters were the harem. With Bonnie the number one slave."

A horrid suspicion crept into my mind. "You're not talking about incest, are you?"

"Oh, God, no," Koenig said. "Not literally. Bonnie was his baby girl, but she was also his big girl. And expected to be everything. She was supposed to be the Miss America who grew up to win the Nobel Prize for physics."

"Tch," I said.

"She told me once," Koenig went on in a flat voice, "that her dad had given her instructions in how to make men *want* her."

"Which were?" I asked, truly fascinated. I hoped that I wasn't subconsciously trying to pick up pointers.

Koenig shrugged. "You know. The whole playing-hard-to-get routine. That men might get mad if you did certain stuff, but at the same time they'd be fascinated and intrigued. Like if a guy asked you to go to a movie, you should say you had to wash your hair, or some fucking thing like that." Koenig paused. "I have to say," he continued. "She could do that routine beautifully. And she was also extremely good at playing dumb. Like if you took her out for ice cream, you'd have to choose the flavor because it was too difficult for her to decide and she had to depend on your superior taste." Koenig took a sip of coffee. "She told me her father said men didn't like women who expressed opinions about anything. That women were for relaxation."

"Yet he expected her to win the Nobel Prize for physics," I said. "Or whatever."

"Shit," Koenig replied. "I don't know how else to explain it." His voice was mechanical and bitter. "She was Big Frank's sweet little princess. His helpless kitten who was supposed to depend on men for everything. But when it was report card time, and Bonnie got a B when she was supposed to get an A, or when she didn't make the girls' basketball team, it was a different story then."

I was silent.

"It was not," Koenig concluded softly, "a particularly happy upbringing for her, as far as I can tell."

"Would it be safe to assume," I said, "that Bonnie's life was a quest to please her father? That never met with success?"

"Yeah," Koenig said. "That sums it up nicely."

There was nothing I loathed more than questions with a psychoanalytic bent, but despite that, I posed one. "Do you think that explains how she acted with other men?"

"It could."

It probably did.

"Dennis," I said.

He was slouched over the counter, staring, staring at the patch of Formica between his forearms. He looked up at me, his face flat and blank.

"The constant pressure to be all things to all men," I said. "Was that what it was that got Bonnie into drugs? Did the cocaine and whatever else make her feel on top of things? As if she could do what was expected of her and be in control?"

"Why ask me?" Koenig shrugged. "I'm no expert on drug abuse."

"That's true," I agreed, smiling slightly. "But you don't have to be one to answer my question."

He looked at me for a moment, hard, and then moved his mouth into a reluctant simulation of my own small, rueful smile. "Yeah."

"So?"

Koenig took a deep breath and let it out slowly. "Bonnie and the coke?" He shrugged again. "Yeah. I suppose it made her feel better about things."

I nodded. "Did her family ever find out about her using drugs?"

Koenig shook his head. "As far as I know, no. She didn't visit them that often. And when she did, she was very careful not to use anything." Koenig grimaced. "Big Frank would have killed her."

"I see." I took a sip of now-tepid coffee. Then I asked my last and in some ways roughest question. "Were the drugs why you and Bonnie broke up?"

"How'd you guess?" Koenig said bleakly.

I nodded, a meaningless gesture.

Koenig reached into his hip pocket and extracted his wallet.

"Oh, let me get this," I said.

He shook his head quickly, almost angrily. He took four ones from the wallet and laid them back on the counter along with some change.

"I have to get back to the office," he said.

"Thank you for seeing me."

He gave me another faint smile.

We left the luncheonette and walked without conversation back to Clark, DeAngelis Associates. At the door, we shook hands.

"I'll let you know what happens," I said.

"You do that," he replied.

I watched him as he went up the front steps of the office building. His shoulders were hunched slightly. It made him look as if he'd lost an inch of height.

19

What I'd heard from Dennis Koenig had enlightened as much as it had depressed me. It had also given me an idea that I was very eager to confirm. I walked quickly back to Harvard Square in search of a working public phone in a relatively quiet place. The nearest one was just inside the entrance to the Harvest Bar.

I called Christine Cameron at Thatcher College. A secretary answered her phone and informed me that Professor Cameron was working at home today. I tried there. I don't know about the working part, but Christine was certainly home.

"A cryptic question for you," I said.

"What're you, a student?" she replied.

I laughed. "Yeah, of life. Do you know if Carl DiBenedetto and his wife ever had any children?"

"That's a cryptic question all right," Christine said.

"Well, did they?"

"Yeah. One. A daughter."

"What's become of her?"

"She died very young," Christine said. "Meningitis, I think it was."

I grimaced reflexively into the phone. "How awful."

"Yeah, I know," Christine said. "I don't think *he* ever got over it."

"Did he talk about it much?"

"Well, sometimes. I remember when I first started working at Thatcher, the DiBenedettos had Tom—that's my husband—and me over to dinner one evening. And afterward, when we were sitting around having coffee and liqueurs, Carl asked us, right out of the blue, what our plans were for having a family, and said that we shouldn't wait for too long, and that if we didn't have kids we'd regret it as long as we lived, and all that. And then he told us about how they'd lost their own little girl. Andrea, I think her name was."

"I see," I said.

"He told everybody in the department that story at one time or another."

"Including Bonnie?"

"Oh, sure."

"Poor man," I said.

"I know," Christine said. "Every time he does something to infuriate me, which averages maybe five times a day, I think of the little girl. And then I feel guilty for getting angry at him."

"I would, too, I suppose," I replied.

"The really ironic part," Christine continued. "Is that the one thing DiBenedetto does that drives me the most crazy is to treat me as if *I'm* his little girl."

"Funny how I guessed you'd tell me something like that," I said. "Does he do the same thing to Linda?"

"Oh, sure. Makes *her* crazy, too."

"I can see that."

"Why is this important?" Christine asked.

I put another dime into the coin slot of the phone box. Then I told her what Dennis Koenig had told me about Bonnie's father complex.

"My God," Christine said. "She and Carl were made for each other. A *folie-a-deux.*"

"In the grand style," I said.

She laughed.

"Still, it's sad, isn't it?" I said.

"Uh-huh."

We talked about nothing in particular for another few moments. I reminded her that she and Linda Rosenberg were supposed to have dinner with me, and we set a date a few weeks hence. Then Christine went back to correcting student essays and I went back to detecting, or at least to my version of it.

What I had to do next was talk to DiBenedetto himself. The conversation I'd had yesterday with Joe McFadden bothered me a little. I wasn't altogether sure the cops weren't semi-seriously considering DiBenedetto as a candidate for Bonnie's murderer. Ludicrous as the notion seemed to me, whose money at this point was on Gayle Lydecker anyway, I could perceive that in the cops' view it might have a certain credibility. Bonnie had, after all, bilked Carl of a considerable sum and, worse, made him look like a fatuous old fool in the process. That could be a motive for murder.

But only if you didn't know Carl.

I walked over to Garden Street. It was as sunnily affluent as it had been on my last visit. The squirrels hadn't lost their smiles. But what did they know?

DiBenedetto, clad in a Yale sweatshirt and a pair of baggy old grass and paint-stained chinos, was clipping the yew hedge in front of his house. He stopped when he saw me and stood very still, the giant scissors raised at a ninety-degree angle.

"Hi, Carl," I said.

He looked at me very hard for a moment and then resumed chopping at the yews, with somewhat more vigor than before.

"Grow fast, don't they?" I remarked, in conversational tones.

No reply.

Well, I hadn't thought this would be easy. I had, after all, by Carl's lights betrayed him. As had Bonnie. And maybe even Andrea, by dying so young so long ago.

"Hey," I said. "Talk to me."

He looked up briefly from his clipping. "Do we have anything to say to each other, Elizabeth?"

"Well, now, Carl," I said. "Of course we do."

He snapped the clippers at one last six-inch fugitive sprout of yew, turned, and walked toward the house.

I zipped around the hedge and up the path that led from the sidewalk to the house. DiBenedetto went up the front steps to the porch. I quickened my pace, feeling the way I had the day I'd chased Gayle Lydecker.

I was about five feet behind DiBenedetto when he opened the front door. He'd have shut it in my face, except that I managed to insert my right foot between it and the jamb before he could. Nonetheless, he gave a token shove to the door. Thank God I wasn't wearing sandals.

"Ah, come on, Carl," I said, leaning against the door.

He released it so abruptly I almost fell across the threshold. Then he stepped back a pace and gave me another hard stare. He set the hedge clippers on a small table in the foyer and walked toward the back of the house, where his study was. I followed him. My foot felt a little squished, but I didn't limp.

I wondered if, in the strictest legal sense, I were trespassing. I had not, after all, been precisely welcomed into *Chez* DiBenedetto.

When we got to the study, Carl deposited himself heavily in the swivel chair behind the desk. Without waiting to be invited—it would have been a long wait—I plunked down on the camelback sofa. DiBenedetto looked at the bookcases. I looked at him.

His appearance was not terrific. There were dark smudges beneath his eyes and his skin had an oystery cast. His goatee was ever so slightly ragged. He might even have lost a few pounds, but not from diet and exercise. The grubby clothes didn't help, of course.

I caught him glancing at me out of the corners of his eyes, and I smiled. He shifted his gaze back to the bookcase hastily.

"I'm here to give you an update," I said.

"I didn't ask you to do that," he replied stiffly.

"No, you didn't," I said equably. "But it's all part of the service."

He grunted something unintelligible and gave me another quick, sidewise look.

I leaned back on the couch to make myself comfortable, inhaled strongly, and started talking.

DiBenedetto kept his eyes on the bookcase and his face carefully expressionless. But I could tell that he was absorbing every word I was saying. Some of it must have been painful for him to hear. I didn't exaggerate anything, but I didn't understate anything, either.

I decided that it would upset him to no good purpose if I even hinted to him that the cops might consider him a suspect in Bonnie's murder.

He was silent after I finished speaking. Then he swiveled his chair so that his back was to me. He set his elbows on the desk, leaned forward, and put his head in his hands.

A few moments passed, in which the only sound was the muffled one of traffic on Garden Street.

DiBenedetto spun around from the desk to face me. His face was flushed and his eyes were wet.

I gave him the faintest of sympathetic smiles.

When he spoke, his voice was a little clogged.

"That girl," he said. "That girl was like a daughter to me."

"I thought it might be something like that," I said softly. I was *very* glad I hadn't breathed a word to him about my suspicions about the cops' suspicions.

"I had another daughter once," DiBenedetto continued. "She died, too."

"I know," I replied. "I'm very sorry."

DiBenedetto closed his eyes and nodded. Then he twisted around in his chair and pulled open the top right desk drawer. He took from it a small leather object, held it tightly for a moment, then held it out to me. I leaned forward and took it. It was a small folder, like a wallet.

"Open it," DiBenedetto said.

I did.

It was a photograph case with two compartments. The compartment on the left held a black-and-white photograph of an infant in a long white dress. The compartment on the right contained a color picture of a smiling blonde child, perhaps three years old, dressed in a plaid pinafore and puffy-sleeved white blouse. The girl was clutching a large red rubber ball to her chest.

I closed the album, feeling my throat tighten.

"That's my Andy," DiBenedetto said, in a quiet, uninflected voice.

I handed him the album and he replaced it in the desk drawer. He shut the drawer very gently.

There was something terribly moving about his composure. Much more so than there would have been in flailing and uncontrolled weeping.

"I always thought," DiBenedetto said reflectively, "that my Andy would have looked a little like Bonnie, if she'd lived to grow up."

I nodded, and sucked in my lower lip and bit it.

DiBenedetto looked me full in the face. "I know a lot of people think I'm a fool for doing what I did," he said. "You probably do, too, Elizabeth."

I started to deny it, but he cut me off.

"Sure you do," he said. "And it's true. I am. A useless old fool and a buffoon."

"Oh, come on, Carl—"

"No," he said. "I could tell, when the police came to see me, they were wondering what kind of old sap would give thirty-five hundred dollars to a golddigger with a drug habit. Why shouldn't they? What kind of sucker would do what I did?"

"You were generous," I said.

He shook his head. "I don't blame them. How could they know the circumstances?"

"Even so . . ." I began lamely.

He smiled sadly. "That's all right, Elizabeth." He let out a long sigh. "You know, it wasn't just for myself that I didn't want the police in on this, at the beginning." He raised his right hand a few inches from the arm of the chair, held it motionless in the air for a few seconds, and then let it drop.

"I knew Bonnie was in trouble. I thought if I brought the police into it, at that point, that she'd only be hurt worse, to be treated by them like a thief." He glanced away from me, back to the bookcase. "I was wrong."

"You did what you thought was right," I said strongly.

He raised his hand again and waved it dismissively. "I thought I could save her," he said softly. "I thought maybe my little girl wouldn't have to die again." He gave me a pained, quirky smile. "But it didn't work out that way, did it?"

I swallowed hard. Then, with some effort, I said, "We can't go back and fix that, Carl."

"No," he agreed. "So what else is there to do?"

"We can find out who killed Bonnie," I said. "And we will." I paused a second and then repeated, with an assurance I hoped wouldn't prove unfounded, "We will."

20

I recalled Bonnie's Huron Avenue landlord telling me that, prior to last September, Bonnie had lived somewhere in the Back Bay. Which meant she'd lived there when she'd applied for her teaching job at Thatcher College. I got out the copy of her personnel file and looked at the resumé stapled to it. The address under Bonnie's name at the top of the first page was a Beacon Street one in Boston.

The following afternoon, I took the Red Line subway from Harvard Square to the Park Street station. Despite the fact that it was a twenty-minute walk to Boston from my house,

I didn't get in there much above once or twice a month. Too firmly settled in my Cambridge rut, I supposed.

Bonnie's former apartment was a block and a half down from Dartmouth Street, on the side of Beacon nearest Storrow Drive and the Charles. The building was a four-story brownstone that had obviously begun life as a townhouse and then been cut into perhaps eight or nine apartments. According to her resumé, Bonnie had lived in number three.

Parked in front of the building was a battered green pickup truck, its bed loaded down with lumber and various other items of construction material. The front door to the house was open, and I could hear, faintly, the buzz of a power saw. Somebody had left a paint-spotted drop cloth folded neatly over the iron railing on the front steps.

It didn't require much in the way of deductive ability to figure out that the building was being renovated, perhaps by someone with an eye to condo conversion.

A tall, lean young man in filthy cut-off jeans and gray tee shirt emerged from the dark foyer of the building and came down the front steps. Probably one of the construction workers. He went around to the rear of the pick up truck and opened the gate.

"Excuse me," I said.

The young man was sliding some two-by-fours from the bed of the truck. He looked over at me and said, "Yeah?"

I tilted my head at the brownstone. "The landlord or the super around?"

"Third floor," the kid said. "Apartment six."

"Thanks." I went up the steps and into the foyer, which was large and would probably be handsome when refurbished. The drop cloth on the parquet floor and the pile of Sheetrock remnants in one corner didn't do a lot for it at present. I went up the staircase that ran along the right wall.

The door to apartment six was open, and I could hear someone moving around within. I rapped on the doorjamb.

"Come in," a woman's voice said.

I pushed the door the rest of the way open and walked into what was clearly the apartment's living room. It was about twenty by fifteen, with a bay window that looked down onto Beacon Street and a ten-foot-high ceiling. Nice.

A short, rather plump mid-thirtyish woman in denim overalls and white tee shirt was standing before the rear wall. She had a can of spackle in one hand and a plastic chisel-like gadget in the other, and was daubing away at a small hole in the wall. She was meticulous about her work, I noticed.

When she'd finished, she set the can of spackle on the floor and turned to me. A startled expression flashed across her small round face.

"Oh," she said. "I thought you were one of the carpenters."

"No." I smiled and shook my head. "Just somebody looking for some information. Are you the super or the landlord here?"

"Both," she replied. She bent down and set the plastic chisel on the spackle can. As she straightened up, she added, "If you're looking for an apartment, I'm sorry, but nothing's available at the moment." She waved her right arm at the wall she'd been repairing. "You can see we're right in the middle of redoing the place."

"It looks like it'll be very nice when it's finished," I said.

"Thanks."

So much for the amenities; it was time to get down to business. "It's not an apartment I'm after," I said. "The information I'm looking for concerns a person who used to live here."

The woman raised her eyebrows.

"My name is Liz Conners," I said. "You are . . . ?"

"Daisy Jacobsen." The look she gave me now was compounded of eighty percent puzzlement and twenty percent uncertainty.

"Nice to meet you." I held out my right hand. After a moment, Ms. Jacobsen wiped her own right hand on her overalls and took mine. We shook. When I pulled my hand back, there were flecks of spackle clinging to the palm.

"Were you the landlord here last year?" I asked.

She nodded, still giving me that slightly wary look.

"Okay, then you probably *can* help me," I said. "The person I'm asking about is a woman named Bonnie Nordgren."

The wariness on Daisy Jacobsen's face deepened into suspicion. She took a step toward me, as if to study me at closer range. "Why?" she said. "Who are you, anyway?"

I ignored the question, which Jacobsen was certainly well within her rights to ask. "You *did* know Bonnie?"

Jacobsen nodded automatically, then caught herself. She frowned at me, hard. "What is this about?" she demanded. "Bonnie Nordgren is dead."

"Yes."

"Are you a reporter?" Jacobsen asked.

I guess I didn't look like a detective to her.

"No," I replied. "Although I am a writer. I'm not doing a story about Bonnie, though."

"Then—"

I held up my right hand. "Let me explain. If you don't like the explanation, then you can tell me to go and I will. But could you hear me out first?"

Jacobsen pursed her lips and gave me a very steady look that lasted for perhaps ten seconds.

"It'll be a *good* explanation, I promise you," I said.

"Oh, hell," Jacobsen said, letting out a long sigh. "All right. But I'm very busy."

"It won't take long," I said.

Jacobsen bent down and picked up the plastic chisel and spackle can.

"If you have another one of those doodads," I said, gesturing at the chisel, "I'll help you."

She shook her head, scooped a small amount of spackle from the can, and began dabbing at a dime-sized indentation in the wall.

I gave Jacobsen an absolutely accurate synopsis of how I'd come to be involved in the affairs of Bonnie Nordgren, and of the reasons why I was still involved in them. At the end of it, Jacobsen glanced at me briefly and said, "That's one of the nuttier stories I've heard recently."

"Yeah," I said. "Me too."

Jacobsen permitted herself a tiny grin, one that came and went so quickly that I almost missed it. "So what do you want from me?"

"Whatever help you can give. First off—how long did Bonnie live here?"

Jacobsen scowled thoughtfully. "About a year, maybe."

"Good tenant?"

"Sure, she was fine. Not noisy or dirty. Paid the rent on time."

I nodded. "Did you see much of her?"

Jacobsen scraped delicately at some excess spackle around the edges of the nail hole she'd just filled. "Occasionally, going in and out."

"How did she seem to you?"

"What?"

I'd phrased the question too ambiguously. "How did she act when you met her? I've talked to several other people who knew Bonnie fairly well, and they all told me that she had a tendency to behave oddly at times. *Spacy* was one of the words used to describe her."

"You mean do I think that Bonnie acted like someone on drugs?" Jacobsen asked.

Her directness was refreshing. "Well, yes."

Jacobsen dug into the spackle can. "She seemed a little weirded-out to me at times, yeah. About the drugs, I don't know. It could be. She died of an OD, didn't she?"

"Uh-huh."

"Well, all I can say is that if she *was* doing drugs while she was living here, she wasn't doing them heavy. She had it under control. At least, as far as I could tell. And I've known my share of druggies."

"All right." I paced slowly around the room, thinking up my next question.

"Did she ever have anyone living with her?"

"You mean a roommate?"

"Whatever."

"Not that I know of. And I probably would have noticed if she had."

"I see." I nodded. "What about visitors? Did she have many of those?"

Jacobsen leaned forward to inspect a hairline crack in the plaster of the wall. "Not lots. She had some."

"Okay. The person I'm interested in would be a woman in her mid- to late thirties. About five-foot eight or nine. Very fair skin. Prematurely gray hair. Very well groomed, very conservative dresser. Attractive, in a prim sort of way. Ever see anyone like that with Bonnie?"

"Nope," Jacobsen replied, still studying the crack in the wall.

"Oh," I said, a little crestfallen. My pacings had brought me to the bay window. I looked down at Beacon Street. The kid in the cut-off jeans was tossing some busted-up pieces of lathing into the back of the pickup truck.

"There was a guy I saw her with a lot."

I swiveled slowly to face Jacobsen. "Oh?" I repeated, but in a completely different tone.

"Well, maybe not a lot of times," Jacobsen said. "But pretty often."

"Who was he?"

"Don't know," Jacobsen replied. "I guess I figured he was her boyfriend. They held hands when they came in or went out, anyway."

I felt a little surge of excitement. "Could you describe him to me?"

"Sure." Jacobsen spackled another nail hole, then stepped back, head cocked, to study the effect. "He was, I don't know, maybe in his mid-forties. Maybe about five-ten. Very broad shoulders. Good build, what I could see of it in a suit. Dark hair, kind of cut like . . ." Her voice trailed off, and she frowned a little, concentrating.

"Like what?" I prompted, after a moment.

"You ever seen a bust or a picture of Julius Caesar?"

"Sure."

"Okay. Well, this guy had those little like bangs, you know? He had a like Julius Caesar haircut."

"Beard?" I said. "Mustache?"

"Nope." Jacobsen squinted at the wall. "He wasn't a bad-looking guy."

"Would you recognize him if you saw him again?"

Jacobsen shifted her gaze away from the wall and gave me an amused look. "Of course."

"And you have no idea what his name was?"

"Sorry."

I shook my head. "You've been a tremendous help. I want to thank you for your time and trouble."

"It wasn't all that much trouble," Jacobsen replied judiciously.

"Well, thank you again, anyway."

Jacobsen nodded absently, her gaze once more fixed on the wall.

"Bye-bye," I said. "Hope the renovations go smoothly."

"Yup."

When I was at the door, I had another thought. One that puzzled me. I paused on the threshold and looked back at Daisy Jacobsen. She was still deep in contemplation of the wall.

"Excuse me," I said.

"Wha—oh. Yes?"

"You haven't told the police about Bonnie's friend, have you?"

Jacobsen wet her forefinger with the tip of her tongue and pressed it against one of the spackled indentations. "Nope."

I blinked. "Why not?"

She gave me a bland look. "They haven't been here to ask me about her."

"Ah," I said. "Well, that makes sense. But how did you know Bonnie was dead, then? Did you see an item in the papers?"

"I never read 'em."

"Then . . ."

"One of my tenants who lived here when she did mentioned it to me."

"Oh."

When I left, Jacobsen was on her knees, picking at a paint blister on the baseboard. I don't think she noticed me go.

As soon as I was outside, I got an index card from my bag and wrote down Daisy Jacobsen's description of Bonnie's apparent boyfriend. Then I reread it. Whoever he was, he sounded a hell of a lot more appetizing than the thug I'd heard about from Dan Fowler.

I rode the subway to Porter Square, disembarked, and walked the five blocks to Jack's place.

Lucy met me at the front door. I bent down to pat her and she jumped up, sliding her forelegs over my shoulders in a kind of hugging gesture she's carefully cultivated.

"That's you, I assume," Jack's voice called from the kitchen.

"It's me," I confirmed, disentangling myself from the dog's frenetic embrace and rising. Lucy raced into the kitchen and I followed her. Jack was at the counter, making himself a drink.

"Get you something?" he asked.

"Sure. You know what."

He nodded, and took the vodka and vermouth from a cabinet next to the refrigerator.

"How was your day?" I asked.

He turned to me and grinned. "We caught the bank robbers."

"Oh, well done," I cried. "Congratulations." I hopped up from the table and went over to give him a hug and a kiss. "That's great. Good for you."

"Well, I had some help," he said modestly.

I made a face at him and he laughed.

"Where were they from?" I asked.

"Charlestown," Jack replied, putting some ice in a glass. "Where else?"

"Uh-huh." Jack had once told me that all local bank robbers came from Charlestown. Or at least, the ones who got caught did.

He handed me my drink and I raised it in salute. "Here's to you," I said, and sipped.

He smiled and picked up his own drink. I leaned against the counter, crossing my legs at the ankles. "What do you want to do for dinner tonight?" I asked.

Jack glanced reflexively at the refrigerator. "I hadn't thought about it. Want to go out some place?"

"Sure," I said. "If you'll be my guest. In honor of solving the bank robbery."

"Oh, now—"

"Nope." I shook my head vigorously. "My treat, Sherlock. You pick the place. I'll pick up the tab."

He looked as if he were about to object, then laughed a little. "Okay."

"Good." I patted his shoulder.

We went into the living room. A copy of the *Globe* lay folded on the coffee table.

"You think about where you want to dine," I instructed. "I'll catch up on the news."

We sat down side by side on the couch. I set my drink on the end table, picked up the paper, and unfolded it. The headlines were generic: more crisis in the Middle East, eructations at a Boston City Council meeting. I skimmed the world news, wished I hadn't, and turned the page.

At the top of page three was an article entitled, "Kin of State Senator Dies in Crash." Next to the article was a photograph of the accident victim. I glanced at it casually. Then I *really* looked at it, and felt myself begin to go into shock.

The face of the dead man was the face of the man who'd attacked me on my doorstep five nights ago.

21

Neil A. Levesque—cousin of Alan P. Levesque, state senator—was, at the time of his death, twenty-six years old. He'd been brought DOA to Symmes Hospital in Arlington after losing control of his 1973 Buick on Route 2, jumping the median, and piling into an oncoming eighteen-wheeler. The truck driver suffered a fractured right leg, three broken ribs, and a concussion.

Levesque's blood alcohol level had been point-twenty. In Massachusetts, if your blood alcohol level is point-ten, you are legally incapable of operating a motor vehicle.

According to the information the Arlington police had gotten from Symmes, Levesque was five feet seven inches tall and had weighed one hundred seventy pounds. He had reddish-brown kinky hair, blue eyes, and a mustache and short beard.

There was no doubt in my mind that he was the man who had assaulted me. There wasn't any doubt in Jack's mind, either.

I went with him to the police station the following morning. Jack made a call to an acquaintance of his on the Arlington PD, which was how we got Levesque's vital statistics. Then Jack punched the kid's name into the CPD computer, to see if he had a record of any prior arrests and convictions.

I was sitting in Jack's office, sipping a Styrofoam cup of CID coffee and gazing idly out the window at the Division of Employment Security when Jack returned from his computer search. I looked at him with raised eyebrows, and he shook his head.

"Nothing," he said. "Just a couple of outstanding traffic warrants. Running lights. Speeding. Crap." He shook his head again, like someone profoundly puzzled.

"What's the matter?" I asked.

He tossed the computer printouts onto his desk and sat down behind it, rather heavily. "It's just that this frigging thing makes no sense whatsoever."

I frowned at him. "What do you mean?"

He gestured at the printouts. "Levesque not having any prior record for rape or attempted rape or purse-snatching or assault or mugging . . . or whatever the hell he was trying to do to you."

"So?"

He sighed and rubbed his forehead. "Guys that do stuff like that, they start early. Usually. Like when they're about fifteen. They have *some* kind of record, anyway."

"Always?"

He looked up at me. "Well, no, Liz, not always. Maybe just ninety percent of the time."

"Oh."

"Yeah, oh." There was a note of irritation in his voice. I knew it wasn't directed at me.

"Maybe he *did* do stuff like that before," I offered. "And he just never got caught."

"Maybe."

I went over to him and put my hand on his shoulder. "You don't sound absolutely convinced. That could be the case, I mean."

He shrugged, and looked broody. "Guys who have the habit of attacking women, they're such stupid degenerates, they usually do get picked up somewhere along the line. At least for questioning. Even if there isn't enough evidence to nail them."

"And nobody here or anywhere else has ever picked up Levesque on suspicion of committing some kind of street crime?"

"No." He had his hands folded together on the desk and was inspecting them very closely, as if on his knuckles were imprinted an encoded message.

"It *was* Levesque who attacked me," I said.

Jack glanced up sharply. "That isn't in doubt."

I gazed at him for a moment, and then grabbed the visitor's chair from alongside the desk and drew it up next to his. He had gone back to contemplating his knuckles.

"I think this was the kid's first time out," I said. "Why he did what he tried to do to me, I can't say, but he was most definitely a beginner in the game."

Jack looked up at me again, but not quite so sharply as before.

"The moment I saw Levesque's eyes," I continued. "I knew, without any question, that he was as scared of what was happening as I was. I know that, Jack. I was there. It was happening to me."

"Okay."

I leaned closer to him. "Even the cop who drove me around to look for Levesque afterward didn't think the whole thing made any sense. He just about said as much. He wasn't being stupid. What happened to me just didn't fit into any kind of rational crime pattern."

"Rational crime pattern," Jack repeated. "What's that?"

I gave an exasperated sigh. "You know what I mean."

He smiled at me, a bit reluctantly I thought, and said, "Yeah. I do."

"When I thought about the whole thing the next morning," I said. "It was very clear to me that this Levesque not only didn't know what he was doing, he didn't even know how to do it. If he could even figure out what it was that he wanted to do." I shook my head, bewildered by my own locution. "You follow that?"

"Yes," Jack said. "I think so. You didn't use any hard words."

I poked him in the ribs with my elbow. "I'm serious, dammit."

He gave me another of those quick, sharp looks. "So am I."

I sat back in my chair. "What it was like was—it was like Levesque was playing things by ear."

"Mmm?"

"Well, yes. It was as if he had this sudden blind, stupid impulse to attack a woman, and I happened to be there and available, so he just acted on the compulsion." I shrugged. "But he couldn't follow through. Why, I don't know. Maybe because he didn't have his plan of attack mapped out beforehand. Somebody who'd never committed a rape or a robbery or a mugging wouldn't, would he? He'd almost *have* to play it by ear."

"You may have a point there," Jack conceded.

"I think so."

Jack looked thoughtful. "Also, Levesque might not have anticipated that you'd resist. Maybe he figured that as soon as he grabbed you, you'd be so terrified that you'd just lie down on the sidewalk or something."

"Could be."

Jack gave me another grudging smile. "Well, if that was the case, he figured wrong, didn't he?"

"Apparently."

Jack reached over and ruffled my hair. "Lady, you are one tough lady."

I frowned. "Is that supposed to be a compliment?"

"Of course it is."

"Then, thank you. But—"

"But what?"

I gave him an owl-eyed look. "If I'm so tough, then how could you possibly find me feminine and desirable as well?"

"Oh, bullshit," he snorted. "You think you'd be more attractive to me if you'd gotten raped or murdered?"

"Well, I don't know."

"Jesus," he said. He looked at my empty coffee cup. "You want some more of that?"

"Is that your final comment on the subject of my femininity?" I asked.

He laughed.

"Sure," I said. "I'd love some more coffee."

He pushed back his chair, got up, and left the office. I resumed looking out the window at the Division of Employment Security, and resumed thinking about Neil A. Levesque. Neil A. Trashbag. The only reason I was sorry he'd been killed in that accident was that his death deprived me of the supreme satisfaction of seeing him arrested, tried, and convicted for doing what he'd done to me. The rotten little flabby son-of-a-bitch.

Jack returned to the office with a cup of coffee in each hand.

"Top of a fresh pot," he said.

"Great," I said, taking the cup he held out to me. There was already cream in it. I dosed the coffee with some artificial sweetener.

"I've been thinking," I began.

Jack leaned against the windowsill and sipped his coffee. "You do a lot of that."

I wrinkled my nose at him. "Thinking about Levesque."

"Yeah?"

"Well . . ." I tasted my coffee. Very fresh, just as Jack had guaranteed. "Remember what I said to you a little while ago? About how I thought he was acting on some sudden impulse when he jumped me?"

"Uh-huh."

I took another sip of my coffee, then put the cup down on Jack's desk. "Even blind impulses have to be rooted in something. I mean, they have a cause."

Jack nodded. "Sure. So?"

"Well, I really wonder what made Levesque do what he did."

"How so?"

I got up, shoved my hands in my jeans pockets, and began ambling around the office, the way I always did when I was cogitating fast and furiously. "Levesque was waiting outside my door. But even so, I can't believe it was me he specifically wanted to attack."

"You don't know that for sure, Liz."

"What?"

Jack shrugged. "Maybe he'd been in your neighborhood before this. And he noticed you and fixated on you. For whatever reasons."

I stared at him. "Jesus," I said softly. "What a horrific thought."

"Well, things like that happen. You know they do."

I did indeed know. I was silent for a moment. Then I said, "Well, be that as it may. Whether it was me or just any woman he was waiting for. I want to go back to your original point. Why the hell would this jerk embark on a street crime career at his advanced age?"

Jack sighed. "I don't know, sweetheart. I wish I did."

"Was Levesque married?"

"No." Jack looked at me curiously. "Why?"

"Oh." I walked over to the window to join him. "I was thinking he might've had a fight with his wife, and stormed out of the house, and decided to vent his anger on the nearest available female."

"No wife."

I nodded. "Maybe a girlfriend, then."

"Possibly."

I was hunched over, staring at my toes. "That's the only explanation I can think of."

"Uh-huh."

"Where did the kid live, anyway?"

"Everett."

I looked up at Jack. "That's a few miles from here, isn't it?"

"About five."

I ran my right hand back through my hair. "So why would Levesque come all the way to Cambridge just to find a woman to assault?"

"Maybe he thought it would be safer than jumping one in his own home town."

"In that case, he could've gone to Chelsea or Revere. They're closer to Everett than Cambridge is."

"True."

"Wait a minute."

"Yes?"

I slumped against the wall and crossed my arms over my chest. "Whatever town Levesque decided to go girl-hunting in, that argues at least some degree of premeditation or forethought on his part."

"Uh-huh."

I scowled at Jack. "But I know—I *know*—Levesque was acting on impulse when he jumped me. He didn't premeditate shit."

Jack nodded.

I looked at him for a moment longer. Then I pushed myself away from the wall and went back to the desk to pick up my coffee.

"You're right," I said. "This frigging thing doesn't make any sense whatsoever. None at all."

22

"Well, we do know one thing for sure," Jack said.

"What's that?"

He gave me a wolfish grin. "Levesque won't be attacking any more women."

"How true," I said, finishing my coffee. "How true."

It was quite obvious to me, and no doubt to Jack, that, on the basis of what little we knew about Levesque now, we weren't going to be able to figure out why he'd done what he'd done. So it didn't seem as if there would be much point in discussing the matter further. In any case, you can only ponder the imponderable so long before your brain gets fed up and goes on strike. I know mine does.

Besides, there were other, more fruitful lines of inquiry I wanted to pursue this afternoon.

I was about to say something to this effect when the captain of detectives appeared in the office door. He smiled at me and nodded, then said to Jack, "When you got a minute."

"He has one now," I said. "I'm just leaving."

Jack looked a little startled. I rose, gathered up my handbag and the linen blazer I'd slung over the back of the visitor's chair.

"You don't have to rush off," Jack said.

I shook my head. "Nah. I have some errands to run. And you have work to do. I'll see you tonight, okay?"

"Of course."

"We need anything from the grocery store other than stuff for dinner?"

Jack frowned slightly. "I think we're a little low on milk."

"Okay. I'll pick some up on the way home." I leaned across the desk and gave him a kiss. "See you later."

"Yup. Stay out of trouble."

I paused at the door, looking back over my shoulder. "Why ask the impossible?"

He grinned. "My kind of girl."

When I left the police station, it was with a very clear idea of what errand I was going to discharge first. A visit to Bonnie's place on Huron Avenue. I wanted to talk to the little old lady who lived on the first floor. The odds were good she'd be home at this time of day.

She was.

I rang the bell for apartment one and then positioned myself for inspection in front of the lower left window. Sure enough, a moment later, a panel of the curtain moved aside and the wrinkled, bright-eyed face I remembered from my first trip here peered out at me. I smiled and waved. The woman's eyes widened in recognition. She mouthed, "Just a minute,'' at me and let the curtain fall back into place. I leaned against the porch railing.

I heard some faint shuffling noises and then the sound of bolts being drawn and chains unhooked. A security symphony. The oak door opened about three feet. In the opening stood the sparrow-lady. She blinked at the sunlight and gave me a tentative smile.

''Hello,'' I said.

''I gave that book you gave me to Bonnie's roommate,'' she said quickly.

''Thank you,'' I replied. ''But that's not why I'm here. May I talk to you for just a moment?''

The expression on her face became speculative. ''About Bonnie?''

''Yes.''

''Well . . .'' The woman shifted from one foot to the other, as if the request made her physically uneasy.

''Just one or two questions,'' I said.

''Well . . .'' the woman repeated. ''Seeing as how you were Bonnie's friend.'' She scratched her head, ruffling the pixie's cap of silver hair. ''I guess so.''

''Thank you.''

''Such a terrible, terrible thing, what happened to that poor girl.''

''I know.''

''Were you a very close friend of hers?''

''Not exactly,'' I said. ''But I'm trying to locate someone who was, and that's where I think you might be able to help me.''

''Oh?''

''The person I have in mind is a man,'' I continued. ''In his mid-forties, about as tall as I am, with very broad shoulders. Dark hair, short, with little bangs. Clean-shaven. Well-dressed, usually. Good-looking. Does that sound familiar?''

''You want to know if I ever saw someone like that with Bonnie?''

''Yes.''

The woman pursed her lips in concentration. "Dark hair," she murmured. "Broad shoulders. Let's see . . ."

I smiled at her encouragingly.

"You know," she said. "That *does* sound familiar."

Hot damn, I thought. Aloud, I said, "Then you do remember seeing a man of that description with Bonnie."

"I think so." She paused, then nodded decisively. "Yes. Yes, I did. I'm sure of it." She gave me a shrewd look. "Was that her boyfriend?"

"I think he might have been," I replied. "Did you see them together often?"

"Oh, no," the woman said. "Just a few times. I believe," she added in a disapproving tone, "that he had a key to this house."

I raised my eyebrows.

"I saw him let himself in one night," she added, the disapproval in her voice stronger.

"When was this?"

She frowned. "I couldn't say for sure. Sometime last fall, as far as I can remember."

Thank God for stay-at-home, sharp-eyed, sharp-witted old ladies. They didn't miss a trick.

"You didn't ever happen to hear this man's name, did you?"

She looked regretful. "No," she said. "I never did."

Too bad. Oh, well. I hadn't really expected she would have.

"Did you tell the police about this man?" I inquired casually, positive she hadn't.

The woman's eyes widened and her mouth made a small "O." "I can't . . . no, I don't think I did." She bit her lower lip. "Oh, dear, this is terrible. One of them even *asked* me if I knew if Bonnie had a boyfriend." Distress was written all over her small, wrinkled face. "You know it just slipped my mind completely. I don't think I'd have remembered today if you hadn't jogged my memory. Oh, how awful."

"Don't worry about it," I advised. "The police'll be back to talk to you again, probably."

"Oh." The woman nodded. "Then I'll tell them then."

I smiled, and glanced at the nameplate above the buzzer for apartment one. It read "Gallagher."

"Mrs. Gallagher," I said, holding out my hand. "Thank you very much for your time. You've been a tremendous help."

She shook my hand lightly. "Oh, you're welcome, dear."

"Hope to see you again sometime. Bye-bye."

She smiled at me. I started down the porch steps.

All the way up Huron Avenue, I could barely refrain from hopping and skipping. I now had all the confirmation I needed of the existence of the mysterious boyfriend whom Mrs. Nordgren had mentioned. And that the relationship between him and Bonnie had been of at least two years' duration. You could get close in that time. Jack and I had.

So where the hell was this joker?

I was sure Joe McFadden didn't know about him. Perhaps I should give McFadden a call. Or tell Jack, and he could transmit the message.

It occurred to me, as I was prancing up Concord Avenue, that Bonnie's long-term intimate relationship with a man probably precluded a sexual involvement on her part with Gayle Lydecker.

Maybe it didn't.

Whichever, the issue was far less pressing than was that of the whereabouts of either the boyfriend or Gayle.

If Gayle had had nothing to do with Bonnie's death, why had she dropped out of sight? And ditto Mr. Broadshoulders? Why hadn't *he* come forward?

Well, I could think of some *fairly* reasonable explanations for the latter. Such as the existence of a wife, who might object to her husband's carrying on a torrid affair with a gorgeous blonde. Her lover's being married might also account for Bonnie's secrecy about his identity.

The possibilities were intriguing, I reflected as I crossed the Cambridge Common.

I looked at my watch. It was a little after two-thirty. Plenty of time for me to go back to my apartment, pick up some fresh clothing and collect whatever mail had accumulated, do the grocery shopping, and get back to Jack's place in time for the cocktail hour.

On impulse, I stopped at a public phone in Harvard Square, called information, and asked for the number for the Middlesex County District Attorney's Office. When I got through to them, I asked to speak to Sergeant McFadden. He wasn't in and wasn't expected back that afternoon. I said I'd call again in the morning. It was too complicated to leave a message.

I caught a bus home from the stop across the street from Holyoke Center. My apartment had that vaguely musty air of stillness they all do if left unoccupied for more than twenty-four hours. The mail was bills and a complimentary copy of *The Watchtower.* Whoopee. I tossed it on the coffee table and went into the bedroom.

I was putting some clean underwear and shirts into a canvas drawstring bag when the phone rang. The sound seemed louder than usual in the quiet apartment. I dropped the shirt I was folding onto the bed and went to answer it.

A woman's voice said, "Is this Elizabeth Connors?"

"Yes."

"I've been trying to get you for two days," the voice continued.

Reflexively, I started to explain that I'd been away, then stopped after three words. I didn't recognize the voice on the other end of the line. So I sure as hell didn't owe it any report on my comings and goings.

"To whom am I speaking?" I asked.

There was a moment of silence. Then the voice replied, "This is Gayle Lydecker."

"Holy God," I said. The words exploded out of my mouth before I could swallow them. I pressed the receiver closer to my ear. "Sorry," I added quickly. I took a deep breath and willed myself to composure. "Yes?" I said. "Can I help you?"

"Oh, God," she said, and suddenly her voice quivered. "I wish you could. I wish you could."

"Maybe I can," I replied, a lot more steadily than I felt. "What is it?"

I heard her inhale shakily. "It's—I can't handle this anymore. It's out of—I can't deal with it."

What shocked me was not that this woman would call me in her hour of need, but that someone of her chilled and remote self-control would have an hour of need. It was . . . incongruous. Like hearing a statue laugh or burp.

"What is it?" I repeated.

"I have to talk to someone."

If I were the best receptacle for her confidences she could come up with, she was indeed in a bad way.

"I'll talk to you," I said. "Now?"

"No, no," she said hastily. "I have to get off the phone. I'll meet you somewhere. Later."

"Do you have a place in mind?"

"Oh, God," she repeated. "Wait a minute. Let me think."

"Take your time." The frayed desperation in her voice appalled me.

"There's a place on Hampshire Street," she said. "A few blocks up from Prospect."

"Morin's?"

"Yes, that's it."

"I know it," I said. "Shall I meet you there?"

"Yes. Is—can you be there at five-thirty?"

"No problem," I said, and realized a split second later that that probably wasn't the choicest phrase to use to someone who apparently had a very *big* problem.

"I'll see you." She broke the connection.

I called Jack.

23

"I'll be fine," I said, for what was no doubt the tenth time. "What could possibly happen to me?"

Jack stopped pacing around the office and stared at me. "A lot."

"Oh, honey. Come on. Like what?"

"You want me to count the ways?" He stared at me again and shook his head, as if exasperated by my apparent slowness. "I don't like this. It stinks. In fact, it sucks."

I sighed.

We weren't alone in his office. McFadden was leaning against the file cabinet, his left elbow resting on a stack of arrest-incident reports. Bernie Carr was perched on the windowsill. Bill Wallace was in the visitor's chair, his feet on the desk, crossed at the ankles. The magic of police communications had summoned them from wherever they'd been less than an hour ago.

They'd spent most of that time as audience to the little drama Jack and I were enacting.

"We can go to Morin's and pick her up," Jack said. "There's no reason for you to be there."

"Now of course there is, Jack. I don't care what you do with her after I've talked to her. But I *am* not going to set that woman up for a fall and walk away for it."

"Jesus, Liz, she could be setting *you* up."

"Oh, for God's sake." My level of exasperation was fast approaching his. "What reason would she have for doing that? Because I've been messing around with the Bonnie Nordgren business?" I broke off speaking and glanced around the room, letting my gaze rest on Wallace, then McFadden, then Carr. "The *cops* are messing around in the Bonnie Nordgren business. You guys are a hell of a lot bigger threat to Gayle than I am. She's bright enough to know that." I shrugged. "And, who knows? Maybe she wants my advice on how she should turn herself in."

"Liz." McFadden's quiet, measured voice broke into the dialogue.

I glanced back at him. "Yes?"

"How did Lydecker get your name and phone number, anyway?"

"I wrote a note to Bonnie a few days before she died. I put my name, address, and phone number on that."

McFadden looked at Carr. He shook his head slightly. McFadden looked at Wallace. He shrugged.

"We didn't find anything like that in Bonnie's apartment," McFadden said to me.

"No?" I was a little surprised. "It was tucked inside a book of poems by William Carlos Williams. I gave it to the old lady downstairs, Mrs. Gallagher, to give to Bonnie. She said she did."

"Well, we didn't find it."

I frowned. "Could it have been thrown away?"

"We went through the uncollected trash," McFadden said.

What a charming task, I thought. "Well, then, I guess Gayle must have taken it with her."

"Why would she have done that?" McFadden and Jack asked simultaneously.

"I haven't the vaguest idea," I said. I smiled at Jack. "But I can ask her later, if you'd like."

"Oh, fuck," he said.

Wallace looked as if he were suppressing a laugh.

"Do you remember the wording of the note?" McFadden asked.

"Oh, sure," I said. I furrowed my eyebrows. "Ah, okay. Ah—it went something like, 'Professor DiBenedetto asked me to get in touch with you. Maybe I can help if there's a problem.' " I looked up at McFadden. "If that's not the exact wording, it's very close."

"Okay."

Carr slid off the windowsill. He pushed back the sleeve of his poplin windbreaker to check his watch. Then he looked over at McFadden with elevated eyebrows. "If we're gonna get this show on the road," he said. "We'll have to do it now."

McFadden undraped himself from the filing cabinet.

"Catch you guys," Wallace said.

McFadden gave me his pensive smile. He and Carr left the office.

"Where are they going?" I asked.

"Where do you think?" Jack replied.

I felt my mouth tighten. "They'll go sit in Morin's. And the moment Gayle walks in, they'll jump at her from both sides. Swell."

"Oh, Christ," Jack said. "I give up. You want to go there that badly, then go."

There was a brief but heavy silence. Wallace relieved it by ripping the cellophane wrapper from a cigar. He put the cigar in his mouth and struck a match.

"What do you say we work out the *de*tails of this here CIA operation," he suggested through a cloud of blue smoke.

The details of the operation were relatively simple. At least, it only took Jack and Wallace five minutes to come up with an action plan.

"Gee," I said. "don't you have to coordinate with Bernie and Joe?"

Wallace gave me a strange look. Then he heaved himself up from the visitor's chair, reaching across the desk to tamp out his cigar in the office ashtray. He struck the butt in the inner pocket of his suit coat. I hoped it was completely extinguished.

"See you in a bit," he said, and ambled out of the office.

Alone at last.

"Happy, darling?" Jack asked.

I burst out laughing. "Oh, Jack," I said. "What can Gayle do to me in a public place? Shoot me? Stick a needleful of heroin in me? Poison my drink?"

"You have no idea what's possible," he replied.

I sighed. "Jack. Sweetheart. *You're* going to be there. *Joe's* going to be there. *Bernie's* going to be there. *Bill's* going to be there. I couldn't be safer than if I were in the middle of a platoon of marines."

"I wouldn't go that far."

"I said marines, not sailors."

We went back and forth like that till it was time for us to leave.

"Lighten up," I said as we walked out of the CID and down the stairs.

"Yeah," he said.

His car was in the subterranean parking garage beneath the police station. As we got into it, I said, "Is Gayle going to be arrested? Or just taken in for questioning?"

"Just to be questioned," Jack started the car.

"I see."

"Which is not to say, depending on how she answers the questions, she might not get arrested later."

We drove out into the Central Square gridlock.

"God," I said, looking out at the snarled traffic. "I hope we get to Morin's before five-thirty. I could walk there a lot faster."

"Well, you're not going to."

I gave him a sideways look. "I wouldn't dream of it."

Morin's was a neighborhood bar, neither a true dive nor the Ritz. It was three-quarters Irish and the remainder Italian and Portuguese. The combination was a volatile one, but the three ethnic groups seemed to be able to manage drinking together in peace. At least, the cops didn't get called down there every Saturday night to break up a knife fight. And if it was a numbers parlor, which it probably was, then it was a discreet one.

Morin's was also, I thought, a peculiar place for a *haute* yup like Gayle Lydecker to have chosen to meet me. Then it occurred to me that she might have picked that particular bar because she'd be extremely unlikely to run into anyone she knew there.

The action plan was that Carr and McFadden would be in a booth right near the entrance to the bar. Wallace, having cruised the neighborhood with an eye peeled for anything that looked suspicious or funny or even slightly out of place, would be by himself at a table at the back of the pub, by the rear exit. Jack was going to drop me off at the intersection of Prospect and Hampshire. I'd go the rest of the way on foot. He'd park, keeping close watch on me till I got in Morin's. He'd follow me, after about five minutes, and take a seat at the bar. A fifth cop would remain in an unmarked car on Hampshire, in case Gayle came along, changed her mind about talking to me, and took off. Another cop would be stationed on the street behind Morin's for the same reason. And another on the cross street.

Of the eight of us, I was the only one who'd ever actually seen Lydecker. The other seven were relying on her driver's license photo and my description.

Seven cops seemed like more than enough to put the drop on one lady consultant. But that was the way they worked. And I had to admit they had good reason for so doing.

The light at the intersection of Prospect and Hampshire was red. I looked over at Jack.

"See you later, cookie," I said. "Any parting words of wisdom?"

"Yeah. Don't order a vodka martini in that place."

"I'll remember that," I said as I got out of the car.

I strolled the rest of the way down Hampshire, pausing occasionally to glance in a shop window. If anyone other than the good guys were watching me, I hoped I wasn't being too ostentatiously footloose and fancy-free.

Morin's didn't have sawdust on the floor, but it should have. Instead, it had a floor of six-inch wide oak planks scarred and mellowed by a half-century of beer and whiskey spillage. The walls were paneled in dark wood, with a row of booths running up the right side of the room. The bar ran up the left.

The lighting was dim, but even so, I noted that Carr and McFadden were seated in the booth nearest the door. They didn't acknowledge me; I didn't acknowledge them. Wallace was at a table under the rear exit sign, drinking a glass of beer and reading the paper. As per instruction, I took the table for two nearest the center of the room.

The waitress was fat, fifty, and falsely blonde, the kind who calls even the customers she doesn't know "honey."

There were two guys at the bar. They were wearing striped overalls with "Parilli Construction" scroll-stitched across the back.

There were two other non-cop patrons, one a little white-haired man in a garish plaid flannel shirt buttoned up to the neck and a green bow tie, and the other a morose-looking kid with a long brown pigtail and a gold hoop ring in his left earlobe.

I hoped that Gayle, when she arrived, wouldn't try to order Perrier with a chunk of lime.

"What can I getcha, honey?" the waitress said.

"Vodka on the rocks," I said. There was no way I could stomach a boilermaker, which was probably the *specialité de la maison.*

I looked at my watch. Five after five. I put my elbows on the table and my chin in my hands and glanced around the room. The geezer in the plaid shirt gave me an alcoholic smile. I nodded back at him pleasantly, but not too pleasantly for fear he might be encouraged to join me.

The waitress brought McFadden and Carr another glass of beer each. Then she came over to my table, said, "Here ya go, hon," and plunked a dripping glass down in front of me. It was a fairly large glass. I picked it up, and noticed that the rim was at least a quarter of an inch thick. The bottom was easily an inch thick. For two-and-a-half bucks, I was getting cracked ice and a half ounce of liquor. I tasted the drink. A quarter ounce of liquor. Oh, well—I needed to keep my wits about me.

The door opened and Jack came into the bar. Hastily, I looked down at the tabletop. An ice cube in my glass popped. I glanced up cautiously. Jack was sitting with his elbows on the bar, apparently contemplating his reflection in the mirror behind the row of bottles. I supposed that what he was really doing was watching the room behind him.

I peeked at my watch. Five-twenty. I took another sip of my drink.

The coot in the green bow tie pushed himself up from his table and started toward me on unsteady legs.

Oh, Christ, I thought. Just what I need.

I stared rigidly at my drink as he approached my table.

The blast of beery breath from my right forced me to look up. The old man's face was about five inches from mine. He put a thin, veined hand on my shoulder.

"Pardon me, miss," he said. "I just wanted to tell you that you're a very pretty girl."

"Thank you," I said.

He gave me a flash of dentures, straightened, and tottered off to the men's room.

I finished my drink. The bartender brought Jack a beer. Behind me, Wallace rattled his newspaper.

The waitress waddled over to my table. "Getchu a refill, honey?"

I nodded.

Five-twenty-six.

McFadden slid out of his and Carr's booth, went to the bar, and bought a bag of potato chips. He ripped it open as he returned to his seat. Jack sipped his beer.

The waitress brought me my drink.

The old guy returned from the men's room.

Five-thirty-five.

I wished I'd brought a book, or something to write.

The door to the bar opened. I tensed. A fat guy in jeans and a blue tee shirt came in and went up to the bar. I relaxed. Somewhat.

Bill Wallace ordered another beer.

I took a swallow of my drink. It seemed even weaker than the first, if that were possible.

Five-forty-five.

Maybe Lydecker had gotten held up in traffic. No matter where you were coming from, it was atrocious at this hour.

I went to the bar and bought a bag of peanuts, less for something to eat than for something to do.

Five-fifty.

I ate the peanuts one by one.

Jack ordered a second beer.

Carr got up to go to the men's room.

I drank my drink, and ordered a third. At that point, I must have had a whole ounce of vodka sloshing through my system.

Jack got up to go to the men's room.

Six-fifteen.

Maybe she'd had a flat tire.

I bought some popcorn.

McFadden got up to go to the men's room.

Wallace rattled his newspaper.

At six-forty-five, it was eminently clear to me that I'd been stood up. That upset me, and my mood wasn't improved by the consumption of three lousy nondrinks and two bags of stale junk food.

I put some tip money on the table, rose, and marched out of the bar to Hampshire Street.

I looked to my right, and then to my left. No Gayle Lydecker hoving into view.

If the others wanted to sit in Morin's for the rest of the night, that was their affair. In any event, it was something they got paid to do. I didn't.

I got suckered for free.

24

Jack had caught up with me by the time I'd located his car.

"Now that whole episode was just fraught with incredible danger, wasn't it?" I snapped.

"Calm down." He patted my shoulder, unlocked the passenger door of the car, and held it open for me. I sat down on the front seat hard enough to bounce. Jack was so obliging as to slam the door for me.

"What are you upset about?" he asked as he slid behind the steering wheel.

I flicked him a brief incredulous look. "I just love being stood up."

He started the car. "Well, you weren't the only one."

"That's part of why I'm upset." I scrunched down a bit in the seat and put my right hand up to my mouth and bit my thumb. "God!" I mumbled through my fingers. "I'm so embarrassed."

"Why?"

"Oh, Jack. I just dragged seven cops out on a wild-goose chase. Isn't that a good reason to be embarrassed?"

He smiled. "You didn't do it deliberately. Besides"—he took his hands off the steering wheel and shrugged—"we're always going out on wild-goose chases. You know that."

"Yeah," I said. "But I hate to be the one to initiate them."

"In this case, you didn't," Jack said placidly. "We did. So it didn't work out. So what? A lot of stuff like that doesn't work out the way we want it to. That doesn't mean it isn't worth doing."

"I suppose." The reasonableness of what he was saying made me feel less cranky.

We made a right turn onto Prospect Street.

"Where are we going now?" I asked.

"Your place."

"What for?"

He smiled at me again. "Don't you think you ought to be available this evening in case Gayle decides to call you back?"

I smacked my forehead with the heel of my hand. "God. Of course. What a dummy."

"Nah," Jack replied. "You're just not up to speed on all the latest criminal investigation procedures, that's all."

"I hate people who say things like 'up to speed.' "

"I know you do. I only said it to annoy you."

I laughed and felt the last vestiges of my anger and embarrassment dissolve.

"I don't have anything for dinner at my place," I said.

"I can go out and get something. I have to go pick up the dog, anyway."

"Okay."

"In fact," he continued. "Why don't I just drop you off and do both things now."

"Sure."

"Anything in particular you want for dinner?"

I thought for a moment, then shook my head. "No. Whatever looks good to you."

I half-expected—I certainly *wanted*—the phone to be ringing when I walked into my apartment, but of course it wasn't. I dropped my handbag on the couch and went to the kitchen. I poked in the refrigerator till I found a can of diet ginger ale, popped the top on it, and sat down at the table.

What had gone wrong earlier this evening?

I was still pondering that question when Jack and Lucy appeared. The dog galloped over to me, put her forepaws on my knees, and licked my chin. Jack was carrying a brown paper bag. He waved it at me and said, "Sandwich stuff."

"Oh, good." I gave Lucy a little shove aside and wiped the dog spit off my face with my shirtsleeve.

Jack put the bag on the counter, got a beer from the refrigerator, and joined me at the table. "What's up?"

"No word from Gayle. If that's what you're asking."

He nodded and drank some beer.

"I think my temper got the better of me before," I said. "I shouldn't have assumed that she stood me up deliberately, just for the hell of it, should I?"

Jack smiled slightly. "No harm done."

"While you were out, I was trying to think of other reasons why she didn't show."

"Yeah?"

"They're all bad."

He set the beer can on the table. "Tell me."

"Well, she was semi-hysterical when I talked to her on the phone. I mean like distraught."

"But she wasn't specific about why."

I shook my head. "No. All I could gather was that it was her circumstances or situation that had gotten out-of-hand. And I automatically figured that whatever it was that was scaring her so badly, it had something to do with Bonnie's death."

Jack narrowed his eyes. "She didn't mention Bonnie, did she? Not even indirectly?"

"No."

The look he gave me was very focused. "So what are you driving at?"

I sighed. "Well, you know how I thought that there was a good chance that Gayle had killed Bonnie?"

"Uh-huh."

"I've reconsidered."

"Yeah?"

"What I'm starting to think now is that maybe, yes, she *was* involved in Bonnie's murder, but only peripherally."

"Like an accessory before or after the fact."

"Well, that. Or maybe she came home very late the night Bonnie died, and found the body, and guessed not only that Bonnie'd been murdered, but who'd done it as well. And that scared her, so she took off."

"Could be."

"And now," I continued. "Gayle's being threatened by whoever killed Bonnie."

Jack picked up his beer. "So why doesn't she just turn herself in to the cops and ask for protection?"

"That'd be the logical thing to do," I agreed. "But people who are terrified out of their wits aren't often thinking logically."

He nodded.

"Jack?"

"Yes?"

"If what I'm saying is true, then Gayle's in real trouble, isn't she?"

He nodded again.

"Oh, boy," I said. "Well, then, that probably explains why she never turned up at Morin's." I picked up my empty ginger ale can and tapped it lightly against the tabletop. "Whoever it was who had her so scared got to her before she could get to me."

"That's possible," Jack temporized. "But it may not be quite that bad. Maybe she just got cold feet at the last minute. Or decided it was safer to stay in hiding and not talk to anyone. For whatever reason." He smiled at me. "Hell, maybe she had a flat tire. It could be something as stupid as that."

"Yeah, maybe. But in that case, wouldn't she call me and say so?"

"The night's young, sweetie. Maybe she will."

But she didn't. Jack and I stayed up until one A.M., talking, reading, and eating roast beef and turkey sandwiches. I worked for a bit on the pillow I was making. At one point, we even turned on the television. And turned it off almost immediately when we realized simultaneously that there was nothing on it that either one of us could stand to watch.

The phone rang at nine. I almost tackled it. The caller was someone trying to sell me a subscription to the *Globe*.

At one o'clock, Jack closed his book with a snap and tossed it onto the coffee table. He looked over at me and said. "What do you say we call it quits?"

I nodded gloomily.

"Should I take Lucy out again?"

"No. I think she's settled down for the night."

"Okay." He stood up, yawning and stretching. I gave one last lingering glance at the phone and went with Jack into the bedroom.

As we were undressing, Jack said. "I hope you're not going to lie awake all night letting this bug you."

"I hope not," I replied, writhing out of my jeans. "But I bet I will."

He unbuttoned his shirt. "I can do something to take your mind off your troubles," he offered. "Relax you, even."

I smiled at him. "I thought you'd never ask," I said. "But don't you have to get up early?"

"Oh, sure. But it'll be worth losing some sleep."

"It certainly will," I said, and tossed my underpants into the corner.

An hour later, I was dead to the world. So much so that I didn't even stir when Jack left that morning. When I did wake, at nine, it took me a minute to remember what had been bothering me the night before.

I was drifting around the apartment in my robe, trying to decide how to occupy myself for the rest of the day, when the phone rang at ten. I stood very still and stared at it, saucer-eyed, as it rang a second and third time. Then I grabbed the receiver and said "Hello" with great urgency.

It wasn't Gayle Lydecker. It wasn't even the *Globe* subscription department. It was Dan Fowler. I tried not to sound too disappointed.

"You've been a very elusive butterfly these days, angel," he said.

"I've been staying with Jack for a few days," I replied. I thought briefly of telling Dan why I'd done so, then decided against it. The story was too complicated to be told at this hour of the morning. I'd save it for when we were having a drink together.

"What's new?" I asked.

"Nothing much," he replied. "Classes are over, thank God. I may go to P'town for a few weeks to recover."

"That sounds nice."

"Yeah, a friend of mine just finished building a house down there. I'll probably stay with him. Hey, you and Jack ought to come down for a few days. My friend could put you up. He's got a lot of room."

"I'd love it," I said. "But I don't know if Jack can get any time off till July."

"Oh, is that when all the bad guys take *their* vacations?"

"No." I laughed. "That's actually one of their busier seasons."

"Yeah, well, speaking of bad guys, that's one of the reasons I've been trying to call you."

"Oh?"

"It's probably nothing. But . . ."

"Yes?"

"Did you see in the paper a couple days ago that story about how that cousin of a state senator, I forget his name, got killed in a car crash?"

I felt a jangle of shock in my guts before they tightened and grew cold.

"Liz?"

"I think so," I said quickly, yet in carefully casual tones. "Yeah, I remember reading something about that. Why?"

"It's the damnedest thing," Fowler replied. His voice was slow and just slightly troubled-sounding. "They ran a picture of the kid along with the article."

"I saw it."

"I'm probably hallucinating all this—"

"But?"

"The kid looked a hell of a lot like the guy I used to see with Bonnie. A *hell* of a lot."

"God," I said.

"I could swear they were the same person. Isn't that weird?"

It was more than that.

I didn't say as much to Dan. Instead, I agreed with him that the coincidence was indeed a bizarre one. After that, I ended the conversation as quickly and as politely as I could.

Then I curled up on the couch to try, as calmly as possible, to align my thoughts. Not hard to do so. All the random bits and pieces of information I'd accumulated about Bonnie had just, by the merest happenstance, been linked together. At least, by my lights they had.

I consulted my notebook to verify what I was remembering. According to what was written there, my memory—so bad for things like when to pick up the drycleaning—hadn't played me false.

I added up the facts one way, and then another. And then sideways. No matter how I did it, I ended up with the same answer. Well, maybe not so much an answer as a pattern.

Item: Bonnie Nordgren had been involved with a man who "worked in government" in Massachusetts. Item: Gayle Lydecker, before her disappearance, had worked as a political consultant. Item: A few days ago, I'd been attacked on my doorstep by the cousin of a state senator. Item: The man who'd attacked me had also been a cohort of Bonnie Nordgren.

That morning I broke the land speed record for showering, dressing, and putting on eye makeup. I decided exactly how it was I was going to spend the rest of the day. I was going to get hold of, by whatever means necessary, a photograph of State Senator Alan P. Levesque. And show it to one or two select people. The rest I'd play by ear, including calling the cops. Despite the reassuring things Jack had said, one wild-goose chase was enough for me. I wasn't going to kick off another.

But deep down in my bones, I knew this wasn't going to be a wild-goose chase.

This would be chasing the dragon.

25

Senator Levesque represented one of the Boston districts. I didn't know which one, since I have about as much interest in politics, particularly local ones, as I do in mink ranching. But I did know that most politicians were lawyers, and that most of them kept up their practices in case they got voted out of office or indicted by a federal grand jury.

I consulted my favorite research tool, the phone book. The law offices of A. P. Levesque and G. C. Porter were located on State Street in Boston. There was also a listing for a Committee to Re-elect Alan Levesque situated in Oak Square in deepest Brighton. I made a note of both addresses and phone numbers in my little notebook.

The campaign headquarters would probably be far more likely to have the kind of material I was looking for than would the law offices. Besides, there was a bus every half hour from Central Square right into Oak Square.

Waiting for a bus or a cab or a subway in Central Square is always a fun experience. With that in mind, I timed myself to get there no earlier than eleven-twenty-seven. Even so, in the three minutes that elapsed between my arrival at the bus stop and that of the bus, one guy offered to sell me some pharmaceuticals and another offered to screw me. I rejected either proposition.

The streets leading into Oak Square were quiet and tree lined, perhaps with a preponderance of oaks, and half-residential, half-commercial. It was hard to believe that only a few years ago, the square had been one of the major drug-trafficking sites in Boston. One of the tv news teams had done a report on the activity down there during a heroin shortage. I recalled having seen an amazing videotape of about twenty or thirty desperate junkies milling around down by the street-car stop, all hoping against the odds that maybe today nirvana would finally arrive. What got me was how blatant it all was. The junkies apparently had no idea they were being filmed. Or if they did, they didn't care.

I got off the bus and walked back up Tremont Street. The block I was on was all commercial. One of the establishments was an antique store much fancier-looking than the immediate neighborhood seemed to warrant. Well, this part of Brighton was very close to the Newton line. The Levesque campaign headquarters was next to a laundromat. One of your storefront operations.

In the center of the plate glass window had been hung a poster-sized photograph of the man himself. I took a deep breath and moved in to study it closely.

Daisy Jacobsen had been right; Levesque was a good-looking guy. I remembered thinking so myself when I'd seen him on tv. His hair was dark and straight and cut in short bangs across his forehead. He had very broad shoulders. He was wearing a sincere grin. Be still, my heart.

The door to the campaign headquarters was wide open and held thus with a rubber stop to catch the late spring breeze and fugitive traffic emissions. I put a foot over the threshold. The office was perhaps fifteen feet wide and forty deep. The furnishings—file cabinets and uneven rows of metal desks—looked as if they'd been purchased at a fire sale at a discount office-supply house. Most of the available surfaces were weighted down with stacks of brochures and pamphlets. I wondered why it was that all campaign offices were always so messy. Probably to create the impression that politicians had their minds on more cosmic concerns than keeping house.

There was one person in the room, a sixtyish-year-old woman with blue hair and eyeglass frames to match. She rose from behind her desk, smiled at me, and said, "Can I help you?"

I could hardly reply, "Just give me a photograph of Senator Levesque, preferably full-length, and I'll be on my way." So I smiled at her and said, "I'd like to see some of the senator's campaign literature."

"Do you live in the district?" she replied hopefully.

"Yes," I lied.

"Oh, well, then, perhaps you'd like to be on our mailing list."

She looked like a fairly nice woman and I hated to disappoint her. "Sure," I said. I gave her a fake name and a real Brighton address and she wrote them down on a lined yellow pad.

There was a pile of bumper stickers on her desk. They had a blue background with white lettering that read: MAKE IT SENATOR LEVESQUE! I took one of the bumper stickers, folded it, and put it in my bag.

The woman handed me a sheaf of pamphlets and bills. One of the bills reproduced the photo of Levesque that appeared on the poster in the window. One of the pamphlets was illustrated with a picture of him and two other guys at what seemed to be some kind of ribbon-cutting ceremony.

I looked up from the brochure, smiled at the blue-haired woman, and said, "Thanks."

She nodded and returned the smile. She looked as if she were about to say something, but before she could, the phone on her desk rang. As she picked up the receiver, I waved good-bye to her and left, clutching my booty. I wanted to get out of there before I got invited to be a campaign worker or something.

I walked back down Tremont to the streetcar stop in the square. No junkies. No streetcar, either. I sat down on the curb to wait. And to read Senator Levesque's campaign literature.

It was the usual generic political crap. Levesque was on the side of the poor, the elderly, the handicapped, the ethnic, the gay, women, low unemployment rates, and lower taxes.

He favored cutting back on government spending and establishing more wide-reaching social welfare programs, a neat trick if I ever saw one. He came out firmly against graft and bureaucracy.

Carefully, I tore the two photographs from the bill and the pamphlet. Then I got up and stuffed the remains into a wire wastebasket attached to a maple tree.

A streetcar came along about five minutes later. I boarded it and rode in town to Copley Square.

The same battered green pickup truck was still parked in front of Daisy Jacobsen's townhouse. The front door was still open. I bounded up the steps.

Daisy Jacobsen was on a stepladder in the foyer, fiddling with the overhead light fixture. She had on the same overalls she'd been wearing the last time I'd seen her, but a different tee shirt. She looked down at me, blinked, and said, "Well, well, the return of Lois Lane."

I laughed. "I told you I'm not a reporter."

"That's what they all say," she replied, and squinted dubiously at the coil of dusty black wiring that dangled a few inches away from her nose. She shook her head at the condition of it and climbed down from the stepladder.

"Now what?" she said.

"I'd like to show you a picture."

She shrugged. "Why not?"

I handed her the poster photo of Levesque. She peered at it, then went over to the open door where the light was better.

"Recognize him?" I asked.

Daisy studied the picture, then glanced back up at me. "Yup."

I felt a huge internal jolt of excitement. "And he is . . ."

She handed me back the picture. "The guy that went with Bonnie."

"Ha!" I said exultantly. "Got you, you bugger."

Daisy gave me a strange look.

"You'll have to excuse me," I said. "I'm the excitable type."

She raised her eyebrows. "Doesn't take much, does it?"

I let that pass.

Daisy took the picture back from me and gazed at it again. "You know, this dude looks vaguely familiar for other reasons. What's his name, anyway?"

"Alan Levesque," I replied. "Ring a bell?"

She frowned thoughtfully. "Sort of."

"He's a state senator," I said. "Represents part of Brighton and a couple of other places."

"I wouldn't know," Daisy said. "I don't keep up with local politics anymore than I read the papers."

"Probably wise," I said.

I thanked her and hotfooted it out of there to find a public phone. I located one in a coffee shop on Newbury Street and called the woman who wrote the gossip column for the *Herald.* If anyone would have the real dirt on Levesque—the hell with his voting record or any bills he'd sponsored—she would.

"Hiya," I said, when she picked up the phone. "It's Liz."

"Baby," she shrieked happily. "How are you, darlin'?"

"I'm fine," I said. "How about you? You had lunch yet?"

"No, I haven't," she said. "Do you want to meet me somewhere? In about a half an hour?"

"That'd be great. Where?"

"The Premier?"

"Sure."

"Okay, well, I just have to finish writing this one little piece and then I'll be out the door. Oh, I can't wait to see you. It's been so *long*."

"It'll be soon," I replied, laughing. Her exuberance was irresistible. "Oh, and Edie?"

"Yes?"

"Have I got a story for you."

The Premier Restaurant is in the shadow of the Dover Street el station. It was the kind of neighborhood where the local merchants sold their wares out of car trunks. Half the pedestrians had a tendency to vanish mysteriously when a police cruiser drove by.

I beat Edie to the restaurant. It was a fairly large place,

and there was, unbelievably, a grand piano in the middle of the room. A young black man sat at it playing "The Shadow of Your Smile" with great intensity. I went to the counter and ordered a chopped chicken liver sandwich on an onion roll and iced coffee. Then I took a booth by the window. The pianist segued into "Someone to Watch Over Me." He was very good, but the music was a trifle too loud for comfy listening. It would have been fine in Symphony Hall.

I was picking up my coffee and sandwich when Edie appeared, somewhat out of breath. I grinned at her.

"Darlin'," she said. "I'm late."

I made a dismissive gesture with my right hand. "What'll you have to eat?"

She pursed her mouth. "Reuben," she announced. "On dark rye." The counterman was hovering, waiting for the rest of her order. She gave him a dazzling smile. "And a club soda," she added.

Edie was in her late forties, a thin, small-boned woman of medium height. She had brown hair, blunt cut to about two inches above her shoulders, and very large blue eyes. They gave her face a soft, ingenuous look. People who didn't know her assumed she had a personality to match. They were wrong.

We collected our food and went back to the booth. The pianist crashed into "Strangers in the Night." Over the din, Edie said to me, "So what's this hot news item you have for me?"

"Before I tell you, can I ask you a question or two?"

"Sure."

"What do you know about State Senator Alan Levesque?"

Edie looked a little startled. Then her face cleared and she said, "He's an asshole."

I laughed. "Well, that's succinct."

"And a crook."

I widened my eyes at her.

"Oh, well, sure, baby. Everybody knows that."

"I didn't." I picked up my sandwich.

"Well, you don't follow politics."

"No," I agreed. I ate some chicken liver. "If he's a crook, why isn't he in jail?"

Edie gave me an amused, tolerant look and said, "Is that supposed to be a serious question?"

"I guess not."

She peeled the top layer of bread off the top of her sandwich and inspected the pile of sauerkraut beneath it. She poked at the meat and melted cheese with her fork, then replaced the bread.

"Everything okay?" I asked.

She nodded.

"So tell me," I said. "How does Levesque's crookedness manifest itself? According to his campaign literature, he's a cross between Saint Francis of Assisi and Abraham Lincoln."

Edie snorted. "More like Warren G. Harding and Reverend Moon."

I smiled. "Go on."

She wiped some sauerkraut juice off her fingers with a paper napkin. "He's been involved in some shady real estate deals. Plus there was something funny about the circumstances under which he got a big loan from one of the banks."

"That's dirty," I said. "But not filthy."

Edie ate a small forkful of sauerkraut. "He's connected."

I looked up from my sandwich. "To organized crime?"

"No, baby, to the Lowells and the Cabots and the Lodges on his mother's side. Of course, to organized crime."

"And is this also one of those things that everybody knows?"

"Oh, sure."

"Uh-huh." I finished my sandwich. "Edie, when people say that somebody's mob-connected, what exactly does that mean? I hear the phrase all the time, but I've never known what it was supposed to entail. Does it mean that whoever it is, is actively engaged in committing crimes?"

"Not necessarily," Edie replied. "Though it depends, I guess, on how you define crime. A politician who's mob-connected has a different relationship with them, sort of, than a businessman who is."

"Sure," I said. "The mob infiltrates a legitimate business, takes it over, and it becomes a money-laundering operation."

"Politicians, they buy," Edie said. "If there's not already some kind of family relationship."

"Which is it with Levesque?"

"Bought," Edie said.

"Are you sure?"

She laughed. "Of course I am, baby."

"So how come he's never been indicted?"

She gave me that same look of tolerant amusement. "This is Massachusetts."

I nodded. "How did Levesque get bought?"

"Initially?" Edie shrugged. "Who knows? Probably a humongous campaign contribution."

"I see."

Edie had completed her top-down demolition of the first half of her Reuben. She leaned back slightly and her expression intensified from low-beam tolerant to high-beam inquisitorial. "So what's this story you have for me?"

"If you'll finish your lunch," I replied. "I'll tell you."

It took me fifteen minutes. Edie listened with her chin cupped in her hand, her sandwich forgotten, her eyes never leaving my face. They grew brighter as I spoke.

"I love it," she said finally. "I *love* it. This is marvelous. Oh, Liz, this is *wonderful.* That asshole."

"Now I have some questions for you," I said.

"Absolutely," she replied, beaming.

"Okay, number one," I said. "Is Levesque married?"

"Divorced. For about ten years. Two kids who live with Mom in a Tudor palace out in Chestnut Hill."

"God, of course, that's right," I said. "Isn't he dating some socialite? I think I saw the two of them on the tv news a while ago. What's her name, again?"

"Camille Frattiani," Edie said. "She and Alan have been, uh, keeping company for the past few years."

"Is it serious?"

"Far as I know."

"I see."

"Camille's the grandest dame in Boston since Isabella Stewart Gardner."

"So what's she doing with a jerk like Levesque?"

Edie shrugged. "Shortage of single heterosexual men over the age of thirty."

"Yeah, so I hear," I said, sipping my iced coffee.

"Anyway," Edie said. "Camille's a very ambitious lady. A nice, nice lady, but an ambitious one."

I raised my eyebrows. "So?"

"Levesque's got ambitions, too." Edie nibbled a slice of Kosher dill. "Wants to be the next governor of Massachusetts, in fact."

"Oh, swell," I said, laughing. "Just what we need, another crook in high office."

"Camille would like to be First Lady of the Commonwealth." Edie crunched another bite of pickle. "And after that, who knows?"

"You think she loves Levesque?" I asked. "Or is she just using him as a means to an end?"

"Oh, *no*." Edie sounded a little shocked. "No, no, no, no. Not at all. As I said, she's a nice lady. Interesting past. I'll tell you about it later. But, no, I think she *does* love him. In fact, I'm sure of it. It's just an extra added attraction that he might have a big future in politics."

"Do you think *he* loves *her*?"

Edie curled her lip. "Not as much as he loves himself. But then, he wouldn't, being a politician and all." Edie set the pickle back on her plate and looked contemplative. "Yeah, I suppose he loves her, by his definition. She's beautiful, and social, and well-bred, and well-known."

"In other words," I said. "She's an asset to him. Politically speaking."

"Uh-huh."

"So," I said. "If what I suspect is true, then Levesque

had Bonnie on the string the same time he had Camille on it.''

''Seems like it.'' There was more than a hint of malice in Edie's voice.

''You really don't like Levesque, do you?'' I remarked.

''As I said, he's an asshole.'' She picked up the second half of her sandwich. ''What you're telling me just confirms it.''

I laughed. ''What have I told you that's concrete, really? A divorced guy was cheating on his steady girlfriend with a beautiful young blonde English professor.''

''Whom you just happened to know,'' Edie continued relentlessly. ''And then Blondie just happened to die of an OD, not self-administered. And then Levesque's cousin just happened to assault you, this in a neighborhood with the lowest street crime rate in the greater Boston area. Meanwhile, Blondie's roommate, who just happens to be a political consultant, just happens to disappear. Pure coincidence. Uh-huh.''

''All right, all right,'' I said. ''I agree. But there's still nothing there we can legally prove.''

She gave me her brilliant smile. ''No,'' she said. ''But we will.''

26

''What do you have in mind?'' I asked.

She set the remains of her sandwich on the plate. ''The senator's holding a fund-raiser at the Royal Sonesta tomorrow night. I have an invitation to it. Why don't you come as my guest?"

"What would I do there?"

"I'll introduce you to Levesque. You can feel him out, you should pardon the expression."

I thought for a moment, then smiled. "I've never been to a political fund-raiser."

"They suck. You'll love it."

"You're on."

"Good."

The pianist thundered into the opening bars of "Hey, Jude." Edie jumped a little in her seat. I couldn't blame her; I was a little jarred myself. Edie turned her head to the right and glowered at the pianist. "If he doesn't lower it, I'll throw the coffee urn at him."

"He thinks it's Friday night at the Pops," I said. "Relax."

She rolled her eyes at the ceiling.

I picked up my iced coffee. "What time tomorrow night?" I asked.

She knitted her eyebrows. "Nine?"

"Okay."

"Wonderful," Edie smiled. "Well, look, they're staging this circus in the Grand"—she pronounced the word *graaaahhhnd*—"Ballroom. Why don't I meet you outside the entrance."

"Oh, good," I said. "I'd hate to walk into something like that alone."

I had no plans with Jack for the following evening, so there was no problem in that regard. The problem was, I reflected on the subway ride back to Cambridge, whether I should tell him what I'd learned today. Part of me wanted to, of course—it felt unnatural keeping information from him. The other part of me was still smarting a little from the Gayle Lydecker fiasco.

In the end, I compromised. I'd see what happened at the fund-raiser tomorrow night. Then I'd pass along to Jack whatever—if any—hot stuff I'd gathered. He could take it from there.

That evening, at dinner, he commented to me that I seemed a little quiet and subdued. I told him I was tired.

For my debut on the political circuit, I wore a green-and-blue linen dress with matching blue shoes and handbag. I almost wore a blue-and-white dress, but decided against it for fear I might be mistaken for a Levesque bumper sticker.

I walked to the Royal Sonesta, and was outside the entrance to the Graaaaahhhhnd Ballroom at five to nine. The festivities were well underway. I took a quick peek inside the ballroom. There were maybe two hundred and fifty to three hundred people in there. A band on a raised platform pounded out swing music loud enough to make the chandeliers quiver. The two cash bars were doing a big business.

Edie appeared at five after nine.

"Don't you look nice," she said, gracious enough not to sound surprised.

I smiled and shook my head. "People are so shocked to see me in something other than jeans, they always say that."

"Well, come along," she replied briskly.

Tables had been set up just inside the entrance to the ballroom. The one on the right had a sign on it that read "PRESS." Behind the table sat a young woman. She smiled at us inquiringly.

"Edith Gold from the *Herald*," Edie announced. She jerked a thumb at me. "My colleague, Liz Connors."

"She didn't check her list to see if we're legit," I whispered to Edie as we walked away from the table.

"They never do," Edie said. "Bimbos. Listen, honey, if you ever want to crash a big party in town, just tell the person at the door you're meeting me there and they'll let you in, no questions asked."

"Right," I said, laughing.

"Now, how do we get a drink?" Edie said.

"There's a bar over there."

Before you could buy a drink, you had to buy a ticket from a young woman with a reel of them and a metal cash box who sat at a card table in one corner of the room. The tickers were color-coded for hard liquor, beer, or wine. Edie got a wine ticket and I got a booze one. We traded them in at the bar for, respectively, a Chablis and a vodka-on-the-rocks.

"Why don't you wander around for a while?" Edie suggested. "I see some jerks I gotta go talk to."

"Have fun."

"Yeh, that'll be the day." She darted purposefully toward the opposite side of the room. No wonder the woman stayed lithe. She never moved anywhere except at top speed.

The room was decorated with blue and white bunting. A cluster of helium-filled blue and white balloons bumped lazily against the ceiling. I was very glad I hadn't worn the blue-and-white dress I'd originally intended to wear.

I wandered over to one of the hors d'oeuvres tables. It looked as if it had been ravaged by a swarm of locusts on a high-cholesterol diet. I cut a sliver from the remains of an Edam cheese and fished the lone cocktail frank from a chafing dish.

The crowd looked to be predominantly fifty and up. There was a lot of polyester and a lot of pastel hair.

I thought of the blue-coiffed woman who worked in the Levesque's Oak Square office. Maybe she'd had her hair tinted to match the campaign colors.

I strolled away from the hors d'oeuvres table and began a slow ramble around the room. On the wooden dance floor in front of the band's platform six or seven couples bobbed and jigged more or less in time to the sound of some Benny Goodman imitators, I smiled as I watched them; they were all obviously having a hell of a time.

I spotted Edie on the other side of the dance floor. She was deep in conversation with a tall and enormously fat dark-haired man. I walked over to them. "Oh, Liz," Edie said. She gestured with her glass at the fat guy. "This is—"

The rest of the introduction was drowned out by the music. I smiled at the fat man and said, "Hello."

He was wearing a gray suit and white shirt that had come untucked from his trousers. There was some cocktail sauce on his tie.

"Pleased to meet you, little lady," he said.

At five-ten, I wasn't used to being called little anything. It was kind of cute. And I sure as shooting was little in comparison to *him*.

"I *know* you've heard of Vin, Liz," Edie said, her voice baby-innocent and her eyes twinkling with good-natured malice.

"Oh, sure," I lied.

"Well, I guess almost everyone has," Vin boomed. "They don't call me the Mussolini of Middlesex County for nothing."

"Have you made the trains run on time?" I inquired.

Edie threw back her head and gave a shriek of laughter. Vin looked blank for a moment. Then he ho-hoed dutifully.

"Just teasing," I said.

"You gotta good sensayuma," Vin said. "I like that."

"Thank you," I replied.

Edie said something about Ward One, whatever that was, and Vin gave his attention back to her. I listened for a moment, but the dialogue had no meaning and even less interest for me. I raised my glass to Vin, winked at him, and said, "Good luck with the trains." Then I moved off to try my luck at another buffet table.

The one at this side of the room had apparently been replenished. I speared a piece of rumaki with a toothpick and ate a miniature eggroll.

As I was contemplating the cheese tray and adding up the calories it represented, a tallish slender woman in a black dress drifted alongside me. I looked up automatically. The woman smiled politely and said, "Excuse me." She picked up a broccoli floret from the *crudités* tray and nibbled it delicately. She said, "Lovely party, isn't it?"

"Very nice," I agreed, trying not to stare at her.

"Enjoy yourself," she said, and wafted off into the crowd.

I knew who she was; I'd seen her briefly on a television news show—and had probably also seen, without particularly noticing, her picture in the newspapers and in *Boston Magazine*. Camille Frattiani. A photographer's dream, she was even lovelier in person. She was also a local legend.

Edie had told me the whole story. She had been born Camille D'Alessio, above her father's bakery in the North End, the fifth of seven children. Her talents as a musician and as a graphic artist had first manifested themselves in a parochial elementary school. She'd graduated from Girl's Latin with a full scholarship to the New England Conservatory. From there, she'd gone as a flautist to the New York Philharmonic. In the two years she was with Bernstein's orchestra, she'd kept up with her drawing and painting. Enough to have had several one-woman shows at Soho galleries.

At twenty-four, she'd met, at a party, an attaché to the Italian diplomatic corps named Giorgio Frattiani. They married two months later. Camille left the Philharmonic and traveled to Italy with her husband. They settled in Rome.

After two years of marriage, Camille gave birth to a son. He was christened Alessandro.

After three years of marriage, Giorgio died in a plane crash on his way to a NATO conference in Paris.

The year after that, Camille and her son returned to Boston and moved into a townhouse on Beacon Hill. In due course, Camille was appointed a trustee of the Conservatory. She became honorary chair of the Italian-American Cultural Exchange. She was named to the board of governors of three major charities. She received an honorary doctorate from the University of Massachusetts of Boston, for "outstanding public service."

Alessandro was on the soccer team at Choate.

Camille's drawings and paintings still continued to be featured at Newbury Street art galleries.

She had never remarried, although she had accumulated some pretty heavy-duty escorts.

All this flashed through my mind as I watched her float through the crowd of Levesque supporters, pausing every few feet to smile at or speak to someone.

She was perhaps five-seven, willowy, with a perfectly oval face dominated by very large, melted-chocolate brown eyes. Her black hair was drawn into a coil at the nape of her neck.

Her skin was antique ivory. A quattrocento *principessa* in a Halston shift.

Whatever you could say pro or con Alan Levesque, you had to admit that he had a good eye for fine-looking women. I resumed my inspection of the cheese tray.

The chandelier lights blinked on and off three times, very rapidly, as if it were the last call for drinks. The band burst into "Happy Days Are Here Again." Somebody turned the chandelier rheostats down completely and a single spotlight, focused on the center of the dance floor, came on. The room quieted.

A young man in a dinner jacket bounded into the spotlight. He was carrying a hand mike that trailed a long cord.

"Ladies and gentlemen." His amplified voice reverberated around the room. "And now the man you've all been waiting to see. I . . . give . . . you . . . Senator Al Levesque!"

There was a crash of cymbals. Alan Levesque emerged from the shadows at the fringe of the dance floor and walked into the spotlight. The audience shrieked and whistled and clapped its welcome. A man beside me cupped his hands around his mouth and bellowed, "Hey, Al, looking good."

I hoped I'd have the hearing in my right ear tomorrow.

The applause grew more tumultuous. Levesque grinned and held up his hands. The kid in the dinner jacket handed him the microphone.

"My good friends," Levesque said. "I can't tell you how much it means to me to see you all here tonight."

About fifty grand in the old campaign chest was what it meant, I figured.

Levesque started to say something else, but was interrupted by another burst of cheers and applause. I decided it was time to visit the ladies' room. I'd seen and heard enough.

When I returned to the ballroom, ten minutes later, the lights had been turned back up and the band was playing a medley of fifties show tunes. The waiters were restocking the buffets. I fetched myself another drink. A guy in tartan-patterned slacks and red sportcoat asked me if I wanted to dance. His eyes had a glassy unfocused look and he swayed as he spoke. Before I was able to reply, a middle-aged blonde women in ruffled black taffeta rushed up to him, grabbed his elbow, and hissed something in his ear. She didn't look at me. The drunk yanked his arm free and shook his head in boozy irritation. I left the two of them to their altercation.

As I turned, I saw Edie by the bar. I caught her eye and she waved at me to join her. I maneuvered myself through the crowd toward her.

"You want to meet the man of the hour?" she asked.

"That's what I'm here for."

Edie set her empty wineglass on the bar. "Well, let's catch him while he's relatively free."

I trailed after her, feeling in my stomach a little flutter of nervous anticipation.

Levesque and Camille Frattiani were standing shoulder to shoulder chatting with a tall, lean, balding man in a blue suit. Actually, Levesque and the balding guy were doing all the chatting. Camille was listening and wearing a fixed, polite smile.

You could quite easily imagine her moving gracefully in and out of diplomatic circles. Political circles, on the other hand, didn't seem like her milieu.

Edie charged right up to the trio.

Camille's smile lost some of its fixed quality. She looked at Edie with genuine warmth and said, "Hello, I was hoping you'd be here this evening."

"Wouldn't have missed it, darlin'," Edie replied. She must have liked Camille; she never addressed anyone as "darlin' " or "baby" whom she didn't.

Levesque's face broke into its sincere grin. "*E*die Gold," he exclaimed. He reached out and clasped both of Edie's hands and drew her to him. She tilted her face and he kissed her on the cheek.

"Hi, Al," Edie said. "No "darlin' " or "baby" this time, I noted.

"I love your column," the balding man said. "I read it every day. I wouldn't miss it."

"Ooohh, thank you," Edie replied, in what was almost but not quite a girlish squeal. I bit the inside of my lower lip to keep from laughing.

"I'm Bob Fenster," Baldie said. "Of Fenster, McDougall, and Levine."

I waited for a flourish of trumpets, but there wasn't any.

"I'll be doing strategy for Al's next campaign," Fenster added. He was clearly hoping for Edie to whip out a notebook, transcribe everything he'd said, and run it in her column the next day.

It may have been projection, but I thought that Camille looked faintly embarrassed.

"Camille," Edie said. "Al." She touched my shoulder lightly. "This is my friend, Liz Connors, the writer." She said it as if I were Eudora Welty or Anne Sexton.

Camille held out her hand. "Didn't we meet at the buffet?"

I smiled and shook hands with her. "Yes. And it's nice to meet you a second time. I've heard so much about you."

"You sure have," Baldie said. He looped an arm around Camille's waist and squeezed. "Let me tell you, this is one terrific gal."

If I'd had food or drink in my mouth, I'd have gagged on it.

Levesque gave me a toned-down version of his campaign-trail grin and said, "What is it you write about, Liz?"

"This and that," I replied. "Usually, whatever catches my interest. I don't have a specialty."

"Ever do any political stories?" Fenster asked.

"No," I smiled at him. "But after tonight, I may."

I heard Edie snicker through her nose and simulate a sneeze to cover it. "Damn pollen," she remarked. "Gets me every time this time of year."

Camille looked at her with concern.

"Well, let me tell you," Fenster said to me, slapping Levesque between the shoulder blades. "You got one hell of a story here in old Al."

I looked at Levesque. "I'm sure of that."

Camille was telling Edie about a wonder-working allergist she knew. They drew off to the side a bit to continue the discussion.

"Enjoying the party?" Levesque asked, with every appearance of being interested in my answer.

"Very much," I said. "It's my first political fund-raiser. It's . . . quite an interesting occasion."

"Well, I think I'll go get another drink," Fenster said. He smiled at me. "Real pleasure to meet you, Miss Conran."

"You, too, Mr. Fenwick," I replied.

If he heard me, it didn't register. But I don't think he *did* hear me; he was halfway to the bar as I spoke.

Levesque sipped at what appeared to be a weak Scotch and soda and glanced around the room. If I didn't in the next five seconds think of something fascinating to say, I'd lose him.

I wasn't emboldened by the two vodkas I'd consumed. It takes more than that. I think it was the thrill of the chase.

"Senator," I said.

He glanced back at me, eyebrows elevated, glass raised to his lips.

"I think you and I have a mutual acquaintance," I continued.

"Oh?" Levesque looked pleasantly curious.

"Well, I'm almost sure of it," I said. I smiled expansively. "Woman named Bonnie Nordgren."

He was very good; I'll give him that. His face remained pleasantly curious for a half-second, then became pleasantly thoughtful. "Nordgren?" he repeated.

I nodded.

He frowned, then shook his head. "Gee, I don't *think* so." He sipped his drink and again looked meditative. "No, that doesn't ring a bell." He smiled. "Sorry. Maybe you have me mixed up with someone else."

It was my turn to assume phony mystification. "That's funny," I said. "I could have sworn . . . well, never mind. I probably *am* mistaken."

He smiled at me.

I smiled at him.

But we both knew I wasn't mistaken.

27

The next morning, bright and early—by my standards of early, at least—I was ringing the doorbell to apartment one in the brown frame house on Huron Avenue. Then, as per our established routine, I moved over so that Mrs. Gallagher could peep through the curtain and inspect me. When I saw the nylon drapery flutter, I grinned and waved.

A moment or so later, Mrs. Gallagher was at the door. She had a dish towel in her right hand.

"Me again," I said, quite unnecessarily. I glanced pointedly down at the dish towel. "Am I disturbing you? You look busy."

"Well, I can spare a minute, I guess."

"That's all it'll take," I said, smiling. I reached into my handbag and fished out the picture of Senator Levesque, I offered it to Mrs. Gallagher. "Does this person look familiar to you?"

The woman's birdlike eyes narrowed as she looked at the picture. She cocked her head and pursed her mouth. After about thirty seconds, she glanced back at me, her face thoughtful. "I think . . ." she began.

"Yes?"

Mrs. Gallagher held up the photo and peered at it again. Then she shot me another look, bright and shrewd. "You want to know if this is the man I saw with Bonnie."

"Well, yes."

She held the picture out to me and I took it. "They do look a lot alike. I think they could be the same person."

It wasn't the kind of ID you'd want to take to court, but it was enough for me. I replaced the photo of the senator in my bag and took out the one of his cousin I'd clipped from the newspaper report of the kid's death. I handed it to Mrs. Gallagher. "How about this guy?"

She looked at the picture for a few seconds and then shook her head, very decidedly. "No."

"Okay," I said, and replaced the picture in my bag. I was pretty sure that neither she nor Daisy Jacobsen had seen the kid before; if they had, they'd have mentioned it to me. But there's no harm in betting on a long shot, especially if it doesn't cost you anything.

"I want to thank you for all your help," I said to Mrs. Gallagher. "I don't think I'll have to bother you again."

"Oh, you haven't bothered me, dear."

We shook hands. The worn skin of hers was warm and dry.

"Bye-bye," she said, and shut the door.

I had a cup of slightly less than mediocre coffee at the luncheonette up the street. Then I went to the police station. I was ready to dazzle the CID with my investigative expertise and its results.

Jack was just emerging from the captain's office when I arrived. He grinned at me and said, "My favorite writer. What's up?"

"Can I talk to you for a minute?"

"Sure."

We went into his cubby. I flopped into the visitor's chair and put my feet on his desk. Jack took his own seat, and leaned back, and linked his hands behind his head.

"What's up?" he repeated.

"I think I know who murdered Bonnie Nordgren," I said.

Jack was too old and too experienced to let anything in the way of a reaction show on his face. Or maybe he was just used to me and my penchant for high drama. After a moment, he raised his eyebrows and said, "Oh?"

I produced the photo of Senator Levesque from my purse, flourished it, leaned forward, and slapped it down on the desk blotter. "Ze villain of ze piece," I said.

Jack studied the photo for a moment and then raised his eyes to mine. "Fascinating," he said.

"You wanna hear my, uh, theory?" I asked.

"Cookie, I wouldn't miss it for the world."

The recital took me five minutes.

"Now *that*," Jack said, "is ingenious."

"You like it?"

"Oh, it's great. It explains everything. Unfortunately, you don't have a shred of evidence to support it."

"What're you, the DA?" I said, mock-waspish.

He laughed.

"Anyway," I said. "You're wrong about there being *no* evidence. There *is* evidence that Bonnie and Levesque were having some kind of relationship."

"So what?"

"Huh?"

"Doesn't mean he killed her. And, by the way, why would he *want* to kill her? What do you think his motive was? You really haven't explained that to me, Liz."

"All right," I said. "According to all I've heard, Bonnie was a flake with a drug problem."

"So?"

"So that made her dangerous to Levesque. To his political career." I made a face. "God, Jack you know what those guys are like. They'd strangle their own grandmothers to get elected or reelected. Levesque may be only a state senator now, but he has his eye on something bigger."

"Rumor is he wants to be the next governor," Jack said.

"Oh. You heard that."

Jack gave me his lupine grin. "Honey, I hear almost everything."

"Never doubted that for a moment," I said. "Have you also heard about his alleged mob connections?"

"Sure."

"Is it true?"

"Probably."

"Dandy," I said.

Jack laughed again.

"Okay," I said briskly. "What you've just told me only adds weight to my argument. What I'm saying is that I think it's very possible that Bonnie might have stumbled, somehow, it doesn't matter how at this point, on some really intense dirt—I mean something *bad*—about Levesque's, uh, connections. Or his private life. And he, knowing how unstable she was, didn't want to run the risk of having her blab to someone. So he shut her up, or had her shut up, permanently, and tried to make it look like suicide."

Jack looked thoughtful. "I don't know," he said finally. "Still sounds a little thin to me. What awful thing could Bonnie find out about him that would make him run a risk like that?"

I shrugged. "How would I know? Maybe he's a closet child molester. Maybe he's a drug distributor. Now there's an interesting thought. Maybe he's in the pharmacy business with the Colombians or the boys from Sicily. That would explain where he got the drugs to kill Bonnie."

"You want me to ask him?" Jack said.

"Oh, stop making fun of me. This is serious."

"I agree," Jack said. "And I'm not making fun of you."

I looked at him.

"All I'm doing is pointing out to you that everything you've told me is pure speculation."

"And therefore useless."

"I didn't say that." He leaned forward and put his elbows on his desk blotter, bracketing the photo of Levesque. "You may be on to something. Although it probably isn't what you think you're on to."

I was feeling a lot less confident of my theory than I had

been when I'd waltzed into the CID twenty minutes ago. "So what should I do now?" I asked.

"Tell Bill or Joe or Bernie everything you've told me," Jack replied promptly.

"Oh, God, I can't do that."

Jack looked very surprised. "Why not?"

"They'll laugh at me."

"Okay, I'll tell them, then."

"Would you?" I asked gratefully.

"Sure."

"Good. That way, when they collapse in hysterics, I won't have to be there to watch."

"They won't laugh," Jack said. "In fact, they'll probably want to talk to Levesque. I would."

"Really?"

"Sure."

"What'll they ask him?"

"Well, they won't bust down the door of his office and grab him by the collar and slam him against the wall and yell, 'Okay, maggot, tell us why you killed Bonnie Nordgren.' "

"No, I suppose not."

Jack smiled. "They'll ask him if he knew her, see how he reacts, take it from there."

I nodded.

"You got to be subtle sometimes," Jack said. "Devious, even."

"Bernie'll have to leave his bamboo shoots at home."

"Uh-huh."

"Okay," I said. "Well, that sounds like a satisfactory arrangement to me."

Jack nodded. "Speaking of arrangements, what are we doing for dinner tonight?"

I shrugged. "I don't know. You got any ideas?"

"Let's go out some place."

"That sounds nice." I stood up slowly, stretched, and smiled down at him. "When?"

"I'll come get you around, oh, seven."

"Fine."

The phone rang. Jack picked up the receiver and said, "Lieutenant Lingemann." I looped my handbag strap around my shoulder and mouthed "See you later."

When I was at the office door, he called to me. I turned to look back at him. He had the receiver of the phone cradled in the hollow of his shoulder. His left hand covered the mouthpiece.

"Liz?"

"Yes?"

"With regard to the detective work you've done on this . . ."

"Yes?"

He held up his right hand and made a circle with the thumb and forefinger.

I went home feeling pretty good. I didn't feel so swell at six-forty-five that evening, after Jack phoned to tell me he'd be late because they'd just gotten a call from the Brookline police that the body of a woman named Gayle Lydecker had been found slumped over in the front seat of a silver 1984 Volvo sedan.

28

"Carbon Monoxide poisoning, huh?" I said.

"Well, that was the immediate cause of death," Jack said.

"Uh-huh," I repeated. I gave Jack a beady look. "They don't *really* think she committed suicide, do they?"

"I don't know exactly what they think, Liz," Jack sounded a little weary. As well he might; I'd been haranguing him for the last half an hour.

"Has an autopsy been done yet?"

Jack shook his head. "I think it's been scheduled for this afternoon."

"I'll be fascinated to learn the results."

He raised his eyebrows questioningly.

"I know they're going to find traces of drugs in her system." I sprang out of my chair and paced across the narrow room. "You know what happened to Gayle? I'll *tell* you what happened to Gayle. Levesque doped her and dumped her into the front seat of that car and left the motor running. And then he walked away and let her die. *That's* what happened to Gayle Lydecker."

Jack made a steeple out of his hands and pressed his forefingers against his chin. "Okay," he said. "Say you're right. Why did he kill her?"

I windmilled my arms, nearly knocking a stack of reports off the filing cabinet. "Same reason he killed Bonnie. She was coming apart at the seams. My God, Jack, I spoke to the woman only—what was it—three or four days ago. She was distraught. She sounded as if the hounds of hell were after her."

"She left a note."

I stopped my flailing and stomping and stared at him. "What?"

"There was a note on the dashboard of the car."

"What did it say?"

Jack got up and left the office. He returned a minute or so later with a manila folder. He sat back behind his desk, riffled through the folder, and extracted from it a report form. He glanced it over quickly, then looked up at me. "I'm sorry for everything," he said.

"Huh?"

"That was the contents of the note. 'I'm sorry for everything.' "

"That's all?"

"Yup." He slipped the report back into the folder and placed the folder to one side of the desk.

"That's vaguely enough worded to be subject to a number of interpretations," I said. "Was it handwritten?"

"Typed."

"Signed?"

"Nope."

I felt a slow, nasty smile spread over my face. "I see. Despite that, everybody's still positive Gayle wrote it."

Jack sighed. "Liz, don't argue with me. I'm not investigating this case. If you're not happy with the way it's being handled, go bitch to the DA's office."

I bit my lower lip. "I know. I'm sorry. I wasn't yelling at you. It's just—I'm frustrated, that's all. You get that way sometimes, too."

He nodded.

I sat down in the visitor's chair. "If they think Gayle killed herself, do they have any idea why she did it?"

"That I really don't know either," Jack replied.

"I bet they think Gayle killed Bonnie," I said. "And couldn't live with the guilt, and so committed suicide."

"Well, Liz," Jack said. "Given the evidence, you have to admit that that's a reasonable explanation of things."

"Too pat."

"And don't forget, there was a time when you thought Gayle had killed Bonnie."

"Yes," I agreed. "But that was before the Levesque family came boogying into the picture."

Jack smiled, perhaps at the mental image of the Dancing Levesques.

"Speaking of the senator," I said. "Did you get a chance to mention my theory to Bill or Bernie or Joe?"

"Yup."

"What'd they think?"

"There were interested."

"They going to pursue it?"

"I don't know."

"That means they aren't. *Damn!*"

"Don't underestimate them. What needs to be checked, they'll check."

"Yes," I said. "If only we could arrive at a consensus as to what needs checking."

Jack laughed. Then he put both hands flat on the desk blotter and pushed back his chair slightly. "I'd offer you an early lunch," he said. "But I have to be at the courthouse in fifteen minutes."

"Oh? What's doing there?"

"Gotta testify before the grand jury. About the bank robbers."

"I see. Well, have fun."

"Oh, sure." He straightened his tie and began rolling down his shirtsleeves. "A little song, a little dance—"

"A little seltzer down your pants," I concluded.

"Right. He put on his suit coat. "Liz?"

"Yes?"

He came over to me and put his arm around my shoulders. "Don't get unglued about this, okay? You did what you could for Bonnie and Gayle."

I nodded. He gave me a single pat on the back and said, "Attagirl. See you tonight."

"Yup."

Walking back through Central Square, I had much the same aimless feeling I'd experienced the day I'd learned of Bonnie Nordgren's death. Jack was probably right that I'd done what I could. There wouldn't be much point in pestering Bill or Bernie or Joe. In any event, maybe I *was* totally off-base in suspecting Levesque. Maybe Daisy Jacobsen and Mrs. Gallagher had misidentified his photo. Maybe Dan Fowler had been mistaken in identifying the Levesque kid as the one who'd visited Bonnie at Currier College. Maybe the pattern I'd discerned was nothing more than a series of bizarre coincidences.

No.

I opened my purse and dug out my little notebook. I flipped it open till I came to the page where I'd written down the phone number and address of Levesque's law office. I checked my coin purse for change. The I went into an upscale pizza parlor and fought my way through the hanging plants to their public phone. I dialed Levesque's number.

"Law offices," a female voice said.

"Is Attorney Levesque in today?" I asked.

"Yes, but I'm afraid—"

I didn't hear the rest of what she was saying because I'd hung up the phone. I brushed back through the jungle of Boston ferns and spider plants and ran for the subway. As I got to the platform a train was just pulling out, naturally, but another one came along in five minutes. I rode it to Park Station and walked from there to Federal Street. Chasing the dragon.

The dragon's lair was on the ninth floor of a fairly new office building. I took the elevator up, along with a delivery boy from the Tastee—Temptee Coffee Shop in the lobby and some secretarial types.

The dragon's lair had a blonde wood door. I opened it and stepped into a large, air-conditioned reception room done in leather and tweed and chrome. Masculine. There were two doors in the rear wall. A young woman sat behind a mahogany desk. She smiled at me inquiringly. I smiled back at her and said, "I'd like to see Attorney Levesque."

"Do you have an appointment?"

"Hell, no. But when you tell him I'm here, I'm positive he'll drop everything."

The pleasant, inquiring smile lost about four-fifths of its pleasantness. "I'm sorry, but—"

I went over to the desk. The girl eyed me warily. There was some blank typing paper in a plastic tray by the telephone. Next to that was a ceramic mug full of pencils, pens, and felt-tipped markers. I took a sheet of paper and one of the markers, and with it, block-printed on the paper "I KNOW WHO KILLED BONNIE NORDGREN. BET YOU DO, TOO." I capped the marker and replaced it in the mug. Then I held out the sheet of paper to the receptionist and said, "If you'll give this to the senator with my compliments. My name is Liz Connors."

The girl read what I'd written and her eyes widened slightly.

"Go on," I urged, rattling the paper. "Take it in to him. Shoo. Scat."

She took the paper, holding it gingerly by one corner, rose, and went to tell her boss that there was a madwoman foaming around in the outer sanctum. I sat down in one of the brown leather armchairs.

A minute later, the right-hand rear door opened and the receptionist appeared. She walked back to her desk and sat down behind it, studiously avoiding looking at me. Levesque was behind her. He stood in the open doorway and gave me an expressionless stare. I grinned back at him.

"Hiya, pal," I said. "Nice bash at the Sonesta the other night. Rake in much dough?"

Levesque said to the receptionist, "Hold my calls, please, Doreen." To me, he said, "Come in here."

"What'd I tell you?" I asked Doreen. I got to my feet. She goggled at me. As I passed her desk, I stage-whispered to her, "If I were you, I'd start looking for another job." Then I went into Levesque's office. He followed me, shutting the door. There was a couch across from his desk, and I sat down on it. Levesque remained standing.

"All right," he said, in a hard, flat voice. "What is this bullshit? I told you once, I don't know any Bonnie What's-her-name."

"Oh, knock it off, Senator," I replied. "You were sleeping with her for two years. Does Camille know that, by the way? She's a nice lady. I can't imagine what she sees in a trashbag like you. Even if she does want to be First Lady of Massachusetts.

Levesque's face flushed slightly. "Leave Camille out of this," he said sharply. I repeated the words silently along with him. Funny how I'd know he'd say just that.

Levesque didn't appear to enjoy being made sport of. Not

many people do. "I'm not going to ask again," he said. "What the fuck do you want?"

"If you'll sit down and stop looming over me, I'll tell you," I said. "But first I want to tell you that if you're contemplating doing anything nasty to me here, everything I'm going to tell you I've already told to a Cambridge cop named Lingemann. And he's told another Cambridge cop and two state police investigators." I nodded at the office door. "Plus I wouldn't push Doreen's loyalty too far. If you throw me out a window she might feel compelled to mention it to the police."

Levesque gritted his teeth and said through them, "Jesus Christ." He walked behind his desk, yanked out the chair, and sat down hard.

"You know, you're playing this all wrong," I said. "You ought to be all sweet bewildered innocence."

"Don't tell me how to act, lady."

"Probably wouldn't make much impression if I did," I said. "So I won't."

"Will you come to the point?"

"Okay," I said. "Here's what I think. Excuse me, what I know. You met Bonnie Nordgren two years ago at—what? A party? Doesn't matter. Anyhow, you started an affair with her. You probably found out quick enough that she had emotional problems and drug problems, but so what? She also had a gorgeous face and a great body. Maybe you were even supplying her with drugs. In fact, I think your crappy cousin *was* supplying them to her."

Levesque looked startled at the mention of the kid.

"He was hanging around Bonnie on the Currier College campus while she worked there," I said. "And I know someone who'll testify to that. Stupid, stupid. Well, at least the kid was more discreet about it this year. Nobody seems to have seen him hanging around with Bonnie recently. Well, be that as it may."

"You're out of your mind," Levesque said. "You know that? You're really off the wall on this one."

I held up my hand, gesturing imperiously for silence.

"Let me continue. I think you got pretty intimate with Bonnie. In fact, I think you got pretty obsessed with her. Sexually and in other ways." I paused, and thought of what Dennis Koenig had told me. "I bet Bonnie knew how to make you feel good." I said, stressing the last two words. "She had a father thing. And with you being an older, sort of powerful guy . . . man, I bet she really blew you away, huh?"

Levesque seethed at me wordlessly.

"All right," I said. "Let's take it as a given that she had you where she wanted you. Panting. And you know what, Senator? I think you let slip to her, in the heat of the moment, so to speak, or she found out, because you didn't keep your mouth shut, some unattractive things about your, uh, business transactions with the guys from the North End. Did you think that would make you look like an even bigger guy in her eyes? If she knew you hung out with the hard cases?"

Levesque was breathing very hard.

"On the other hand," I said. "I suppose it's possible that your asshole cousin told her. He struck me as someone idiotic enough to think it was macho to brag about his relative's criminal doings."

"What do you know about my cousin?" Levesque interrupted.

"He jumped me on my doorstep a few nights before he died," I said. "That's why I wouldn't feel sincere offering you my condolences. But we'll get back to that later." I leaned forward slightly. "Okay. Bonnie knew some bad stuff about you. But she apparently loved you and maybe she thought you'd ditch Camille and marry her. At least, she sort of hinted about that to her mother last Christmas."

Levesque had regained his control and was watching me very steadily.

"All right," I continued. "Everybody who knew Bonnie agreed that her condition had deteriorated badly this year. She was able to fool her family from long distance, but the people who saw her every day knew she could barely function. That scared you, didn't it? I mean, God knows what kind of crazy thing she might do or say that would fuck up your life. Enter Gayle Lydecker. Now, I don't know how you met her, but I figure that since she was a political consultant and you're a politician, you got together that way. You worked together on a campaign, maybe. And you learned that she was capable and trustworthy and, best yet, knew how to keep her mouth shut. So you got her to take a leave of absence from Mac-Crimmon—for which you probably compensated her pretty well—and to move in with Bonnie and babysit her full-time till you could think of a more permanent solution to the problem. So that was fine. Or it would have been fine. Then Bonnie really royally screwed things up when she went to her boss and got him to give her that three and a half grand for a phony brain tumor treatment.'' I paused for breath, eyeing Levesque. ''She needed that money to pay a dealer, didn't she? Because you'd cut her off.''

Levesque shook his head in a good simulation of dazed astonishment. ''This is insane.''

I ignored him and went on, relentlessly. ''You tried for another month to keep Bonnie under control, right? But she was becoming completely unmanageable. So . . .'' I shrugged. ''Tell me, Senator,'' I said. ''Did you shoot her up with that OD? Or did you delegate the task?''

''Christ,'' Levesque exploded.

''Probably delegated it,'' I said. ''Doesn't matter. You're still responsible. If I had to guess, it was your creep cousin. I wonder how many drug charges *he* got picked up on that you had buried, Senator? Oh, well, it doesn't matter now.''

''Get out,'' Levesque said. His face was purple.

''When I'm finished,'' I said. ''Let's get back to Gayle. Now Gayle, being as she was an old hand at the political game, probably wasn't too fussy about dirty tricks in the name of the cause. But I think she probably drew the line at murdering your girlfriend. And that's why she took off. She called me a few days ago, you know, sounding scared out of her wits. What did she do, come to you and tell you she couldn't handle it anymore? That she was going to the cops? Or to me? Is that why you killed her?''

Levesque looked as if he wanted to lunge across the desk and rip out my throat. I didn't think he would. He'd send an aide to do it.

''Let's return to your charming cousin,'' I said. ''Delightful lad. As I told you, I made his acquaintance on my doorstep when he tried to mug me. What I figure is that he saw me hanging around Bonnie's, before and after she died, asking questions of the tenants, and that he got my name, address, and phone number the same way Gayle did, from a note that I wrote to Bonnie, which one of your bozos walked off with. More stupidity. The cops were wondering why they couldn't find it.'' I took another deep breath. ''And so Neil decided to take matters into his own hands and beat me up to scare me off or to teach me a lesson. That was a brilliant move on his part. Successful, too, as you can see.''

''Are you finished?'' Levesque said, shooting the words out between his teeth like spit.

''Yeah,'' I replied. ''I think I've covered everything.''

He jerked his head at the door. ''Then get the fuck out.''

''My pleasure,'' I said, rising. ''Would you care to confirm or deny what I've just told you?''

''I don't have to confirm or deny shit, you bitch. Get out.''

''I'm on my way,'' I said. ''One last item, though.''

He stared at me.

''If any of your little helpers ever come near me again,'' I said. ''I'll kill him.'' I stabbed the forefinger of my right hand in the air. ''And that, Senator, is my campaign promise to you.''

29

When I left Levesque's office, I was so pumped up that I briefly considered going over to Boston Police Headquarters and asking them if there were any muggers or rapists available for beating to a pulp. But I decided against it. The BPD, unlike the CPD, wasn't used to my winningly eccentric ways, and they might lock *me* up.

Instead, I went to a Chinese restaurant and had a vodka martini and cashew chicken. The combination of liquor and monosodium glutamate tranquilized me a bit. And I calmed down further as the afternoon wore on, till I got to the point where I was able to step outside myself and study the virago who'd pulled that incredible scene in the dragon's lair.

Was *that* what they meant by the politics of confrontation?

I didn't say one word about the incident to Jack, even when he told me that the preliminary autopsy results on Gayle Lydecker indicated the presence of a narcotic substance in her blood. I contented myself with mildly pointing out that that fact might, just might, give credence to my theory. He said, "Mmph," which constituted a sort of semiagreement.

We had a very nice dinner in an Italian restaurant near MIT and then went to a really stupid science fiction movie at the Harvard Square Theatre. It occurred to me, fleetingly, that nothing I was seeing on the screen was as outlandish as what I myself had done that day.

When we went back to my place, there weren't any mob

henchmen or wardheelers or whatever lurking about to do me in. Not a single one. It was almost a disappointment, after the bloodcurdling oath I'd sworn in Levesque's office.

But not a surprise. I had no great opinion of Levesque's intellect (or of that of any politician, for that matter), but even *he* wouldn't be stupid enough to have me hurt or killed. He had to assume that if anyone so much as jostled me on a subway platform, the cops would be all over him like flies on garbage.

So I was safe as houses.

Jack and I took Lucy for a walk down to Bullfinch Square. After that, we had a brandy apiece in my living room. And so to bed.

If I dreamed anything weird, I had no recollection of it the following morning.

As usual, Jack had left before I awoke. He left a note saying that he'd call later and some coffee on the stove. I reheated it and had a cup with juice and toast.

At ten I got a call from somebody at BU wanting to know if I'd like to teach a journalism course in the fall evening division. I said I'd let them know. A half hour later, the editor of *Cambridge Monthly* called to ask me if I'd do an article on the local singles spots. He wanted the title to be "Bar Wars." He thought I'd provide the proper sardonic perspective. I agreed to both propositions.

I took a shower, got dressed, and asked Lucy what she wanted to do that day. She grinned at me with her tongue out and waved her tail, a response that, like Gayle Lydecker's "suicide" note, was open to a variety of interpretations.

"Let's clean the house," I said, which was fine with her until I brought out the vacuum. Before I'd even started uncoiling the cord, she'd gone into the bedroom and slithered under the bed.

The phone rang just as I'd dispatched the last of the living room dustballs. When I answered it, a woman's voice said, "Is this the public library?"

"Not quite," I replied, glancing at the four hundred and fifty-seven books on the floor-to-ceiling shelves.

The woman hung up without apologizing for dialing the wrong number. Inconsiderate bitch.

I did the domestic bit until one-thirty and then broke for lunch. Lucy came out from under the bed as soon as she heard the refrigerator door open.

I had a cheese sandwich and an apple. Lucy watched me soulfully as I ate, her eyes following each bite from plate to mouth. When I couldn't stand it any longer, I gave her a dog cookie. She'd have licked the crumbs from my plate, but I drew the line there. I read somewhere that labradors or dogs with a heavy Lab strain will eat until they explode. I believe it.

"We're going to have to think about a diet for you, one of these days," I said reprovingly.

I washed and dried the breakfast and lunch dishes. Then I went back to the living room and sat down on the couch, feeling rather at loose ends. I looked at the ceiling, as if I'd find inscribed there a set of printed instructions on what to do next. The ceiling was blank and white. I looked at the floor. The Mexican rug wasn't any help, either.

I had pushed my Bonnie Nordgren investigation about as far as I could. The cops would have to take it from here.

I should get started on organizing the BU journalism course. I knew I'd accept their offer because I needed the money. I could think about what would be a good angle for the article on singles bars. I could find out which bars were currently hot, and why. And who went to them, and with what expectations. And trepidations. Or reservations. Pun intended.

The result of either pursuit could only be a healthier bank account and a widening of my repute as a writer and a teacher of writing. I could use all of those things.

And I couldn't think of a damned thing else I could do for Bonnie. Pointless to brood and stew and fret about her further.

What I should do now would be to go for a long walk. The

exercise would clear my mind. Then maybe I'd be able to turn my attention to planning the journalism course and thinking up a hook for the "Bar Wars" piece.

I got up from the couch. Lucy sprang to her feet and gave me a hopeful look. How she can tell when I'm about to go out someplace is a mystery to me.

I went into the kitchen. Lucy hurried after me. I got a dog biscuit from the canister by the stove.

"Here," I said, tossing it to her. "We'll think about your reducing plan tomorrow."

I got my house keys and some money from my handbag, shoved them into the pocket of my jeans, and left the apartment.

I stood on the front steps of my building for a moment, taking deep breaths of the warm, dry air. Gorgeous day. I felt a little guilty not bringing Lucy with me, but if I did I wouldn't be able to drop into a bookstore or coffee shop if I wanted. Ah, well. I'd make it up to her this evening.

I started purposefully down the sidewalk.

Behind me, a car horn beeped. I glanced automatically over my shoulder.

"Liz," a female voice said. "Oh, Liz."

The voice was coming from a light blue Audi parked with its engine running in front of my house. The sun was bright on its windshield and I could only make out the silhouette of the driver. She was waving at me.

"Liz," she called again, through the open window of the car. The voice was sort of familiar, but I couldn't quite place it. Maybe she was a neighbor.

I turned and walked toward the Audi. The driver continued to wave.

The window of the passenger's side was also open. I braced both hands on the door and bent down to peer inside the car, smiling inquiringly.

The smile on my face turned to a rictus.

The driver of the Audi was Camille Frattiani. In her right hand, she held a gun. It was pointed at my nose.

30

"Get in," she said.

I stood unmoving, staring at her, feeling as if my eyes were about to pop out of my head.

Camille pushed the gun about three inches further toward me.

"Unless you want me to shoot you and leave you in the gutter," she remarked, her voice pleasant, almost conversational, "you'd better get in the car right away."

I didn't see that I had much choice. I opened the door and slid onto the front seat.

Camille nodded. She set the gun in her lap, put the car in gear, and yanked it out of the parking space. My head bounced back against the seat. Camille drove swiftly to the corner and turned right onto Cambridge Street. She let her right hand drop from the steering wheel and come to rest on the gun.

I gaped at her in terrified confusion. She was smiling slightly.

"You silly girl," she said. "Why didn't you leave it alone?"

We rode down Cambridge Street, merged with the traffic at Lechmere Square, and turned right onto the McGrath-O'Brien Highway. Camille fed the Audi quickly and expertly into the stream of cars and trucks and accelerated up the left-hand lane.

"Leave it alone," I repeated numbly.

"I have to give you credit, though," she said. "You figured the whole thing out perfectly. Except for one small part."

I was staring at her the way a snake must stare at a mongoose in the second before the mongoose strikes.

"Alan didn't kill those women," Camille said. She pursed her mouth, then added in offhand tones, "He wouldn't have had the nerve."

I inhaled loudly and sharply.

Camille flicked me another brief, smiling glance. "He told me all about that showdown in his office yesterday afternoon." She sounded amused. "I wish I'd been there to see it."

We were on Route 93 now, heading north. At midafternoon, the traffic was moderately heavy. I looked away from Camille and sat rigidly facing forward, trying to control the panic exploding inside me.

Camille swung the Audi into the passing lane, and we cruised by an eighteen-wheeler and a van full of elementary school-aged children.

"I'm really impressed with the way you put the whole story together," she remarked. "*Of course* Alan was sleeping with that blonde bitch. And the other one, Gayle, she was doing what you thought, too. Trying to keep Bonnie under some kind of control. Pity she couldn't manage it better. If it had been me, now . . . well, in the end, I *was* the one who had to manage things, wasn't I?"

Obviously it wasn't a question to which she expected a reply. Which was just as well, because I couldn't have given her one. I kept my gaze fixed straight ahead at the asphalt ribbon of highway. I pressed my hands together in my lap. My palms were slick with the greasy sweat of fear. Perspiration trickled down my spine.

When Camille spoke again, it was in the same matter-of-fact fashion. "You know," she said. "It was I who killed Bonnie and Gayle."

The words, so dispassionately uttered, seemed to reverberate within the confines of the car.

I snapped my head around and stared at Camille. Her face, in profile, was as calm as her voice.

"God," I said, in a strangled whisper. "My God." And, a second or so later, *"Why?"*

"Oh well," she said. "It seemed necessary at the time. I'd have preferred another solution to the problem, of course. But"—she moved her shoulders slightly, a delicate shrug—"no point in fretting about that now. I did what had to be done."

She wasn't justifying her actions, but merely musing aloud.

I kept staring at her, unable to believe what I'd just heard. This woman whose name was a synonym for taste and culture, this multitalented beauty, this benefactress of the arts and education, was admitting to double murder with the equanimity she might discuss endowing a scholarship at the state university.

It was beyond assimilation. Like being kidnaped at gunpoint was.

I stared at Camille for a moment longer, then looked away from her and back at the highway.

I'd work on assimilating the unbelievable later. When I got out of this. If I got out of this.

How *was* I going to get out of this?

We were in the second lane and rolling sedately and legally along at fifty-five miles an hour. If I opened the door and jumped out, I'd be dead in thirty seconds or less. If I leaned over and wrenched the steering wheel away from Camille, I'd cause an accident that would kill us both and God knew how many other innocents.

We were approaching the Route 128 overpass.

I could throw myself across the seat, grab the gun from Camille, and turn it on her. Which would have the exact same result that grabbing the steering wheel would.

I could stick my head out the car window and yell for help at a passing car.

Camille seemed to read my mind, for she chuckled softly. "Go ahead," she said.

I looked back at her, wide-eyed.

She gave me an indulgent smile.

"Go ahead," she repeated. "Wave, yell, do whatever you like."

I was silent.

"They'll only think you're fooling around," Camille said.

I swallowed. She was right. Nobody would pay serious attention to a woman hanging out a car window screaming and yelling. At least, not the kind of attention I wanted them to pay. They'd think I was drunk or on drugs and they'd either accelerate or drop back in order to lose us. Precisely what I would do under the circumstances.

The last time Jack and I had been up this road, we'd tangled with an enormous Winnebago full of college-aged kids. The Winnebago had been weaving all over the road. As we'd dodged by it at seventy-five miles an hour, I'd caught sight of the driver. She was drinking from a bottle of Jim Beam and had, for some obscure reason, a bra draped over her head like a pair of earphones.

The underwear I was wearing was being worn in its normal place, but that was beside the point.

Whatever escaping I was going to do would have to be done when we got to wherever it was we were going.

"Where are we going?" I said, surprising myself not only with the sound of my own voice but with its relative strength.

"Up country," Camille replied. "New Hampshire. Right up to the middle of deepest, darkest New Hampshire."

Looking at the gun in her lap, I had a clear notion of what her plans were when we got there.

Nevertheless, I said, "Why?"

She looked at me with that same expression of benign tolerance, the way a patient teacher might look at a slow student who'd asked a question she'd answered innumerable times before. "You have to be taken care of," she said. "When you went to Alan's office, we found out how much you knew. Too much. We can't take any chances on what you might find out next."

"No?"

"Oh, no indeed," Camille replied. Her voice was light.

I felt a tiny flare of anger. I didn't like being patronized much more than I liked being kidnaped. "Maybe," I said. "But as I told Levesque yesterday, there are at least four cops who know the same things as I do."

"So?"

I took a deep breath. "So if anything bad happens to me, they'll know who did it."

"They will?"

"Well, of cour—" I broke off in midword.

Camille gave me a smile broader than all the previous ones she had. "Really, Liz? do you *really* think the police will come looking for *me* if something bad happens to *you*? Would anyone have any reason to suspect *me* of committing any crime?" She paused a beat, then added, "Would *you*?"

She had me there. Of course I wouldn't. Doyennes of café society simply didn't go around murdering people or forcing them into cars by pointing a Smith and Wesson .38 in their faces. No. Never.

I groped for a suitable comeback. After a moment, I thought of what might be one. "The cops will go to Levesque. And he might point them at you."

Camille laughed. "I doubt it. I very much doubt it."

I looked at her.

"I sent Alan on an errand to New York last night," Camille said. "He'll be there until the day after tomorrow. It's just barely possible the police might question him when he gets back, but—so what? He'll be able to account for himself and his time."

I said nothing.

"But I'm sure he won't have to," Camille continued. "As far as I can tell, the police don't really share your theories, do they, Liz? From what I've heard—and correct me if I'm wrong—they tend toward the belief that Gayle committed suicide, don't they? And I'm sure no one but you seriously believes Alan had anything to do with Bonnie's death."

"So what harm am I to you then?" I asked.

Again, the lizard smile. "There's simply too much at stake for me to permit you to keep on poking into this business."

"Oh."

"All this is beside the point, anyway. Whatever happens to you, no one will find out about it for a long time, if ever."

We were in Andover now, where Route 93 narrows from a four- to three-lane highway.

"Think about it a moment," Camille said. "You're an adult woman. You live alone. You don't have to ask permission to do things. If you take it into your head to disappear for a day or two, who'll notice? And even if they do, will they be worried? Not at all. It's summer. They'll think you've taken off for a few days' vacation."

"You're wrong there," I said.

The statement didn't seem in the least to disturb her. "Oh?" she said. "How so?"

"One of the cops I've talked to is a—uh, a very close friend. I'm having dinner with him tonight. If I'm not home when he comes to pick me up . . ." I let the sentence trail off into pregnant silence.

"That doesn't concern me in the least," Camille said. "Your friend won't have the remotest idea where you've gone. Maybe he'll think you've stood him up."

Well, no, Jack wouldn't think that. Still, Camille's point was well taken. Even if I committed the completely out-of-character act of not calling Jack to tell him I wouldn't be home to meet him when I'd said I would, he'd let a few hours pass before he grew really concerned about my absence.

Camille finished the thought for me. "By the time your friend gets worried," she said. "If he indeed *does* get worried, you'll be dead. And suppose he decides to look for you? You'll be in a place where he'll never find you. If he even knew where to begin searching, which he won't. He can suspect whatever he likes. But that's *all* he'll be able to do."

She was exactly right. But I couldn't let it go.

"My neighbors," I argued weakly.

"What about them?"

"Some of them probably saw me get into this car."

"And?"

"Well, maybe one of them noticed the license plate."

"Do you think that's very likely?"

Certainly it wasn't.

"We're going to some woods I know," Camille said. "And I'm going to take you out of the car and shoot you and leave you there. Maybe in a few months or a year from now some hikers or the forest rangers might stumble over what's left. But at that point, it won't matter."

My eyes stung. The tears weren't so much those of fright as those of frustration and fury. I was being ferried to my death and there didn't seem to be a damned thing I could do to stop it.

Maybe I *should* try to grab the gun or the steering wheel. Better to go out fighting your destruction rather than submitting to it.

The cooler side of me—amazing that I still had one—cut off that thought as soon as it flashed through my brain. If I were going to do something drastic, I might as well do it after we'd pulled off into a secondary road and I had a better chance of not causing a multiple-car accident in the process.

We drove over the bridge spanning the Merrimack River. A minute later, we were in New Hampshire.

31

The first town over the border on Route 93 is Salem. Salem, N.H., doesn't have witches. What it does have are a racetrack, a state liquor store, factory outlets, shabby little shops that sell paperback books with their front covers ripped off and cigarettes for a buck and a half cheaper a carton than you can buy them in Massachusetts, and a prolixity of Zayres, K-Marts, and Bradlees. Add those to the Tri-State Lottery and you found everything in Salem necessary to sustain the human spirit. About one half the cars in the parking lots had Mass. plates.

Jack and I often made a run "up the line" when we ran low on vodka and bourbon.

A lot of the traffic that had followed or accompanied us up 93 turned off at the Salem exit. When we passed the Wyndham and Londonderry exits, we'd lose even more. The remainder at Manchester and Concord. And so on up into deepest, darkest New Hampshire.

So absorbed was I in my thoughts of escape that when Camille spoke again, I jumped.

"We have a fairly long ride ahead of us," she said. "Would you like to hear the rest of the story? I can tie up the loose ends for you, if you want."

She sounded as if she were offering me sherry and biscuits. I didn't answer her.

"You deserve to know," she added.

I gave her the nastiest look I could arrange on my face, but she only smiled.

"In the first place," she said. "There's one thing I want to apologize to you for."

Oh, sure. Like kidnaping me, maybe?

"Neil attacking you outside your house," she said. "Totally unnecessary. I regret that."

I felt my expression change to one of incredulity. Jesus Christ, was she joking?

It seemed she wasn't. "You were absolutely right," she continued. "He had the idea he could scare you off. How he thought he could do that, I can't imagine." She sighed and shook her head. "Maybe he figured if he slapped you around a bit and then said something like"—and here her voice went down a few octaves—"lay off the Bonnie Nordgren business''—her voice returned to its normal register—''that you would. What incredible stupidity.'' She sighed again. ''Ah, well, Neil was never too bright. But I must say he had his uses.''

''Oh?'' I said, coolly I hoped.

''As you thought, he *was* supplying Bonnie with drugs,'' she replied. ''That was Alan's doing, I'm afraid. He was a fool to involve Neil in this. But then, Alan's not very bright sometimes, either.''

Camille had so far made two observations about Levesque. The first had been condescending. This second was contemptuous. For a woman supposedly in love, she didn't sound like it.

''I really can't say I'm terribly sorry Neil's gone,'' she continued. ''With the kind of history of drunk driving he had, it was probably inevitable anyway.'' She smiled at me. ''In any case, I'm sorry you were—um, inconvenienced by him.''

''Gee, thanks,'' I said.

She laughed.

I felt that spurt of anger again. I took a deep breath to tamp it down. Any more patronizing crap from this bloodthirsty bitch, though, and I *would* go for the gun. To hell with the consequences.

''Okay, Camille,'' I said. ''You want to talk? Fine. Talk. Tell me why you killed Bonnie Nordgren.''

''Simple,'' she said. ''She could have wrecked Alan's political career.''

Pity she hadn't, I thought. Aloud, I said, ''So Bonnie *did* get hold of some special information about him being involved with organized crime, right? Is that what you're telling me?''

''On the button,'' she replied lightly.

''How nice,'' I said. ''I really hate like hell to be the one to tell you this, Camille, but practically everyone including the cops and the papers, knows or assumes that Levesque has mob connections.''

''They can assume what they wish,'' Camille replied.

"More power to them. Alan hasn't been damaged by anyone's assumptions. He's the great white hope of the party, you know."

"My congratulations to the party on their impeccable taste," I snapped.

I'd hoped the snottiness of the remark might dent Camille's composure. What I'd said did, after all, reflect badly on her taste in men as well as that of the party.

If I'd annoyed her, she didn't betray the fact.

"I guess that means Bonnie must have heard or found out something big about Levesque," I said. "And I mean really big. You care to tell me what that was?"

"Do you know who Joseph Lanciano is?"

The mention of that name pulled me up short.

"Who doesn't?" I said finally.

Joseph Lanciano—or Joe the Lance, or Joe Lucky, as he was variously known—was reputed to be second-in-command of the New England Mafia. He had been arrested more times than I could count on charges running the gamut from loitering through extortion to attempted murder and conspiracy to commit murder. But they had yet to nail him for so much as a parking violation. The second of his nicknames had a literal truth to it.

Lanciano was in his early fifties. He was of medium height, bulky in the way that men who were muscular and athletic in their youth become when they let themselves go in midlife. His fleshy, rubicund face would have been almost jolly had it not been for his eyes, which had all the warmth and sparkle of volcanic glass.

He lived in Swampscott, in a fine large pseudocolonial house with his wife and four children. Joseph Jr., was at Stanford Law. Mrs. Lanciano was active in various charities and in church work.

When asked, Lanciano described himself as an entrepreneur.

When asked, the cops described him as a pus-pocket.

"Yes," I reiterated. "I've heard of Joe Lanciano. What about him?"

Camille flexed her shoulders and leaned back a little in her seat. "About eight years ago, Alan was on a senate committee to investigate organized crime."

"Yeah?" I said, in my new tough, snotty voice.

"He resigned from it after a few years. But he kept up his contacts with the other members of the committee."

I had a feeling I could predict what she'd say next. "Uh-huh."

"A little after Alan left the committee, Joe Lanciano came to him. He said he had a business proposition that should prove mutually profitable."

Ah, the entrepreneurial spirit. It made America great. "Go on," I said. "I'm fascinated."

"Lanciano was prepared to make a very large contribution to Alan's campaign fund in return for certain information."

"Such as?"

"Alan was to tell Lanciano what the status of any grand jury investigations into organized crime were, or if there were any indictments upcoming against Lanciano and his people. Also the names of the committee's informants, so they could be taken care of."

Like the way you took care of Bonnie and Gayle, I thought. "And of course Levesque had all that at his fingertips," I said. "Because of all those contacts he'd kept up on the organized crime committee."

She nodded.

"And Bonnie knew all this?"

"Unfortunately, yes."

"How'd she find out?"

"Alan made some tapes of some of his talks with Lanciano in his office. One time when Bonnie was there, he left her alone to go speak to his partner. Bonnie went through his desk and found one of the tapes. I guess Alan had left it there accidentally. The fool." Camille gave a ladylike snort. "Anyway, Bonnie took the tape and played it. Then she gave it back to Alan. She also told him she'd made a copy of it and had hidden it away somewhere safe.''

''When was this?''

Camille shook her head. ''I don't know the exact day. A few months ago.''

''Just about when Gayle came into the picture.''

''That's right.''

''And Bonnie started demanding more drugs and money.''

''Yes.''

''Jesus,'' I said. My mental television screen was having trouble focusing on the image of Bonnie Nordgren, literary scholar and blackmailer. ''What happened next?''

''Bonnie just got worse and worse,'' Camille said. ''Finally one day about a month ago, she called Alan and shrieked at him that if he didn't start giving her more money, she'd take that tape to the papers.''

''What did he do?''

Camille shrugged. ''What could he do? He gave her more money.''

''Why didn't he just explain the situation to Joe Lance?'' I said. ''Old Joe's supposed to be very efficient at taking care of that kind of problem.''

''There were good reasons we couldn't do that,'' Camille replied, her tone dry.

I didn't contradict her. If Levesque had indeed gone to Lanciano and asked him to dispose of Bonnie, he'd have had to have also told Joe not only what Bonnie had known, but how she'd known it. I could imagine the kind of response that the Lance would have had to the revelation that his private chats with Levesque had been taped for posterity. Bonnie would have ended up feeding the fish in Boston Harbor and Levesque would have ended up in a car trunk with two bullet holes in the back of his head. *If* he was lucky.

''Was it then that you decided to kill Bonnie?''

''Yes.''

''Are you going to tell me about that?''

''Certainly,'' Camille replied. ''If you want to know.''

"That was a very strong overdose that killed her," I said. "A combination of heroin and cocaine. I think it's called a speedball. Where'd you get it?"

"Neil. I told you he had his uses."

I frowned. "Neil must have been very surprised that someone like you would be wanting something like that."

An expression of distaste crossed Camille's face. "Not really. I paid him well. And I told him it was for Bonnie. To keep her happy so she wouldn't bother Alan. I told him I'd be buying more from him for that reason."

"And he accepted that?"

"Oh, yes."

"Did you tell Neil? I mean about your plan to get Bonnie off Alan's back?"

"Oh, good God, no. That idiot?"

I nodded. "But Neil figured out after Bonnie died what had happened."

"Yes. Even as dim as he was, yes. He did."

Accessory after the fact, I thought. Even further reason for the kid to try to discourage me from poking into Bonnie's death.

"I had Alan phone Gayle and tell her to set up a time when Neil could come to see Bonnie," Camille continued, in her matter-of-fact way. "He told her Neil would be bringing Bonnie more drugs. So of course Gayle arranged it. She herself wasn't going to be there that night. So I, not Neil, went to the apartment, and I brought the drugs and the other things with me. And I showed it all to Bonnie, and I told her that I'd be able to keep her supplied with anything she wanted, as long as she left Alan alone."

"But she was in love with him, wasn't she?"

Camille shrugged. "She had been, I suppose. But the drugs, the cocaine, had become more important than anything else."

"So she agreed to the deal?"

Camille nodded.

"What happened next?"

"Bonnie hadn't been injecting herself with drugs," Camille said. "Yet. I told her that what I had with me was something very special that had to be taken by hypodermic. I told her I could give it to her then and there, if she'd like." Camille paused, and a tiny, wry smile appeared on her face. "She was eager to try it. And it was no problem for me to give her the shot. I knew how to do it. My grandmother was a diabetic. I'd learned how to give injections when I was a teenager."

"I see."

"She lost consciousness very quickly," Camille said. "I put the syringe and the belt and the other things in the bedroom. I thought it would look like she overdosed by accident."

"It might have," I said. "But you made one mistake."

She looked at me blankly.

"Bonnie was left-handed," I explained. "If she'd injected herself, she'd have done it in the right arm. You gave her the shot in her left arm."

"Oh," Camille said, without much show of interest. "Is that so?"

"Yeah, it is."

"Well, that's immaterial now, isn't it?"

I didn't bother to argue.

"Tell me about Gayle," I said. "Tell me about how you killed her."

"Oh, that. Well, she called me the other day. She said she knew how Bonnie had died. She thought Alan had gotten Neil to do it. She wanted to talk to me. She was terrorized. And not thinking straight."

I knew about Gayle's confusion and terror. "What did you do?"

Camille smiled faintly. "It wasn't hard. It never occurred to Gayle that she might not have reason to trust *me*, you know. It probably should have, but in the state she was in . . . well, at any rate, we met at a bar. We ordered drinks. When she went to the ladies' room to try to pull herself together, I put something in her drink. I'd emptied out what was in some capsules I'd gotten from Neil." Camille shook her head. "Poor Gayle. She gulped it down, ordered another, drank that, and then started feeling dizzy. I walked with her to her car to see that she got there safely. She passed out right on the front seat. So I propped her up against the passenger door and took her keys and got the car started and we went for a drive till it got dark."

"What did you do when Gayle woke up?"

Camille chuckled gently. "Oh, Liz. She didn't. She was *terribly* heavily sedated. Don't you think I made sure of that?"

I felt my skin prickle.

"Well, anyway," Camille said. "I found a nice vacant lot behind a construction site in Brookline, and I parked the car there and pulled her over into the driver's seat. I connected a bit of rubber tube to the exhaust pipe and put the other end of it through a crack in the window. The motor was still running. I walked away and caught a cab about a half a mile farther on and went home."

"Did you write that 'suicide' note that was on the dashboard?"

"I had it with me when I went to the restaurant."

"And the rubber tube?"

"That too. In a Bonwit's shopping bag."

"Very clever."

"Yes, wasn't it?"

"Weren't you worried that you might be seen by someone in the bar? By someone who might remember you'd been in there with Gayle?"

"Not at all."

I was silenced. The woman's arrogance was breathtaking.

"The place where we met was one of my choosing," Camille said. "And I chose it because I knew it would be crowded at that hour. The waiters were too busy to notice the people they were serving."

"My," I said. "You thought of everything, didn't you?"

"I almost always do."

We passed the Queen City Bridge exit to Manchester. There weren't many cars on the road along with us now.

I looked at the clock on the dashboard. It was three-thirty. In an hour the commuter rush would begin. I couldn't see what good that would do me. I could be dead in less than an hour.

Best not to think about that, at least for the moment. Better to keep Camille talking. It was a distraction, anyway.

"How'd you know I'd be home today?" I asked. "As you yourself pointed out, I could have been anywhere. Like on vacation or something."

"I checked, first."

"You did?"

"Oh, Liz. I phoned you a few hours ago."

I looked at her, perplexed. The only calls I'd gotten that day had been from the editor of *Cambridge Monthly* and the evening-school guy at BU. Plus the woman who'd wanted to know if I were the public library.

I caught my breath. The woman who'd wanted to know if I were the public library.

Camille must have seen the realization dawning on my face, for she said, "That was me. And I wasn't trying to borrow a book."

I closed my eyes.

"I told you," she said. "I think of almost everything. I got your address from the phone book. I drove over to Cambridge and I stopped at the little variety store a few blocks up from you. They have a pay phone. I called from there. You answered. So I knew you were home. And I figured it was a good bet you wouldn't stay inside all day." She gave her soft laugh. "Not with your record of activity."

I opened my eyes.

"You understand," Camille said. "I really *do* think of everything. How else do you suppose I got to be what I am today?"

Excellent question.

"What are you?" I said.

"A success," she replied promptly. "And I intend to keep it that way." She gave me a fleeting sidelong glance. "You know what I came out of?"

The question was probably rhetorical. Nonetheless, I said, "A bit. Your father had a bakery in the North End, didn't he?"

She nodded, rather grimly, I thought. I wondered why. Was there supposed to be something shameful or bad about being a baker's daughter from the North End?

"We were dirt poor," Camille said. "My father was never able to make a go of the business." She flicked me another sideways glance. "Can you imagine that? An Italian not being able to make a go of a bakery in the North End?"

No doubt that *that* was a rhetorical question.

"We lived in a horrible little dingy five-room apartment. I shared a bedroom the size of a closet with my three sisters. My grandmother slept on the couch in the living room. My mother never left the kitchen except to go to mass."

Camille's tone was no longer light or matter-of-fact, I noticed, but bitter.

"My mother died when she was forty-five," Camille continued. She paused a moment, then added, "She looked as if she were seventy."

I didn't say anything.

"I never had a new dress till I was sixteen. Everything I had was hand-me-downs from my sisters. Even my underwear. Sometimes I'd go downtown or to Newbury Street and stand in front of the shop windows and just stare at them. Or I'd walk up Beacon Hill and look at the rich people's houses." She shook her head slightly. "It seemed unbelievable to me that there were people who lived that way."

"The way you do now," I said.

"Yes, my husband was quite well-off."

We were nearing Concord now. Traffic was slightly heavier.

"You know, Liz," Camille said. "I really invented myself. There were three things I was absolutely sure of from when I was a very small child."

Despite myself, I was intrigued. "What were those?"

"That I had brains, that I had talent, and that I had to get out. And I did. I won a scholarship to Girls' Latin and to the Conservatory, did you know that?''

I nodded.

''Well, that was the start of it. My father, of course, didn't want me to go to the Conservatory. I was supposed to work in the bakery and live at home until I married some boy from the neighborhood and had eight kids. *God.*'' Camille's hand tightened on the steering wheel and she seemed to shiver. ''But I got away,'' she concluded. ''I got away.''

Both of us were quiet as we rode past Concord. To the left, the State House dome flashed gold in the late afternoon sun. The traffic was substantial, but not enough to slow us down. Nor were the work crews at the edge of the highway. Probably widening the road. Concord was up-and-coming. It had a number of restaurants with exposed-brick walls and hanging plants. Once they'd been mills.

I glanced over at Camille. Whatever distress reminiscing about her past had caused her was no longer evident on her face. The lovely features were serene. I thought she might even be humming to herself.

This beautiful, intelligent, talented, cultivated, wealthy, even famous woman had committed two murders on behalf of a man she not only didn't seem to like, but was actively scornful of. And she was about to commit a third murder for him. It made no sense.

''Camille,'' I began.

''Yes?''

''You haven't told me why you killed Bonnie and Gayle.''

She threw me a look of astonishment. ''Of course I have.''

I shook my head. ''No. You told me that they had to be gotten rid of so Levesque's career wouldn't suffer.''

''Well, there you are.''

''No,'' I said. ''That's not what I mean. Why did *you* kill them?''

Her lips parted and her eyebrows drew together in a look of extreme puzzlement.

''You didn't do it for love,'' I said. ''Because you clearly don't have a very high opinion of Alan. And you don't at all seem disturbed that he was cheating on you with Bonnie.''

''Oh, *that*,'' Camille said dismissively. ''Alan has a weakness for younger woman. No harm in letting him indulge it. Except that I *do* wish he'd chosen someone other than a drug addict.''

''But aren't the two of you planning to marry?''

''Within the year.''

''I see. And do you plan to allow Alan to continue, uh, indulging his weakness?''

''If he likes,'' she said. ''He'll have to be more careful. That's all I require.''

I shook my head again, this time in disbelief. ''I don't get it.''

''Get what, Liz?''

''What you see in him. I can understand what he sees in you.''

''I'm an asset to his career,'' Camille agreed.

I nodded. ''But what's in it for you? Levesque is a jerk.''

''Oh, he's not *that* bad. Well, maybe he is. In some ways.''

''You admit that,'' I said. ''Yet you're not only marrying the guy, you're killing for him. Why? You don't need him. You already have everything.''

''Not everything,'' she said quickly.

''Okay,'' I replied. ''Tell me what's missing.''

She smiled. ''Power.''

I stared at her. ''And Levesque has that?''

''No. But he will.'' She gave me another smile, this one very confident. ''You know he's going to be the next governor of Massachusetts?''

''Yeah. I heard.''

''There's already talk of even higher office. Maybe in ten years.''

''The U.S. Senate?'' I said.

''Oh, better than that.''

I expelled a long breath. President Alan Levesque? And

his lovely First Lady, the former Camille D'Alessio Frattiani?

In my mind, I heard an echo of Edie Gold's voice.

Camille's a nice, nice lady. Very, very ambitious, but very nice.

Well, Edie'd had it partially right, anyway.

"Does that answer your question?" Camille asked.

"I guess so."

There seemed nothing else to say. We were about five miles north of Concord now, and it really was getting to be deepest, darkest New Hampshire. Maybe soon we'd be pulling off the highway. There were a lot of woods up here. Camille had her pick.

The panic I'd held down for the past hour came bubbling up again.

We were approaching an overpass. Attached to the railing was a large sign bordered with flashing lights. Automatically, I read it. "SPEED CHECKED BY RADAR."

The New Hampshire State Police were rigorous at enforcing the traffic laws. Speeders paid heavy fines. Well, the state had no income tax and no sales tax, and it had to have a source of revenue other than selling discount booze and cigarettes.

The New Hampshire staties really liked flagging down out-of-state violators. Especially ones whose cars had Mass. plates.

I looked at the speedometer. We were going exactly sixty-five, legal for New Hampshire. Nice to know there were some laws Camille didn't break.

In that moment, I had my idea.

I sat very still for a moment, turning it over in my mind. It was a wild one. Probably it wouldn't work.

But it might.

As unobtrusively as possible, I glanced over my shoulder and out the rear window. A beige station wagon barrelled along about a hundred yards behind us. I looked out my window. A red Nissan to the right. Ahead, two more cars.

Traffic was about as light as it was going to get.

The harness seat belt was dangling next to my shoulder.

Trying not to make a production of it, I reached up, pulled the belt down and fastened it across my lap.

There. I'd taken the only safety precaution open to me.

I counted to ten to compose myself. Then I cleared my throat.

"Camille?"

"Mmm?"

"That's quite a future you have lined up for yourself."

"It certainly is. I've worked for it."

I guess she had, if you counted double murder as work.

"You're really looking forward to the White House, aren't you?"

She smiled. "The thought of it makes everything worthwhile. And more."

"Yes, I can imagine. Being First Lady, meeting all those heads of state—"

"Making all those important decisions," she interrupted.

I was momentarily thrown off the track. "Decisions?"

"Well, yes. Alan will need me for that. He'll have advisors, of course. Even so . . ."

I stared at her.

"What did you think I meant by power?" she said.

I shook my head. "Why don't you just run for office yourself?"

"Quicker this way. And still easier, if you're a woman."

We were getting away from the subject I wanted us to be on. "Yes," I said. "That's true. So you'll be a kind of power behind the throne, then."

"Exactly."

"Well, I grant you, that does sound thrilling."

"Oh, yes."

"Piloting the ship of state, and all that."

"Don't make fun of me, Liz."

"Oh, I'm not," I said innocently. "I'm sure you'll be excellent at running the government." I paused, took a deep breath, and added, "It'll give you something to do those nights and weekends when your husband's off fucking some cute little blonde twenty-five years younger than you.''

The dart struck home. But neither hard nor deep enough.

Camille's face tensed, then smoothed out. ''I told you I can handle that.''

''Now maybe you can,'' I said. ''Might start to get to you later, though.''

''I doubt it.''

''Glad you feel that way,'' I said. ''Me, I don't think I could cope. Knowing my husband was off screwing around like that. Having the word get out. Which it would, of course, in a company town like Washington.''

The tension was back in Camille's face. Good.

''Some people would feel sorry for you,'' I said. ''Others? Well, I don't know. I think they might just laugh. People can be awfully mean that way.''

''Nobody laughs at me, Liz,'' Camille said. Her voice sounded as if it were under rather careful control.

''Oh, I believe that,'' I said. ''They wouldn't dare.''

It wasn't the words but the way I said them that made Camille's lips compress and the lines that ran from her nose to her mouth suddenly appear more deeply cut.

''I told you, Liz, not to make fun of me,'' she said.

''And I told *you* I wouldn't dream of it.''

I glanced at the speedometer. It still read sixty-five. Damn. I'd have to shift my line of attack.

''You know something?'' I said.

''What?'' Camille asked, not *quite* snapping the word.

''I think you had another reason for killing Bonnie,'' I said. ''Oh, sure, maybe the big one was to keep her from blowing Levesque's career. But I bet you wanted her out of the picture for other reasons, right?''

Camille's expression went from tense to clenched.

''I bet you wanted her out of the way because he was obsessed with her. He couldn't stay out of her bed.''

''You bitch,'' Camille said, between her teeth.

It was working.

"I met another guy who knew Bonnie," I said. "He told me she knew how to make men *feel good*. Real good."

Camille drew a deep, harsh breath.

"And you couldn't," I said. "At least, not like Bonnie could."

Camille's face flushed dark. Her hand on the steering wheel was white-knuckled.

"Well, it just goes to show," I said. "You can't have everything after all, now can you, Camille?"

She hunched forward slightly, her shoulders rigid, as if she were unconsciously protecting herself from that possibility.

"What you gonna do in Washington, babe? Wipe out every woman Alan sleeps with? That might be a big job. You might even have to call in Joe Lanciano to help out."

She didn't like being reminded of the connection.

"You think Joe's going to go away? Conveniently disappear once you folks are ensconced in the governor's manse? Or the White House? No way, Camille. He'll be around forever. Guys like him don't go away. They're always around. . . . Tell me, you gonna put him on the A-list for all those White House receptions and dinner parties? You may not have any choice. Oh, well. Maybe you can sit him next to one of Alan's girlfriends."

She flung her head around and stared at me, her face blazing.

"There's another thing, too," I said. "Maybe you ought to take into consideration that you won't make it to the White House with Alan. Maybe you'll have lived out your usefulness to him before then." I shrugged. "Divorce is no big deal anymore, even for a politician and aspiring statesman. Maybe old Alan will shitcan you for another Bonnie, five years down the road."

Camille's whole body had gone stiff. I looked down quickly. Her right foot was clamped to the accelerator. I looked up at the speedometer. The needle was over sixty-five and climbing.

All I had to do was keep it that way till we passed a speed

trap. Easy work. Nothing to it. God, please let the troopers be hungry this afternoon.

"You know," I said. "The more I think about it, the more I'm sure I'm right. I bet Al *will* dump you. You're a terrific-looking woman, Camille, but you're not going to stay youthful and glamorous forever."

She bent further forward in her seat, hugging the steering wheel.

I shot another look at the speedometer. Seventy-five. And rising.

"You'll get old," I droned. "And your body will go, and Al will replace you with whatever piece of jailbait catches his fancy."

Eighty.

"And you know what the worse part of it will be?" I asked. "You'll never be able to get any revenge." I grinned. " 'Cause if you blow the whistle on Al, you'll be blowing it on yourself. Now isn't that a nice prospect to look forward to?"

She wrenched around in her seat and swung at me with her right hand. I jerked my head back and felt her fingernails graze my cheek. The Audi veered crazily into the middle lane.

Behind us, someone blasted his horn. Camille yanked the steering wheel violently and reflexively to the left. I was thrown against the door. A brown Chevy bombed past, still blaring its horn, the driver mouthing curses.

I pulled myself upright and looked at the speedometer.

Ninety.

Camille got the car under control and moved it back to the left-hand lane.

I twisted around as best I could, given the restraint of the seat belt, and peered out the rear window. The highway behind us was empty but for a pickup truck several hundred yards back. *Damn*. I turned back in the seat and stared blankly through the windshield.

The woods were thick on either side of the road. Nice for

a concealed speed trap. Let there be one somewhere along this stretch.

Maybe that trucker behind us had a CB, and maybe he'd radio the state cops that there was a lunatic screaming along ahead of him at ninety miles an hour.

The only trouble was, we weren't going ninety miles an hour any longer. I could feel the car slowing. When I checked the speedometer, it read a relatively sedate seventy-five. Camille had recovered her composure. Or perhaps the near-accident had frightened her into caution.

The gun had fallen to the seat beside her when she'd lunged at me. She picked it up and placed it in her lap. Her hand appeared to be completely steady. Remarkable.

I'd have to intensify my verbal assault. It *did* work. Maybe I should change the angle of attack. The trick would be to sustain the effect of it.

God, what a trick.

"You know," I said, striving for a nonchalant tone. "Speaking of Joe Lanciano, as we were before . . . it's all going to be very interesting, how things turn out."

I might as well not have spoken, for all the reaction I got from Camille. She was quite deliberately intent on her driving. Ostentatiously ignoring me.

"You *don't* think of everything," I said. "Obviously, it hasn't occurred to you that a piece of walking garbage like Lanciano has to be under perpetual surveillance by the feds, not to speak of the state and local cops. Oh, I know they haven't managed to grab him yet. But so what? Maybe they will. Could be any day now." I shrugged. "And then . . . I don't know, Camille. It just seems to me that you haven't given this whole situation quite the thought maybe it deserved."

The corners of her mouth indented. "Your point?" she snapped.

I smiled. "Just this—if Joe goes down, he'll take his pet politician with him. And if Al goes down the tubes, you will too. In one way or another."

Maybe it was wishful thinking, but I could have sworn I felt the Audi pick up speed.

"If Al gets indicted for racketeering, I wouldn't count on him observing the chivalric code. The first thing he'll try to do is cut a deal. And one way will be for him to tell the prosecutors about what you did to Bonnie and Gayle. He'll talk so fast it'll make their heads spin." I sighed heavily. "My God, the only problem they'll have is getting him to shut up."

Camille drew a deep, harsh breath. The red was back in her face. I looked at the speedometer. Eighty-five. Not wishful thinking.

I felt an insane exhilaration. "Boy, did you screw up when you latched onto Levesque," I said. "You thought living in a five-room apartment over a bakery was bad? It's gonna seem like a palace in comparison to a cell in Framingham, babe."

Camille reared back in her seat. "You are dead," she said. "Now."

We hit a seam in the road. The gun bounced from her lap and fell to the floor. It skittered underneath the front seat.

I lurched around and squinted again out the rear window.

About five hundred yards behind us were flashing red-and-blue lights. I made out the shape of a state police cruiser. A moment later, I heard the wail of a siren. Faint at first, and then steadily stronger.

I closed my eyes briefly. When I opened them again, I looked over at Camille.

She'd seen the lights in the rearview mirror. And heard the sirens. The flush in her face had died, leaving it pinched and white. Her eyes were enormous.

She raised her foot from the accelerator and the car slowed quite considerably. The speedometer needle dropped sharply back below seven-five.

The red-and-blue lights were maybe fifty yards behind us now.

"Game's up, cookie," I said.

"The hell it is," she replied.

She turned the steering wheel sharply to the right. The Audi screeched sideways across the travel and breakdown lanes. The troopers seemed to be yelling something at us through the bullhorn on the top of the cruiser. But I couldn't make out what.

Beyond the verge of the highway was a field of waist-high weeds and bushes, and beyond that, some pine woods.

We plunged into the long grass at fifty miles an hour. The Audi bounced so crazily that despite the harness belt I rose up a good four inches in my seat. The brush whipped at the side of the car like angry, clutching hands. We rocked sideways violently. I grabbed the sides of my seat and pushed back into it as far as I could.

What in the name of God did Camille think she was doing? Did she think she could outrun the state troopers? Or was she trying to kill us both?

She might succeed at the latter.

She had both hands tight on the wheel. Controlling the Audi on this kind of terrain was a two-handed job.

We were going about thirty now. Slow enough not to make a drastic move on my part a kamikaze action.

I was just ready to throw myself to the left and scrabble for the gun when Camille rammed the Audi over a small rise in the field.

Whether I heard the crash or felt the impact of us hitting something first, I don't know. Probably they were simultaneous. Then there was a horrendous grinding roar, as if the undercarriage of the Audi were ripped in two. The car shuddered and lurched to a halt. Camille flew forward against the steering wheel. I stopped an inch short of going through the windshield.

I didn't even pause to draw breath and wonder how I'd survived. I tore off the seat belt.

Camille was slumped over the steering wheel. Unconscious or just stunned, I couldn't tell. I leaned over, grappled the gun from beneath the seat, flung open the passenger door, and scrambled out of the car. Then I leaned back into it, pointing the gun at Camille. She stirred and moaned, softly. Her eyes were shut.

To my left, I heard shouting. I backed away from the car a foot or so and straightened up, rather stiffly.

The two staties had abandoned their cruiser in the breakdown lanes and were pushing their way through the brush to the Audi. When they saw me standing beside the wreck, they slowed a bit. And then, so help me God, they unholstered their guns.

I stooped and peered back into the car. Camille was still unconscious. I set her .38 down on the ground next to my feet.

Then I put both hands on top of the Audi.

32

At ten o'clock that night, I was sitting with Jack in one of Concord's hanging-fern-and-exposed-brick restaurants. I was having my first but not my last vodka martini of the evening. Being kidnaped and being in an auto wreck I could handle. Being arrested on top of both was a bit much.

I raised my martini to Jack. "Thanks for bailing me out."

He raised his glass of beer to me. "Think nothing of it."

"It took me two hours to convince those guys to call you," I said. "That's the same length of time I spent with Camille. Oh, well, I suppose they were just doing their job." I sipped my drink. "Does this mean I'll have a criminal record from now on? A sheet?"

"No," Jack said. "It doesn't."

"Oh, good."

"You were never really arrested to begin with."

"Well, it sure felt like it. Although I must say, once you got everything straightened out, those troopers couldn't have been nicer. One of them even gave me a pat on the back."

"Oh, hell," Jack said. "You'll probably be the new pinup girl of the barracks."

"I'll send them a picture of me in my new black bathing suit. The backless one with the high-rise thigh openings."

"Yeah, you do that."

We looked at each other and laughed.

The waitress came to the table and asked us if we were ready to order.

"Another vodka martini for the lady," Jack said. "And I'll have another of these."

"Lady?" I said when the waitress had left.

He smiled. "How you feeling?" he said. "Seriously."

I returned the smile. "A little worn out, I guess."

"You'll feel it more tomorrow."

I nodded, picked up the menu, and opened it. I was too enervated to be really interested in food. But I ought to put something solid in my stomach. I could order a dish that I could pick at, like a chef's salad. I closed the menu and set it to one side.

The waitress brought our second round and hovered smiling, pad and pencil in hand.

Jack looked at me with raised eyebrows.

"The chef's salad," I said. "Roquefort dressing."

"The scrod," Jack said. "Baked potato."

The waitress wrote it all down and sashayed off to the kitchen.

I poured the remains of my old drink into my new one and stirred it with the little hollow plastic tube provided for that purpose. The new drink had an olive in it as well as a twist. I scowled, fished out the olive, and ate it. My first solid food in nine hours. Tasted pretty good.

Camille was being held for overnight observation in one

of the Concord hospitals. She'd be arraigned in her bed tomorrow morning. Then she'd have to be extradited to Massachusetts and rearraigned there. I guessed. I was too tired to ponder the jurisdictional tangle.

I had no doubt that she'd make bail, however astronomical a figure was set. And that she'd retain a lawyer along the lines of Percy Foreman or Edward Bennett Williams to defend her. He might be able to get whatever charges were lodged against her reduced. Or have her plead diminished capacity. Hah.

I figured they had her pretty good on the kidnaping charge. The two murder counts, I wasn't so sure of.

I sighed.

Jack paused with his beer halfway to his mouth and said, "What's wrong?"

"Nothing."

"Something is. Tell me."

I smiled and shook my head.

He set his glass on the table, made a come-along gesture with his right hand, and said, "Give."

"Oh, I was wondering what'll happen with Camille, that's all."

He was silent for a moment, gazing at me over the candle in the middle of the table. Then he said, "Well, I think she's pretty much blown her chance of making it to the White House."

I laughed. "Yes. There's that. I was thinking more in the short-term."

He shook his head. "I don't know. It won't be an easy case to prosecute." He smiled at me. "Except, the state'll have the advantage of you as its star witness, of course."

I made a face. "I can't wait."

"You've testified in court before."

"Yes, I know. But it still isn't something I look forward to."

"A little song, a little dance . . ." Jack began.

"A little seltzer down your pants," I said. "Shit."

He laughed, and reached across the table and patted my hand. ''I'll be there with you.''

''Will the fact that Camille admitted to me that she killed Bonnie and Gayle be admissible in court? Or is that just hearsay?''

''Good question,'' Jack frowned, very thoughtfully. ''Ah . . . this is sort of a legal gray area.'' He rubbed the bridge of his nose between his thumb and forefinger. ''Okay. From what I can figure, it could work like this—if the prosecutor asks you to repeat the conversation you had in the car with Camille, and she told you in the course of that conversation that she'd killed Bonnie and Gayle, and you say so, then that's admissible. Defense will object, of course. But it's still admissible. I think.''

''Well,'' I said. ''Better than nothing, I suppose.''

He smiled. ''Don't worry about it.''

''But there's really no evidence against Camille, is there? For the murders, anyway.''

''Oh, I don't know. The investigators have a direction to go in, now. It'd be funny if they didn't turn up something.''

''Like somebody who saw Gayle and Camille the night Gayle died?''

''That, sure. Or a number of other things.''

I nodded. Then I held up my right hand. The index and middle fingers were crossed.

''Right,'' Jack said.

The waitress brought the food. I looked at the chef's salad and decided that I was, in fact, hungry.

''Can I get you anything else?'' the waitress asked.

I gave her a big smile and pointed at my drink. Then I pointed at Jack and said, ''Nothing for him thanks. *He's* the designated driver tonight.''

The girl laughed and left us.

Jack split his baked potato and tucked a pat of butter between the two halves. I ate the artichoke heart that crowned my salad. And then a black olive, and a strip of roast beef.

''How's your fish?'' I asked.

"Fine. The salad?"

"Fine." I put down the fork. "You know, something weird just occurred to me."

"What's that?"

"Remember how I saved my life today?"

He looked at me curiously.

I picked up the fork and waved it. "It was by staging the kind of catfight I thought didn't exist outside of bad novels written by male writers who hate women."

Jack dropped his fork, snatched up his glass, and took a quick swallow of beer. Then he said, "Well, it worked, didn't it?"

"Oh, sure."

"Sweet Jesus," Jack said. "I hope to hell you don't have any regrets that it did. Do you?"

"No. My God. Of course not."

"Oh, that's good."

From the way he was looking at me, I could tell he didn't understand. I shook my head. "I don't think I've made myself quite clear."

Jack took another sip of beer. "No. You haven't."

"Okay," I set my fork on the table and folded my hands in my lap. "I think . . . you know what was *really* interesting about that whole, uh, dialogue?"

He shook his head.

"Camille got upset when I suggested that Al might trade her in for a younger model. But she didn't absolutely fly off the handle until I suggested she was a bad planner. It was the accusation of incompetence that did it."

Jack smiled. "Does that surprise you?"

"Noooo," I said slowly. "On reflection, no. But then, I must have had a sense at the time that that would be what would get to her best."

"Bitch," Jack said.

I stared at him. He looked as if he were having a very hard time trying not to laugh.

I curled my upper lip at him and went back to my chef's salad. The waitress brought me my third martini. She looked at Jack's beer glass, then at Jack. He shook his head.

"Actually," I said. "Maybe what was more bizarre was listening to Camille's plans for her future." I stopped foraging in the salad bowl and leaned back against the vinyl-padded back of the booth. "On the one hand, they were absurd. On the other hand . . ." I shook my head. "I don't know. She had such *conviction*. Such assurance that she'd get what she wanted." I looked at Jack. "Is it possible for someone to be a monomaniac and still completely sane?"

"Damned if I know," he said.

"Oh, you're a big help."

He smiled. "That's the most honest answer I can give you."

I nodded. "I guess I'm bothered that someone as shrewd as Camille, and as cool and rational, will try to wiggle out of this on some kind of insanity plea."

"She can try. Whether it'll work is something else."

"With her kind of clout? They might even end up dropping the charges."

Jack shrugged. "You never know."

Our dinners were finished. The waitress came to pick up the bowls and plates.

"Coffee for both of us," Jack said to her.

I made a fist and smacked it lightly on the table top. "Damn!"

"Hey, you can have tea if you want. Or another drink. I just thought you'd like coffee, that's all."

I squinted at him a moment, uncomprehending. Then I got the joke and smiled, grudgingly.

"So now what's wrong?"

"Levesque," I said. "That son-of-a-bitch. The courts can't touch him, can they?"

Jack finished his beer. "Why do you say that?"

"No evidence against *him* either. That bastard. He conspired with Camille to kill Bonnie, he's at least an accessory to Gayle's murder, and he's tight with the mob.

And none of it can be proven. Despite what I told Camille. Damn, damn.''

''Well,'' Jack said. ''Even if he walks away from all this, once it gets into the papers, which'll be tomorrow, his political career will be over.''

''But Jack, all the newspaper stories will be about Camille, not him.''

''At first. But the press won't let something like this go. And when the reporters really get to wading through all the slime . . . well, Al can kiss the statehouse good-bye. Not to speak of the gubernatorial manse.

I shook my head. ''I'm not so sure.''

''The waitress brought our coffee. ''Why not?'' Jack said, when she'd left. ''Why won't his career be over?''

''Because Massachusetts has put convicted felons in office before this. Nice precedent.'' I snorted. ''And Levesque won't even be convicted of anything. I *wish*, oh, how I wish, that that tape Bonnie said she'd made had turned up somewhere.''

''Maybe it will,'' Jack shrugged. ''We'll see.''

I stared at him. ''I must say, you don't seem too awfully concerned about Levesque literally getting away with murder.''

Jack looked at me for a moment, smiling. Then he said, ''I know something you don't know.''

''Oh, really?''

''Senator Levesque and his connections have been the target of a federal investigation for over a year now.''

My eyes widened. ''I didn't know that.''

''Not many people do. I'd appreciate it if you didn't spread it around.''

I scowled. ''Of course I won't.''

''I know, I was just kidding you.''

The waitress put the check on the table and wished us a pleasant evening.

''Anyhow,'' Jack said. ''I'm not certain about this, but from what I hear, they may be getting ready to move for an indictment.''

I made an ''o'' with my mouth.
''I thought you'd enjoy that,'' Jack said.
''Enjoy it?'' I said. ''I *love* it. It's marvelous!''
''Well,'' Jack said, ''It's a start.''

About the Author

SUSAN KELLY lives in Cambridge, Massachusetts where she previously taught at Harvard School of Business and presently is a professor of English at a small college in the Boston area. She also teaches classes in communication at the Cambridge police academy.